ASGARD'S
H·E·A·R·T

ASGARD'S
H·E·A·R·T

THE ASGARD TRILOGY
BOOK THREE

BRIAN
STABLEFORD

Five Star • Waterville, Maine

First Edition
First Printing: February 2005

Published in 2005 in conjunction with
Tekno Books and Ed Gorman.

Set in 11 pt. Plantin.

Printed in the United States on permanent paper.

Library of Congress Cataloging-in-Publication Data

Stableford, Brian M.
    Asgard's heart / Brian Stableford.
      p. cm.
    ISBN 1-59414-210-6 (hc : alk. paper)
    Note: "An earlier version of this text, copyrighted © 1982 by Brian Stableford, was published by DAW Books, Inc., under the title Journey to the center"—T.p. verso.
    1. Life on other planets—Fiction.   2. Science Fiction.
I. Title.
PR6069.T17A935 2005
  823′.914—dc22
                                   2004063674

ASGARD'S
H · E · A · R · T

~ 1 ~

I did not set out on life's great journey with the intention of becoming a demigod. Indeed, when I was a boy growing up on Microworld Achilles in the asteroid belt, it had never occurred to me that such a career choice was possible.

Had I known then what destiny had in mind for me, I might have stayed home and spared myself a great many hazards—an exciting life was not something that I particularly craved. On the other hand, now I know how incomprehensively vast the Great Scheme of Things really is, and how very difficult it is for a single individual to amount to anything within that Scheme, I cannot help but feel a certain sense of privilege in having become what I am.

I claim no great credit for the fact that out of all the billions of people who happened to be within Asgard at the critical moment of its history, fate selected me for the crucial role; I was desperately unlucky to be saddled with the responsibility, and fantastically fortunate not to make a mess of things. But the impossible had to be done, and circumstance determined that I was the one who had to do it.

On two occasions in the past I have found it convenient to commit parts of my story to tape, and those earlier slices of autobiography must still exist somewhere in the universe, though I am not sure that it will ever be possible to assemble them in one place to form an eccentric trilogy. I will be brief in summarising the events described therein.

In the first of those accounts I described how my attempts to scrape a living as a scavenger, recovering technological artefacts from the topmost levels of Asgard, were suddenly complicated when my fellow human Saul Lyndrach discovered a shaft which gave access to more than a hundred levels which had never been breached by any member of the galactic community. Saul was prevented from enjoying the fruits of his discovery because he was murdered by some of the more barbaric members of the community, headed by the loathsome Amara Guur, but they in turn were frustrated by their inability to read French, the language in which Saul had kept his notes.

It so happens that I am of French-Canadian descent, and it transpired that I was the one man on Asgard who could read Saul's notes, so the gangsters who had stolen them set out to entrap me. As things turned out, however, I was not delivered into the hands of my enemies, but into the hands of Earth's glorious Star Force, who had a very different reason for wanting to locate Saul's dropshaft. What *they* wanted was to hunt down and kill an android who called himself Myrlin, who had been manufactured for nefarious reasons by the Salamandrans, lately defeated by humankind in a minor interstellar war.

Suffice it to say that our expedition into the lower depths of Asgard culminated in an orgy of murder and mayhem, carefully observed by the technologically-sophisticated inhabitants of a level deep inside the centre of the macroworld. Confused by the discovery that the universe was much vaster than they had previously imagined, and rather different in kind, these super-scientific machine-intelligences then elected to seal themselves off from further contact with the galactic community.

In the second chronicle of my adventures I described how turmoil erupted in and around Asgard when the galactic community's base there was overrun by barbarian invaders from the lower levels, and how the leading citizens of the galactic community, the Tetrax, who were led by the fact that these invaders closely resembled human beings, recruited humans to help them in trying to find a solution to their diplomatic difficulties. Naturally, the double-dealing for which the Tetrax are justly notorious precipitated the helpful humans in question—including me—into very deep trouble. This, however, was only a prelude to the development of much greater problems deeper inside Asgard.

My eventual return to the level inhabited by the machine-intelligences—who called themselves the Isthomi (or, not being very numerous, the Nine)—discovered matters in extreme disorder. Awakened to a new awareness of the mysteries of the universe, the Isthomi had set out to explore the structure of Asgard, trying to make contact with the similar intelligences that they assumed to be running the show. Alas, they suffered considerable injury as a result of the attempt, discovering only the sad truth that if Asgard had ever had great and godlike machine-minds presiding over its vast inner spaces, those minds were either dangerously mad, or embroiled in some kind of conflict whose nature mere humanoids could hardly begin to comprehend.

The war that was raging through the upper levels unfortunately extended its baleful influence to the world of the incapacitated Isthomi, and the reckless stupidity of the warriors in question resulted in my being forced to interface with the machine-mind while a second contact with intelligences closer to the centre was taking place.

After sharing in that moment of contact—and hearing, I thought, an enigmatic cry for help—I was not quite the man I had been before. My mind had not merely been disturbed, but altered in some as-yet-unfathomable way. To say that I was resentful about this invasion of my innermost privacy would have been understating the case, but there was no going back. I knew that I would have to play my part in the interesting times that had suddenly returned to the lower depths of Asgard, no matter what that part might be.

It turned out to be a more vital and more peculiar part than I could ever have imagined.

ᴧ2ᴧ

It began, I suppose, with the haunting.

I had become used to "ghosts" of a certain kind. Following their near-destruction, the Isthomi had found great difficulty in arranging any kind of manifestation of themselves that would present to their humanoid guests a reassuring appearance. Their attempts to produce the appearance of a human face with which to address me had resulted only in blurred images etched in white light upon the night-black walls of their realm: images I could not help but think of as ghosts. But those ghosts differed from the one that later came to haunt me in two very vital respects. Firstly, they were in and of the walls of the worldlet; they inhabited the "body" of the Isthomi. Secondly, their appearance, however confusing or disturbing it may have been at first, was not in any way threatening.

The new ghost seemed very different—and it frightened me very badly.

I had been having a nightmare—one of many which had troubled me since my forced contact with the denizens of Asgard's software space. I can remember certain fleeting details of it: a falcon fluttering helplessly because its leg was caught in the jaws of a trap; a sphinx padding softly across the sands of a great desert, following a guiding star; dark gods and fearsome titans taking formation for some awesome, awful battle. All of these things seemed to my dreaming consciousness to be direly prophetic of chaos to come, of a destruction and devastation which would consume both the

11

universe in which I existed and the private universe which was within my mind.

The memory of a dozen other dreams of like kind was still in my mind as I awoke. I remember being quite certain in my mind that I *was* awake, and that was why I was so very surprised and frightened when I opened my eyes and saw the ghostly entity that was hovering over my bed.

The room in which I was lodged had no windows, but its internal lighting did not fade to pitch-darkness. The artificial bioluminescence of the ceiling retained a glimmer, reminiscent of starlight, even while I slept. Because of that faint radiance, it was not easy at first to see the apparition, whose own glow was very little brighter. It became obvious neither because of its brightness nor its shape—which was not very well focused—but because it was shimmering slightly, like a shifting haze.

I realised immediately that what it was trying to be was a face. I do not speak metaphorically when I say that it was *trying,* for I was in no doubt that there was some kind of intention involved. The face seemed to be about two metres away from me, directly above my head as I lay on my back looking upwards, but I quickly concluded that this was an illusion. It was not a *thing* hovering in mid-air; it was some kind of virtual image, projected there in appearance only.

Only for the briefest of moments did I toy with the supposition that the Nine were at work. Their image-control had increased so wonderfully in recent days that they were most unlikely to present such a weak appearance, and in any case, their phantasmal appearances always remained confined by the walls. This one was obviously different. I quickly came to the conclusion that its source was in my own brain.

In short, I was seeing things.

I did what everyone does when first confronted with such an awareness: I tried to stop seeing it. I blinked, and shook my head, but neither of those feeble gestures accomplished anything, save that they made the image shimmer and waver a little more. Having exhausted that line of approach to the problem I tried the next obvious course, which was to try to see it more clearly, squinting in the attempt to bring it into better focus.

Concentrating hard, I realised that it was a female face, but that something was wrong with the upper part of it. The hair was not right. For a moment, its appearance reminded me of the startling halo of blonde hair which was Susarma Lear's crowning glory, but then I realised that the strands were much too thick—that they looked more like the tendrils of a sea-anemone than actual hairs. Then I looked at the eyes, which were like dark pits, and I felt a distinct thrill of fear.

The darkness of the eyes was surprising. In my painful and enigmatic moment of contact with whatever it was that lurked in the depths of Asgard's software space, the Other had become manifest as a group of four eyes, which burned as though with some consuming fire. Ever since the contact I had occasionally had a curious sensation of being watched, as though I were still somehow open to the scrutiny of those eyes. So why, I wondered, should this new apparition—which surely must be reckoned a legacy of my contact—have only empty holes for eyes. *These* eyes were the very antithesis of those others, which I had called "eyes of fire." These were eyes of vacuum, eyes of awesome emptiness, eyes which promised those whom they beheld a fate so dire and bleak as to be ultimately fearful.

There was no doubt in my mind that this was a threatening ghost, and that its projection betrayed the presence in

13

my brain—in my inmost self—of something hostile, menacing, and dangerous. Something lurked inside of me that seemed to wish me harm, and here it was, struggling to get outside of me in order to look back at me, not merely to see what I looked like, but by the act of observation to transform that which was observed.

The conviction grew in me that this dreadful messenger had come to me with a summons—not the plea for help that I had heard in the moment of my first contact with the gods and devils of Asgard, but a more urgent command. Medusa could not possibly come as a supplicant; she was altogether too stern of countenance for that.

I had no other name to give it but Medusa, and I felt that its gorgon stare was beginning the engagement of a battle of wills whose intended resolution might easily be my petrifaction.

I sweated with the effort of fighting those eyes, gritting my teeth together to express the determination I had to defeat this influence. I did not want to be possessed; I was not about to tolerate the presence of squatters in my inmost soul.

"Damn you," I whispered, thinking to hurt it with sound. "Leave me alone!"

But the sound didn't hurt it, and I realised that it was becoming clearer, achieving better focus. I could see the eyes forming on the snakes that grew from the scalp instead of hair, and I could see the flickering of forked tongues issuing from seams that had not been there a moment before. I could see the line of the cheekbone quite clearly, and knew that its bone-structure at least was modeled on Susarma Lear's—but it did not have her hair and it did not have her eyes.

In fact, it didn't have *any* eyes. Yet.

I felt a shock of panic as I wondered what would happen if those empty eyes should become full, and suddenly the awfulness of their emptiness was nothing to the awfulness of their potential fullness, for if this was indeed Medusa, the addition of those eyes might achieve the threatened end, and harden my own soft features into grey, unyielding stone.

"Get out of here!" I whispered. "Begone!"

But the mere command was ineffective.

Now the snakes were beginning to writhe, and to hiss angrily at one another as if they resented their perverse anchorage and did not love their neighbours. Several of the mouths were gaping now, to expose the needle-sharp fangs, and the snakes' eyes were glowing like red coals. The womanly lips were parting too, very slowly, to expose the teeth within—teeth that were not at all womanly, but pointed like the teeth of a shark. The jet black tongue which lapped over the shark-like teeth, as if savouring the memory of some previous meal, was forked like the snakes' tongues, but much thicker, and there was something curiously obscene about its writhing.

And the eyes . . . the eye-sockets were not as dark now, and there was something in those gloomy apertures that looked like the sparkle of distant stars.

I could not doubt that something terrible was about to happen.

The face moved then, coming nearer to my own. It was no longer hovering close to the ceiling but descending, with that tongue still spreading poisonous saliva upon the jagged teeth, and those snakes seething with frustrated wrath, and the stars in the eyes were beginning to shine. . . .

"Light!" I shouted, breaking the deadlock with a rush of panic. "Light the room, for Christ's sake!"

15

It is said that the story of the universe began with a cry of *"Fiat lux!"* although the story in question has nothing to say on the question of whether there were artificial intelligences already incorporated into the walls which bounded existence, pre-programmed to answer such a call. I had the advantage of knowing that the autonomic sub-systems of the Isthomi were always at my disposal, and I knew that my call would be instantly answered.

It was the right move.

As bright light flooded the room in response to a bioelectric jolt, the gorgon's face—which was composed of a much frailer radiance—was swamped and obliterated.

The monster never reached me. Its eyes were never wholly formed. And I was made of anything but stone—there was no mistaking the frailty of my flesh, which *crawled* as only frail flesh can, when it has had a close encounter with something dreadful.

"Merde!" I said, with feeling, as I sat up and wiped sweat from my brow with the back of my hand. I groped for my wristwatch, though the time that it showed me would be completely meaningless. There was no cycle of day or night here, and for the moment I couldn't quite remember whether the digital display was set to refer to a human twenty-four-hour cycle, a Tetron metric cycle, or the forty-period cycle devised by the Scarid armies that had brought chaos to the corridors of Asgard. By the time I had worked out how long I had been asleep, the datum no longer seemed relevant. I did *not* want to go back to sleep.

I got up and dressed myself, then instructed the kitchen-unit to make me a cup of coffee.

In accordance with the general improvement of the situation, the kitchen-unit that the Isthomi had put together was now quite clever in serving the needs of my stomach and my palate alike. We were well past the stage of supporting life on manna and water, and I hoped that we might soon make progress in synthesizing a reasonable imitation of good red wine. In the meantime, the coffee was a welcome reassurance that the universe was not completely out of joint.

As I sipped it, I contemplated my next move. As was my habit, the first option I considered was forgetting the whole thing, or at least keeping it a dark secret. There were reasons why that might be a good idea. I was hoping that circumstances would soon permit me to gather about myself a few bold companions in order to begin my odyssey through the inner regions of Asgard in search of the final solution to its mysteries. I could hardly expect to attract such disciples—let alone reconcile them to the acceptance of my leadership—if they suspected that I was insane, possessed, or otherwise not to be trusted. No one but me had felt the urgency of that cry for help that had come from Asgard's depths, and no one but me had the strength of my conviction that I had understood it. It was going to be difficult enough to talk Susarma Lear into following my lead—especially in view of the fact that I needed her old adversary Myrlin every bit as much as I needed her—without letting her know that I had been visited by an apparition of a gorgon's head.

On the other hand, I had to concede that I had been way out of my intellectual depth for some time. I am no fool, by human standards—and, despite the opinions of the Tetrax, I believe those to be reasonably good standards—but nothing I had ever encountered in my education or my experience equipped me to come to grips with what had happened to me in my moment of contact with whatever it was that was loose in Asgard's software space. If I wanted to fight this thing properly, I needed the insight and advice of

17

someone much cleverer than I was, and that meant that I had no option but to confide in the Nine. Sick and shattered they might be, but they were the only ones who stood a real chance of figuring out what the hell it all meant.

So when I drained my cup, I turned to the nearest blank wall, and said: "I think we ought to have a little chat."

The grey wall faded away, to be replaced by what looked like another room. Although it was just a surface image, it looked as if it had depth; I had come to think of it as a mirror-world, like the world beyond the looking-glass into which Carroll's Alice stepped. This was partly because it had the colour and sharpness of a reflection, but partly because I knew only too well that the world it represented was not at all like ours, but was instead a mad world where the limits of possibility were very different indeed.

The figure facing me was seated on an illusory chair which looked rather like an ornate wooden piano-stool; it was backless, but had low side-rails. The Nine presented the image of a single person—a female, clad in a somewhat diaphanous garment recalling (and not by any coincidence) my vague memories of ancient Greek statuary. She seemed to be about twenty years of age, and was very beautiful, although the contours of her face, which were partly borrowed from Susarma Lear, now put me disturbingly in mind of the apparition that had recently confronted me.

I coughed, in an ineffectual attempt to hide the embarrassment that her appearance caused me. "I don't want to appear rude," I said, "but could you possibly put some less provocative clothes on?"

The image changed, without a ripple or a flicker, and she was now clad in a severely-cut Star Force uniform; but her hair was black, not blonde, and she seemed less like

Susarma Lear than she had before.

"Thanks," I said.

"Something is wrong?" she observed.

"Maybe," I said, unenthusiastically wondering whether this was, after all, the best thing to do. Now the room was bright and I was face to face with what looked like another human being, my experience began to seem much more like a bad dream, and an alarmist reaction seemed absurdly out of place. "I don't suppose you were monitoring this room a moment ago?" I asked.

"Of course not. Since you expressed to us your anxieties about privacy, we reserve our attention, and take our place only in response to your summons."

I knew that. "I saw something," I said. "I don't think it was real, though. Not *solid*. Perhaps it was just a dream."

Her face reflected her interest and concern. It was odd that her mimicry of human mannerisms went so far, but it was something the Isthomi had very carefully crafted into the programme that produced her. The Nine had taken great care in the rebuilding of their appearances, and took quite a pride in their simulation of expression and non-verbal patterns of signification.

"Please describe it as fully and accurately as you can," she said.

I did my best, stumbling over a couple of details, to give her a complete account of the hallucination. When I had finished, she was radiating puzzlement like an over-enthusiastic method actor.

"Can the silent movie bit," I told her with slight asperity. "We both know it was some kind of residue from that interface when I made contact with whatever it was that nearly took you apart. What I want to know is, was it an attack of some kind? Am I playing host to some sort of poisoned programming or what?"

"Please tell us everything that you know about this person called Medusa," she said calmly.

"I can't remember very much about her at all," I replied. "She was a character in Greek mythology who turned everyone who looked at her to stone. A hero called Perseus cut off her head while watching her reflection in a highly polished shield. That's it."

"Are you sure?" she countered.

The inquiry left me feeling rather helpless. I knew that she was prompting me—trying to make me remember something else. She was an alien group-mind who lived halfway to the core of an artificial macroworld orbiting a star a thousand light-years from Earth, and yet she knew more about the mythology of the ancient Greeks than I did. What made it even more bizarre was that her primary source of information about matters human was an android on Salamandra, whose own second-hand information had been pumped into him by hostile aliens while he was growing at an unnatural pace from embryo to giant in some kind of nutrient bath.

"As sure as I can be," I replied, defensively stubborn. "No doubt there's more locked up in the vaults of my subconscious, but I only have the primitive lever of memory to get me in there. I haven't got your kind of access to stored data."

"Please don't be disturbed," she said softly. "There is a mystery here, but I believe that we can solve it."

She had some of Susarma Lear's features, but she didn't have Susarma Lear's voice—which, as even the colonel's many admirers would have admitted, did tend to the strident. This voice was much more like Jacinthe Siani's. There was no point in complaining—Susarma Lear and Jacinthe

Siani were the only two humanoid females the Nine could use as models. Jacinthe, who still had the trust of the Scarida on account of being their most loyal galactic collaborator, had been brought down by a team of their negotiators shortly after the end of the war.

"It's all very well to tell me not to be disturbed," I told her, "but I'm not sure that I have much control over that any more. This stupid hallucination was a disturbance, and though I'm pretty confident that I'm not going mad of my own accord, I can't help worrying about the possibility of having picked up a little hostile software."

"Exactly what do you mean by 'hostile software'?" she asked, in a painstaking fashion.

I sighed. "As with everything else," I said, testily, "I'm sure you know far more about it than I do. I'm no electronics expert. Ever since the earliest days of infotech on our world we've had things called 'information viruses' or 'tape-worms.' They're programmes that can be hidden on a disc or a bubble, which load into your system along with other software. Once they're established in your equipment they begin intruding bits of random noise into other programmes, and if left to themselves they can turn all your inbuilt software to junk. All our semi-intelligent systems have protective devices—immunizers—which are supposed to keep them out, but the tapeworms just get cleverer and cleverer. They're used mainly by saboteurs. No doubt you and any other machine-intelligences lurking in the depths of Asgard are far too clever to be infected by the kind of tape-worms we produce—but I dare say you have troubles of your own. What I'm asking you is: did I pick up some kind of tapeworm when I was contacted? Is there something in my brain that's intended to destroy my mind?"

She seemed thoughtful, though she'd now corrected the

tendency to overact. "What you're afraid of," she said, "is that when you were forced into the interface with my own software space, where you encountered the alien presence which injured me, your own brain was somehow forced to make a biocopy of an alien programme. You now suspect that the biocopy has become fully established, and is beginning to be active. You think that it might be analogous to one of these 'tapeworms,' and that its purpose may be to disrupt your own intrinsic programming—including that part which constitutes your identity."

"That's about the size of it," I admitted. "I can't shake the feeling that something got into me during that contact, and though I don't know what the hell it is, I don't like it being there. And I certainly don't like the idea of it becoming active. You may be used to the idea of having nine identities in one, but I'm not. I'm a solitary kind of person, and I like to have vacant possession of my own brain. So tell me— have I picked up some hostile software?"

"I cannot be sure," she said, as I'd been fairly certain that she would. "To tell you the truth, despite the success of my efforts at self-repair, I am not altogether certain whether or not I might have acquired some new hidden programming of my own. I still have no very clear idea of what kind of entity it was that I contacted in the deeper part of Asgard, nor what kind of entity it was which subsequently made the second contact within my own systems. Since I began experimenting with the production of the scions— whose minds are, of course, biocopies of parts of my own collective being—I have pushed back my own conceptual horizons quite considerably. I can easily believe that the entity we contacted was capable of making a biocopy of part of itself within your brain, even though it was operating across a primitive neuronal bridge. That does appear to be

23

the most likely hypothesis, which could explain your recent experience. But it is by no means easy to decide whether the entity really had any hostile intent, despite the considerable damage that I sustained as a result of the contact. You have cast considerable doubt on that by your interpretation of the second contact as a cry for help."

"I don't want to be haunted," I said, flatly. "Not by monsters whose *raison d'etre* is turning people to stone. Nothing would please me more than to decide that any software I've picked up is friendly, and that it won't drive me mad—but Medusa is hardly a friendly image, is it?"

"It is not plausible that the entity had any independent knowledge of human mythology," she pointed out. "What you saw just now was mainly your own creation. You were responding to a stimulus, in much the same way that you supplied your own imagery to cope with the contact that you made at the interface. That is why you must ask yourself very carefully what the image of Medusa might mean; it is a symbol which we must decode."

"What Medusa means," I insisted, "is turning people to stone."

"Did you take any special interest in Greek mythology in your youth?" she asked patiently.

I hesitated, then shrugged. "More than some, I guess. Local connections encouraged it. I was born in the asteroid belt, on a microworld. The microworld moved about a bit, but it stayed within a mass-rich region of space at one of the Lagrangian points forming an equilateral triangle with the sun and the solar system's biggest gas giant, Jupiter. For reasons of historical eccentricity, the asteroids near the Lagrangian points are known as Trojan asteroids, and they're named after the heroes who fought in the Trojan War. One group is called the Trojan group, even though it has one asteroid named after the Greek hero Patroclus; the other is called the Greek group, even though it contains one named after the Trojan Hector. Hector was one of two asteroids in our group that had been hollowed to create a microworld; the other—the one where I was born—was Achilles. It was inevitable that a certain friendly rivalry should grow up between the two; at the utilitarian level we were competing for the same resources, but the subtler business of trying to forge some kind of cultural identity for our worlds attached us psychologically and emotionally to the names of our worlds. Achilles and Hector fought a great duel at the end of the *Iliad*, you see—and Achilles won. The Homeric epics were elementary reading for every child on the microworld, and the rest of Greek mythology was a logical extension. The first humans who came out here obviously had a different cultural background, or they'd have translated the name which the Tetrax gave this macroworld as Olympus, not as Asgard."

"In that case," she said, with a hint of irritating smugness, "you did read more about Medusa than you have recalled."

"I know that she never showed up at Troy, and that Odysseus never bumped into her on his travels. Perseus was in a different story. So tell me—what did I forget?"

She didn't want to tell me. She wanted me to remember for myself. After all, understanding my strange experience was a matter of coming to terms with my subconscious.

"Why did Perseus want the gorgon's head?" she asked.

I struggled hard to remember. Microworld Achilles was a long way away, and my years there now seemed to be a very remote region of the foreign country that was my past.

"He'd placed himself under some obligation to a king, and was forced to go after it," I said, eventually. "Athene helped him to trick a couple of weird sisters who had only one eye between them, so that they'd tell him where to get what he needed—winged shoes and a cap to make himself invisible. When he got back with the head he found that the king had done the dirty on him somehow . . . tried to rape his mother, I think . . . and. . . ."

Enlightenment struck as I managed to follow the frail thread of long-buried memories to the punch line. Perseus had used the head to turn the bad guy and all his court to stone.

"You don't think it was aimed *at* me, do you?" I said, softly. "It's hostile software, all right—but you think it may be some kind of weapon!"

"There is no way to be sure," she replied. "But it is a possibility, is it not?"

I looked at her, pensively. Though her hair was dark, her eyes were grey and pale. They weren't Susarma Lear's eyes and they weren't Jacinthe Siani's either. In fact, they were more like mine. It was impossible to think of her, sitting there, as a conglomerate of nine individuals, and it didn't seem appropriate to think of her as bearing the name of only one of the nine Muses after whom Myrlin had impishly named her scions. As she stared back at me, with all the deep concern of a master psychoanalyst, I remembered something else from my reading of long ago.

The mother of the nine Muses had been Mnemosyne. Mnemosyne meant "memory."

Another thought which flitted quickly across my mind was that although the Muses were the inspiration behind the various arts, the supreme goddess of the arts was Athene, who had aided Perseus.

I wondered how I should name the phantasm which faced me now. Should I call her Mnemosyne, or Athene?

But Mnemosyne, I supposed, was a mere abstraction rather than a person, and for all the arbitrariness of her appearance, what I was facing now was a real and powerful being—one who could readily aspire to be reckoned one of the "gods" to which Asgard was supposedly home.

"I have an uncomfortable feeling," I said, "that you might be inclined to find rather more meaning in my little adventure than I want to look for."

"On the contrary," she replied sweetly. "You have already declared your intention of penetrating to the very lowest levels of the macroworld. You are already determined to undertake a journey to the mysterious Centre, and have asked me to try to discover a route that would take you there. It may be that this is a search which will take both of us into unexpected realms . . . let us not discount the possibility that the way to the Centre is already engraved in the hidden recesses of your own mind. Whatever cried to you for help may also have given you the means to supply that help."

I swallowed a lump which had somehow appeared in my throat. "I may be an Achillean by birth," I said, "but I'm not exactly cut from the same cloth as Perseus. His father, as I recall, was Zeus."

"I cannot pretend to have a complete understanding of fleshly beings," she told me, "despite what I have learned from my scions. But I do not think that the paternity of your flesh is of any significance here. It is the author of the software within your brain that concerns us now. The mind which you brought here carries a legacy of knowledge and craft which must be deemed the property of your entire race . . . and what has now been added to it we can only guess."

I wasn't ready for that. I shook my head, and turned away with a dismissive gesture.

"Much more of that," I remarked, and not in jest, "and you'll be scaring me more than the gorgon's head did. Hostile software that wants to drive me mad is something I could maybe be cured of—you're talking about something a hell of a lot more ominous than a tapeworm."

"It is conjecture only," she reassured me. "We must know more before we plan to act, though time is of the essence. We must find out whether anyone else has had such an experience."

Although I was the only one who'd consciously made contact during that dark hour when the Isthomi had come close to destruction, I wasn't the only one who's interfaced. Myrlin had been hooked up too—and so had 994-Tulyar. I wondered what kind of imagery could be mined from the mythological symbol-system of a Tetron mind.

"Do you want me to ask?" I said unenthusiastically.

"The inquiry would come better from myself," she assured me. "It may be necessary to be diplomatic, in the case of the Tetron."

I readily forgave her the impolite implication that diplomacy was not my strong suit. "In that case," I said, "perhaps I should try to get a bit more sleep."

"If you dream," she said, before she faded out, "be sure to pay attention as carefully as you can."

It wasn't the most soothing instruction I'd ever taken to bed with me, but as things turned out, I couldn't obey it anyhow. Whatever dreams disturbed my mind failed, for once, to penetrate the blissful wall of my unconsciousness.

✦4✦

I was awakened from my peaceful slumbers by the delicate trilling of the telephone apparatus that the Isthomi had installed in my quarters. I always hung the mouthpiece above the bed before retiring, so that I could respond to interruptions with the minimum of effort. I didn't even bother to open my eyes—I just fished the thing from its perch, thumbed the ACCEPT CALL button, and mumbled an incoherent semblance of a greeting into the mike.

"Jesus, Rousseau," said the voice at the other end. "You're supposed to be an officer in the Star Force. Why the hell are you asleep at this hour?"

"Time," I said, "is purely relative. "What you call 'this hour' can be any damn hour we care to call it. What do you want, Susarma?"

"For a start," she replied, "I want you to call me 'Colonel.' Also, I would like to invite you to accompany me on a little walk in the garden."

I opened my eyes then and held the phone away from my face, staring at it as one tends to stare at an object that has unexpectedly started behaving in a perverse manner.

"You want me to come for a walk in the garden?" I asked guardedly.

"That's what I said," she confirmed. She sounded slightly bad-tempered, but there was nothing unusual about that. What was unusual was that she was talking about gardens as if I was supposed to know what she meant. I thought about it for a moment, and had little difficulty figuring out

29

which garden she meant, but couldn't for the life of me fathom out her reasons for wanting me to go there. One thing was certain though, and that was the fact that she must have a reason. She was not normally given to circumlocution or to guessing games.

Something was obviously wrong. I wondered whether it was the same kind of something wrong that I had already encountered, or an entirely unconnected kind of something wrong. Troubles seem never to come singly.

"Okay," I said, in an off-hand manner. "The garden. Give me twenty minutes to wake up, and I'll be there."

I was proud of myself for giving no more than the slightest indication that I'd had difficulty working out what she meant, and I further demonstrated my initiative by waiting until I had showered and breakfasted, and was well away from my room, before asking the Isthomi if they could get me to the enclosed region which they'd used as an arena on my first visit to this level, to stage the big fight between the Star Force and Amara Guur's mobsters, and to fake Myrlin's death by fire at the less-than-tender hands of Susarma Lear.

The Isthomi opened up one of their convenient doorways into the hidden recesses of their world, and laid on a robot car which whizzed me away through curving tunnels at breathtaking pace. It was a longer journey than I expected—although it had never before occurred to me to wonder whether the maze in which my last adventure had taken place was geographically close to the essentially-similar one in which I'd found myself on the earlier occasion. I had nothing to do during the journey but worry about the speed at which I was traveling, and wish that it didn't seem quite so much like a kind of repeating nightmare I'd suffered from in my youth—a stereotyped dream from which most microworlders are said to suffer.

Eventually, the car stopped and another doorway opened up beside me, through which I stepped into a hothouse world of gigantic flowers, vivid in hue and sharply scented. They presented a riot of colour—mostly purples and golds in this particular spot, which was dominated by a single vast bush, whose branches were tangled into an inextricable mess, and whose convolvuline blossoms looked like a scene from a surreal bell-factory. Given the host of mythological references that every waking moment now evoked, I could hardly help thinking of the bush as a Gordian knot, though it would have taken a much mightier hand than mine to slash it with a massive sword.

"Colonel Lear!" I called, mindful of her instruction that military protocol was still to be observed between us. I looked in either direction along the grey wall that curved away to my left and right, with a thin green verge which could serve as a path, if only I knew which way to go.

The door by which I had been admitted had closed silently and seamlessly behind me, but now another opened, a dozen metres away, and Susarma Lear stepped through. She was, as always, wearing her Star Force uniform, the black cloth contrasting in a remarkably pleasing fashion with the dazzling shock of blonde hair surrounding her face. She was also wearing a sidearm—one of the guns she'd taken from the Scarida when she'd come to my rescue while I was making my painful contact with the gods of Asgard.

The way she was holding her stern jaw made me wince. It wasn't hard to believe that the icy stare in her bright blue eyes could turn men into stone.

"Hello, Rousseau," she said, soberly. "Thanks for being so quick on the uptake."

"I deduce," I said—having had time to think about it—

"that some unkind person has taken advantage of the fact that the Isthomi granted our request for personal privacy, and has surreptitiously bugged our rooms."

"That's right," she confirmed.

"Finn again?"

"I assume that he's involved. 994-Tulyar is behind it, of course."

"Why?"

"If you mean, why are they doing it, it's probably because they're a bunch of scheming bastards to whom low cunning comes naturally. But I don't like it. I don't know what kind of game Tulyar's playing, but I think it's something I ought to find out about."

"Why did you want me to come all the way out here so you could tell me about it?"

"I don't know where else they've distributed their little listening devices. Since the Tetrax from the prison camp came down here with the Scarid delegation, the entire level is lousy with people I don't like and don't trust. The only other authentic human here is Finn—and he's got the kind of coat that's ready cut for turning at the slightest provocation. It looks to me like you and me against the universe, Rousseau, and this is the only place down here that none of the other guys have been."

She hadn't included Myrlin in her list of potential enemies, nor had she included him while numbering the tiny clique that knew about this little Eden. I gathered that she still had him on her list of unmentionable topics, even though she'd made no attempt to wipe him out for a second time.

"So this is a council of war?" I said.

"If you like," she said. "I never expected to end up in a situation where the only person I could trust is you, but that's where I am now. Read this."

She drew a flimsy out of her pocket and passed it over to me. I scanned it quickly. It was in English, and was signed by Valdavia, the diplomat who's been sent out from the solar system aboard *Leopard Shark* to represent the UN in negotiations with the Tetrax. The document was an order to Colonel Susarma Lear to return as soon as possible to Skychain City. It was embellished with firm statements to the effect that in the meantime she was still to consider herself, and all her subordinates, to be under the orders of 994-Tulyar, and that she was to co-operate in every possible way with the Tetrax. It did not say in so many words that Valdavia knew how cynically the Tetrax had used us to spread their plague for them, but he was obviously assuming that we might have fallen out with Tulyar, and was telling us in no uncertain terms that we were not to take offense at what had happened.

"He's got a hope!" I muttered. "The Scarida have been telling us for days that the chaos caused by that damned influenza makes it impossible to transport anyone up or down above level fifty-two."

"They got *that* down," she pointed out, drily. "And they also brought down a group of top-flight Tetron scientists. Mostly electronics men, plus a couple of bioscientists. They arrived during the night. Our old friend 673-Nisreen is one of them. The Tetrax used us as weapons of war, but now it seems that we're definitely surplus to requirements. They want us out."

"Not exactly," I said. "They want *you* out. There's no mention of your bringing me with you—or Finn for that matter. I have a nasty suspicion that Tulyar might have other plans for me, and that I won't like them one little bit."

"What do you mean?" she asked.

33

It wasn't necessary to tell her about Medusa. "I'm the one who made the contact with whatever godling kicked the shit out of the Nine," I pointed out. "Tulyar can't begin to understand the situation which is now unfolding, and there's nothing a Tetron high-number man hates worse than not understanding. What's more, the fact that he can't understand doesn't affect his ardent desire to *control* things. I think he's almost as far out of his depth here as the Scarid commanders, and I have a feeling that, for all his velvety Tetron manners, he might react to being out of his depth in much the same panicky fashion. One thing I'm sure of—he means me no good. I never thought I'd say this, Colonel, but I think I'm going to miss you."

"Like hell you are," she said. "I'm not going."

I was mildly surprised. I knew how seriously she took the Star Force, and I couldn't quite see her in the role of mutineer.

"Do you have a choice?" I asked, raising the paper slightly.

"Valdavia doesn't understand the situation," she said. "My duty is to protect the interests of the human race, and if I can make a better estimate of what those interests are than he can, I'm the one whose obligation it is to make policy."

"What policy did you have in mind?" I asked. I remembered, without much enthusiasm, her approach to the problem of finding Myrlin when she'd first arrived on Asgard. She had been making her own policy then, and she hadn't impressed me with her style. In fact, she'd shown all the sensitivity and diplomatic flair of a wolverine.

"That's a little hard to say," she retorted, "unless I have rather more information at my disposal. You're the one who knows more than the rest of us, Rousseau. As I said, I never expected to get to the point where you were the only person I could trust, but here we are. What do *you* think we should do?"

I was less surprised than I might have been a day earlier. After all, I'd already been presented with evidence that the Age of Miracles had dawned again. Unfortunately, I didn't have any pat answer ready to hand.

"That's a difficult question," I parried.

"Well," she said testily, "if it was an easy one, I sure as hell wouldn't have to ask you, would I?"

I suppose it was a compliment of sorts, though she hadn't quite intended it that way.

"I think you ought to know," I said, after a brief pause for consideration, "that the situation may be a lot more complicated than you suppose. It seems that while I was interfaced with the Isthomi, and they were involved in some kind of life-or-death struggle, something got into me. Something may have got into Myrlin and Tulyar, too. I think something's happening deep inside Asgard which makes the Scarid invasion look like a very trivial nuisance. The macroworld itself might be in danger—I can't say for sure. One thing I am sure of, though, is that if the beings we're involved with now are determined to make pawns of us, we could be in for a far rougher ride than the Tetrax gave us when *they* hired us as catspaws. There's no way out for me— I'm in too deep—but if you aim to come out of this mess alive, you might be better off obeying this order and getting the hell out of Asgard. You'd be safer out of the system."

She looked at me with an expression that was far less easy to read than those which the Nine's simulacrum had worn.

"You're going to try to make a run for the Centre," she said, "aren't you?"

"Yes I am," I told her. "I guess I've been here too long—I've made myself a thoroughgoing sucker for the big mystery. Anyhow, I don't want to consign myself entirely to 994-Tulyar's tender care. If I need any other reasons, I also suspect that whatever's got into me isn't going to let me rest unless I do try to get to the heart of the matter."

"You were planning to go alone?"

There was no point in dissembling. "Actually," I said, "I was hoping to take Myrlin. I figured he's the only one *I* can trust to the hilt. I think some of the scions will come, too. I did intend to ask you, because I figured we might need your firepower, but I wasn't sure you'd be willing. I've asked the Isthomi to build me a vehicle—a robot on wheels, capable of taking me safely through the levels. They've started work already."

"You hadn't bothered to take into account, I suppose, that you're a star-captain in the Star Force, and that I'm your commanding officer?"

"I guess I'm a deserter through and through," I confessed—not without a pang of uneasiness. "But I was going to tell you."

"Jesus!" she said, with more tiredness in her voice than disgust. "What the hell did I ever do to deserve this command? Poor Serne got blasted, and all I have left is you and that creep Finn. We might be standing on the very spot where Khalekhan got killed in action, you realise that? Where you go, I go. All the way. Got that?"

I found that my mouth was a little bit more open than it should have been, though not so much that you could say that my jaw had dropped.

"You want to go to the Centre?" I said.

"I think that if *you* have to go, you surely need someone to look after you. You're not exactly my idea of a hero,

Rousseau. Anyhow, running away to the surface would look like cowardice in the face of the enemy, and that's not my style. We'll go to the Centre, Rousseau—the Star Force way."

I wondered which of us was volunteering for the mission; everything seemed slightly cock-eyed, if not entirely upside down. But what can you expect, when you go through the looking-glass into the magic world? I had my reservations about the Star Force way, but it was a way that had saved my neck before.

"994-Tulyar's not going to like it when you tell him you're not going up," I said.

"The hell with 994-Tulyar," she retorted. "In fact, the hell with Tetra and everything it ever spawned. From now on, the ambassadors of the galactic community are you and me, and whatever treasure we find at the bottom of the hole belongs to humankind. When were you thinking of starting out?"

"The robot should be nearly ready," I told her. "The main problem is knowing which way to go. We've got no map of the levels. The Nine have thrown out a few dark hints about there being more than one way to get to the Centre, but they haven't explained exactly what they mean. I'm hoping they'll be able to figure out a way to guide us, but. . . ."

I never got the chance to discuss the doubts and uncertainties of the matter. The wall behind me exploded, and the shockwave hurled me head over heels into the meshes of the Gordian knot.

⋏ 5 ⋎

Although the gravity was low, I wasn't exactly feather-light, and I hit the plants with a lot of momentum. But the tangled branches turned out to be so tightly interwoven that I didn't get stuck—in fact, they were so rubbery that I bounced. I was able to roll forward as I hit them so that I was tumbling like an acrobat as I continued on my ungainly way.

Shards of the broken wall were flying everywhere, showering the bell-like flowers and lacerating their petals. I felt a prickling sensation in my back accompanying the sensation of being hit by the shock-wave, and knew that I'd been cut in a dozen places. The rolling probably didn't help, but at least I didn't drive anything between my ribs to administer a fatal stab in the back.

The noise was tremendous—the big flightless insects that roamed this overgrown wilderness always screamed with panic when they were disturbed, and they were certainly disturbed now. I felt them struggling to get out of the way as I landed on a softer spot, crushing the vegetation down upon them.

When I stopped rolling I was sprawled on hands and knees shaded by a huge palmate leaf. I came to my feet as quickly as I could and looked back at the spot from which I'd been hurled. What kind of petard had been used to blast the hole I couldn't imagine, but I saw immediately that it hadn't been quite big enough, because the thing which was struggling to get through wasn't finding it at all easy.

It wasn't immediately obvious whether it was a living

38

creature or an artefact. In a bizarre fashion it didn't seem completely out of place in this world of enormous insects and elephantine flowers because if it resembled anything I could put a name to, it looked like an immense praying mantis, with great long legs, a small head carried high, and groping arms, though the "hands" on the end of the arms looked like a cross between a crab's pincers and one of the articulated graspers they put on robots designed to explore places where no human being can go.

It seemed to be made of metal and plastic, but its joints were as flexible as the joints of a living creature, and the way that the head was moving from side to side as it tried to get its legs through the jagged split in the wall was surely suggestive of something searching for a sight of its prey. The head could swivel through three hundred and sixty degrees, and it was mounted with four shiny black lenses which probably gave it vision in depth in all directions. It also had a rigid proboscis that looked ominously like the barrel of a gun.

But it didn't have vision in depth in all directions for long, because Susarma Lear had been far enough away on the curving path to be shielded from the blast, and she already had the Scarid crash gun in her hand. Whether it was a lucky shot or whether she'd been practising I didn't know, but the first bullet she fired hit one of those black lenses smack in the centre, and blew it to smithereens.

One of those grasping hands immediately reached for her, striking with awesome speed. I had the uncomfortable feeling that if it had grabbed her it could have broken her in two with its clutch, but the act of turning sideways jammed the thing firmly in the narrow fissure through which it was trying to haul its ungainly body, and when the pincers clicked shut at the limit of the arm's expansion, she was all of ten centimetres out of reach. The monster spat fire, dragon-fashion, revealing that its proboscis was some kind of flamer, but the firebolt missed by a couple of metres.

Anyone with an ordinary capacity for fear would have run like hell, but the colonel was anything but ordinary. She watched the groping hand close and withdraw, not moving her feet at all, and as soon as she had the space she put her gun-hand forward again, supporting it at the elbow with her left, and took a quick but careful sight of that wheel-mounted head.

Her second bullet hit the skull-cap a mere half-centimetre away from the rim of a second eye, and ricocheted harmlessly away. I couldn't hear her because of the cacophonous complaints of the insects, but I saw her lips move and I could easily imagine the manner of her cursing.

I saw—as she must have seen—that the colossal mantis had taken advantage of the miss to haul a bit more of its bulk through the scissored cleft in the wall, and that it only needed one last wriggle to get its entire carcass into the garden. I think I shouted at her to run, but there was no way she could hear me. As usual, it was an utterly futile gesture, because she was undoubtedly better at judging these circumstances than I was, and she wasn't about to hang around for the next flame-bolt or the next attempted snatch at her midriff. She was already backing away, although she had the gun raised, anxious to try a third shot if she could balance herself—the Scarid gun wasn't an easy weapon to use because of the recoil kick.

While I was watching, fearful for *her* life, I'd carelessly forgotten my own troubles, and it was with a sense of desperate astonishment that I noticed the second arm flashing out in *my* direction, ambitious to grab my shoulder and pluck me out of my hidey-hole in the bushes. Even with its eyes at seventy-five-percent strength, the monster was obviously capable of paying attention to two targets at once.

I ducked, wishing fervently that for once my reflexes wouldn't let me down—I had long ago come to the conclusion that I was at the end of the queue when instincts were handed out, and that the stupid set I'd been born with was absolutely not to be trusted. But my luck was still holding; like Susarma, I was just out of reach, and the mechanical grab went back empty-handed.

Knowing only too well that it would get me next time, I turned and ran. A purple flower to my left suddenly turned into a firework, and I knew that the head was pointing my way now. Panic spurred me on, but running wasn't easy. The plants were just too tightly-packed, and even though their stems and branches weren't woody at all, they were still capable of getting in the way.

There was only one thing I could do, and that was to dive down to the region where the insects lived, beneath the lowest leaves. There was a narrow space down there where even a man might crawl, if he'd a mind to. Doing snake-imitations is not usually my kind of thing, but when death is only a few metres away you have to improvise as best you can.

Flattening myself out, I tried to pull myself along with my arms and scramble with my feet, almost as though I was pretending to swim. It was pretty crowded at ground level, because the entire space was seething with panic-stricken insects that didn't know which way to run, but were totally committed to the project of getting somewhere fast. They were still shrieking their hymn of complaint from all sides. I hated the noise, but I could sympathise with the way they felt.

As I did my silly parody of the breast-stroke I could feel

the muscles in my back protesting. I could feel the sticki-
ness of my shirt, but couldn't make a guess as to how badly
I was bleeding. I took a little comfort from knowing that the
Isthomi were top-flight medical men when it came to re-
pairing bodies and making people immortal, and that they'd
already made me a promise that they'd wrought some considerable improvements in the quality of my flesh, but as
the pain built to an excruciating level that comfort seemed
to fade away.

It faded away even further when the question rose belatedly
in my mind as to why there was an enormous mechanical
praying mantis trying to destroy me in the Isthomi's own
back garden. The fact that it had been able to make its
grand entrance at all suggested that something was yet
again amiss in the state of Isthomia. If it was not, the Nine
would surely have managed to give us a little notice of im-
pending danger, even if they didn't have the heavy metal to
nip it in the bud.

As I continued crawling, I began to feel that I was in a
uniquely awkward situation. I had no idea where I was
going, and no way of knowing whether the monster mantis
was right on my heels. I had no weapon of my own and was
well and truly separated from Susarma Lear. The indigenous
insects didn't seem to want me in their underworld, and
didn't seem to want to get out of my way to ease my passage.
Fortunately, I had every reason to think that they were not
given to biting, stinging, or otherwise being nasty, though
the repulsiveness of their touch made their company quite
unpleasant enough. I imagined that they were tolerated in
this garish scheme of things because they pollinated the
flowers, but I couldn't help feeling that a tastefully designed
and suitably-programmed robot could have done the job
more economically.

I got to a place where even the space beneath the foliage became unbearably constricted, occupied by a tangle of what looked to me like surface-lying adventitious roots. They fanned out from a central stem, and I had moved into a closed V-shaped space, cornering myself. I had no alternative but to stand up, and was glad to find that the leaves above my head were fern-like, and that they parted easily. Unfortunately, their delicacy was compensated by profusion, and when I was drawn up to my full height they were still clustered above my head. When I looked up I could catch a glimmer of light filtering through the translucent foliage, but could see almost nothing.

The insects were quieter now, and when I rose to my feet the ones I had been disturbing with my snake-act decided that I was no longer a threat to their sanity and well-being. They gradually ceased their awful keening. I was able to stand still and listen.

I didn't know what kind of sound would be made by a mantis-dragon stomping through a giant's garden, but I figured that its progress would probably alarm the insects just as much as mine, and once I had ascertained that there was no cacophonous whistling in the neighbourhood, I came to the conclusion that I was relatively safe.

Because I wanted to see where I was, I decided to climb a tree. This wasn't easy, because there were no authentic trees in the place—merely overgrown bushes with limp branches. Nevertheless, the topmost parts of the canopy, which extended all of ten metres into the air to bask in the glow of the fifteen-metre ceiling, were borne aloft by relatively sturdy stems, and I was able to pick my way through the ferny stuff to a stem bearing a particularly solid leaf.

There was an insufficiency of decent footholds, and the stem swayed alarmingly when I shifted my weight. The pain in my wounded back didn't help, either, and I had a fearsome headache caused by a combination of shockwave concussion and screeching insects. But I managed to climb, drawing on those hidden resources of strength that our bodies prudently save for moments of terrorized hyperactivity.

When I got to a reasonable vantage point, with my feet on one leaf-stem and my hands clutching another, balanced as safely as I was able, I looked around—and promptly wished that I hadn't.

Big the monster mantis might be, but it obviously wasn't very heavy. Its great long legs were protruding in every direction—I could count ten of them now I could see the thing in all its hideous glory—and it was moving three or four of them at a time, finding new purchase wherever it could. It was coming over the top of the canopy, and it was already turning from its previous path to head straight for me, having caught a glimpse of me with its three remaining eyes the moment I stuck my head out into the open.

I wasted no time in clambering down—I jumped, half-falling and half-sliding through the thick vegetation. But with the ground still cluttered by the root-ridges there was no way I could hug the turf and crawl, so I ended up in a furtive crouch, trying to step over the ridges as fast as I possibly could, hoping to reach a space which I could share with the inhospitable insects.

One of the great pincers smashed down beside me, trying to stab rather than to grab, missing me by a margin that was far too small for comfort. There was a tearing sound from above as the other grabber began tearing at the foliage, trying to get a sight of me. I jinked to the left, then to the right, trying to confuse any extrapolation of my path its mechanical brain might be making, but it obviously got another brief sight of me because the hand came groping through the vegetation again, closing with a vicious snap no more than a dozen centimetres from my left ear.

The insect chorus was in full swing again now, filling my ears with raw sound lacking even that elementary aesthetic propriety that one might imaginatively credit to the last trump.

I stumbled over a root, but thrust myself instantly to my feet again, and ran on as fast as my feet could carry me across such disadvantageous territory. The arm reached out for me just once more, unsuccessfully, and then I suddenly found myself confronting an open space—a clearing where the only things which grew were no higher than the top of my boot. It was star-shaped, and maybe twenty or thirty metres across. When I saw it my heart leapt, as I realised that here was somewhere I could really run, but almost immediately it sank again as I realised that it was somewhere that the gargantuan predator could see me clearly as I ran, and get a clear shot with its flamer.

It was too late to change my mind—my legs had already carried me out into the open—but in trying belatedly to alter the direction of my charge I turned my ankle, and fell, rolling as I did so to look back at the thing which was looming far above me, its head seeming tiny now because it was so high, its legs lashing out in search of purchase so that it could anchor itself for one final, fatal grab.

I saw its swiveling head rotate and stop, so that two good eyes stared down at me, and I saw the barrel of the proboscis come into line as the arms pulled back, ready to thrust.

And then the thing stiffened, as though struck rigid by some inner convulsion. A curious shiver passed along its body, and then it collapsed, falling all in a heap like an unreasonably complicated puppet whose strings had been simultaneously sheared.

I shielded my face as it fell, and ducked towards the ground because I feared that it would fall on top of me and crush me, but its loathsome head came down to one side, missing me by a metre or more. I stood up again, and looked around—feeling slightly foolish, although I didn't know why.

Myrlin was standing on the far side of the clearing, with something on his shoulder that looked like a bazooka with a slender, solid barrel. Susarma Lear was by his side, looking uncannily neat and trim. She was still holding the crash-gun in her hand, and she used it to beckon me urgently.

"Come on, Rousseau!" she yelled, audible even above the sound of the insects. "Let's get the hell out of here!"

I picked myself up, knowing that I was filthy, ragged, and bloodstained, feeling as if I had just been stamped on by a giant boot. I limped across the open ground. The news that my life no longer seemed to be in imminent danger must have been transmitted to my hormone system, because all the adrenaline seemed to drain away, and my limping gait became a drunken stagger. I felt as though my legs had turned to rubber.

Incongruously, I fell over. I remember thinking, dimly but clinically, that I must have lost a lot of blood.

Myrlin shrugged the silent weapon from his shoulder and let it drop. He took three titanic strides forward and picked me up as though I were a rag doll. Then he threw me over his shoulder where the weapon had rested, and set off at a run.

Inexpressibly glad that someone else had finally taken responsibility for my poor battered body, I thankfully blacked out.

～6～

Inevitably, I fell straight into the grip of a dream.

I express it thus because that is precisely what it felt like. It was as if something had been there, forming and growing according to some inner process of its own, ready and waiting for whatever it was that constituted the essential *me* to lose its grip of consciousness. When I blacked out, it was as if a great cold pool of darkness sucked me in and gobbled me up, consuming me more completely than any mammoth-sized mantis-machine ever could have.

The sensation of falling didn't last long, and there was no jarring end, but I found myself suddenly alone, standing on an infinite plain as featureless as the surface of Asgard. The stars were bright in the sky, and I knew that a cold wind was blowing though I could not feel it on my skin. It was as though it blew straight through me.

I looked down at myself, and was unsurprised to find that I was a phantom—a pale, glimmering, translucent thing. My ghostly form was clad in a phantasmal tunic cut in a style which I associated with ancient Greece, but the cloth was torn and stained with blood and I knew that I had been mortally wounded by the thrust of some savage blade—a sword, or the head of a spear.

I was dead, and waited for my journey to the Under-world to begin.

There came to meet me, riding across the sky on a great night-black horse with shadowy wings, a woman in quilted armour. Her hair was very pale, but there was no colour in her, and I could not tell whether her piercing eyes were blue. I knew, though, that something was wrong, and that the imagery was out of joint, for surely this was a valkyrie come to carry some fallen Norseman off to the halls of Valhalla, whereas I had been slain without the walls of beleaguered Troy, and was destined for a very different kind of paradise.

When the night-mare landed beside me, and she reached down her tautly-muscled arm to lift me up, I raised my own hand in protest, as though to tell her to go away, but she only gripped my arm in hers, and pulled me to the saddle behind her, as effortlessly as might be imagined, given that I seemed to weigh almost nothing.

I had no time to discover whether I could speak my protest aloud, because the huge creature launched itself forthwith into the firmament, and carried us up into the starry night, where we grew in size so vastly that the stars seemed mere snowflakes gently flowing through the wintry air.

I looked down, expecting to be giddy, but there was no particular sense of height—it was as though I looked through a godly eye which could capture all Creation at a glance, and I saw what I took to be the whole great world of men, which consisted not of one meagre Earth and a handful of microworlds, nor even all the worlds of the galactic community, but something immeasurably vaster, growing even as I watched in a futile attempt to fill the limitless expanses of the infinite and the eternal. I was inexplicably unmoved by the incalculable profusion of it all, but while I watched, and the winged horse soared above the very rim of the cosmos, I saw patterns of change which worked in me like pangs of anxiety and knots of fear.

Despite the vastness of everything there was no detail which I could not comprehend, and I *might* have seen a single sparrow fall if I had not been so disturbed by other things that tormented my attention.

I saw a land all a-tremble with the paces of a giant hungry wolf, which led a pack of dire shadows to a feast of blood.

I saw a world that was a mighty twisted tree, ravaged by a blight which ate up its vitality from within, desiccating its foliage and shriveling its multitudinous fruit.

I saw a great ship whose hull was made from the growing nails of the coffined dead, whose sails were their silvered hair, riding on massive waves stirred by the roiling of a serpent greater than galaxies, its crew of skeletons armoured for war.

I saw a traitor with eyes like red coals, making magic to draw the shadowy wolf-pack to the field of slaughter.

I saw a monstrous army whose troops were made of fire, which marched like glowing lava from a wound in the fabric of time, its banners of lightning streaming proudly in the radiant breath of countless dying suns.

I saw a bridge like an infinite rainbow, extending from the world below to some other mysterious realm outside the range of my miraculous vision, its colours livid as it cracked and splintered, presaging in its shattering the death of all the gods, the desolation of that Valhalla where—after all—I did not really belong.

And I saw a face, which stared at me from the starry firmament, and knew it for the true possessor of that godlike sight I had borrowed for an instant. It was a face full of sorrow and concern, a face where mercy was mingled with wrath, whose sight could penetrate every atom of my being, every secret of my soul, and I knew that this was a god which men had made, and a god which had made man in his turn, and a god which now faced destruction, and was desperate enough to seek his heroes wherever he could find them, whether they belonged to him or not. . . ..

And then the god who held me in his guardian hand was forced to let me go, and I fell again, and fell, and fell, all the way back to consciousness.

⌃7⌄

I opened my eyes, and looked up into the ungodlike face of my old friend Myrlin. I was flat on my back and he was kneeling over me, peering at me with a measure of concern.

My back was hurting, but not so very badly. It was cushioned by something soft and yielding. I was slightly surprised to find that I was not in one of the Isthomi's healing eggs being quietly restored to full fitness, but it seemed to be a time for counting my blessings and a quick survey of the relevant referents assured me that my body was still in one piece and that my mind, so far as I could tell, was still my own.

I looked around, and saw nothing but grey walls. The ceiling was rather ill-lit and there was a distinct lack of furniture and fittings. Susarma Lear was sitting on the floor with her back to the wall, watching me, with less apparent concern than Myrlin. The upper half of her was clad only in a light undershirt, and I guessed that her Star Force jacket was what was providing my injured back with a modicum of comfortable support.

"Where are we?" I asked, hoarsely.

"Safe, for the time being," said Myrlin. "How do you feel?"

"Not so bad," I said. "Just had a hell of a dream, though."

"You'll be okay," he assured me. "The way the Isthomi have fixed us up, we heal quickly. The cuts and bruises won't trouble you for long."

I sat up, then reached behind me with tentative fingers to see what sort of damage I'd sustained. There was no moist blood, and the wounds didn't complain too terribly about being touched. I looked down at the colonel's jacket, and saw that it wasn't badly stained. I picked it up and threw it to her.

"Thanks," I said, as she caught it. She put it on, but didn't fasten it. She looked rather tired.

"Anything to drink?" I asked Myrlin. "Even water would do."

He shook his head.

I looked at the weapon which was propped up in a corner of the tiny room. "What is that thing?" I asked—unable to figure out how it had felled the dragon without so much as a bang, let alone a bullet.

"It's some kind of projector," said Myrlin. "I don't understand the physics, but it creates some kind of magnetic seed inside a silicon brain, which grows—or explodes—into something disruptive, wiping out most of the native software in a fifth of a second or so. It's a kind of mindscrambler, I suppose, except that it's for artificial minds instead of fleshy ones."

It was a gun that shot hostile software. The Nine were clever with that sort of thing. It crossed my mind, though, that it was a dangerous weapon to keep around the place. Presumably, it could be turned on the Nine just as easily as their enemies. I knew that they could trust Myrlin, but the thought of a Scarid regiment equipped with such weapons rampaging around the Isthomi worldlet was one that might make a lovely goddess frown.

"I don't want you to think that I wasn't impressed by the trick with the bazooka," I said, "but how the hell did the Isthomi manage to let that thing into their garden?"

"The Isthomi have problems," he answered. "Your dragon wasn't the only thing that went on the rampage around these parts. The attack was sudden and surprising, and the Nine's ability to oppose it was severely restricted by the fact that somebody had just switched the power off."

I looked at him, blinking to clear my vision and working my tongue over my salivary glands to try to spread some moisture around my mouth.

"You mean," I said, slowly, "that someone pulled the plug on the Nine's hardware?"

"Not exactly," he said. "I mean that as far as the Nine can tell, someone pulled the plug on the levels. All of them."

I hadn't quite recovered complete control of my faculties, so I stared helplessly at him for a minute or so. It was a fairly mind-boggling item of news. We knew that there were at least two thousand levels, each one containing anywhere between two and ten independent habitats—the equivalent of ten thousand habitable worlds. Some of those habitats were dead, others decaying, but most of the inhabited ones depended to a large extent on power drawn from the walls—power that was presumably generated by a starlet: a huge fusion reactor in the core of the macroworld.

Switching off that power wouldn't mean that all the lights in Asgard had instantly gone out. Most of the habitats had bioluminescent systems that could run for a while without input, and some of the inhabitants had technical know-how adequate to the task of generating their own electricity to feed electric lights. Nor did it mean that every information-system in the macroworld had crashed; a great many of them would have some kind of emergency system to prevent their going down. The Nine would have had support systems to preserve themselves against accidents

53

even of that magnitude—but the vast majority of their subsidiary systems and peripheral elements would have run on power drawn from the central supply. When the central supply went off, the Nine would have had to shut down ninety percent of their capacity—and if they had a physical invasion to fight off at the same time, they must have been stretched to the limit. They'd already been weakened twice by serious injury to their software; now, it seemed, someone or something was bent on smashing up their hardware. The software saboteurs of inner Asgard had turned Luddite.

"You're saying," I said, to make sure I had it right, "that in order to attack the Isthomi, someone has cut off power supplies to the entire macroworld."

"Not necessarily," he said. "I think we can rule out coincidence, but it's possible that the enemy simply had advance notice of the power being cut off, and decided to plan his assault on the Nine accordingly. The power-cut might be part of a grander campaign. If there really is a war going on in Asgard's software space—and the Nine are convinced that there is—that war seems to be getting hotter by the hour."

I looked around again, at the blank walls. Susarma Lear was still watching us, her eyes attentive despite her tiredness.

"We're sealed off in a hidey-hole," Myrlin told me. "The Nine have put solid walls around us; hopefully no more robot dragons will be able to find us, let alone break through to us. The real fight is going on back at the living-quarters. We three were lucky to be away from there for various reasons—we may yet turn out to be the sole survivors. The Nine don't have many robots with fighting capability, nor any substantial store of weapons. The Scarida will fight, and the scions with them, but they may be up against overwhelming odds.

"It will take time to get power back to all the peripheral systems, and to get vehicles like the ones which brought you here on the move again. They'll send something to pick us up when they can, and will activate the wall to talk to us once they're certain that it won't attract hostile attention. They didn't know what they were up against when they last got a message to me, and they didn't dare take too many chances."

"Well," I said, "so much for our fond hopes that the software damage they sustained in their contacts was just an unhappy accident. We really are caught up in a shooting war, and it doesn't look as if the guys doing the shooting are prepared to consider us innocent bystanders. If the power doesn't come back on. . . ."

I remembered that Sigor Dyan had casually mentioned the total size of the Scarid population. There were tens of billions of them, without counting the members of races they'd displaced or conquered. Their tinpot empire had already been laid low by the plague that the Tetrax had loosed on them; now the power supplies which they believed to have been left to them by their kindly ancestors were suddenly gone. People were going to die. Lots of people. If the power didn't come back on soon, every single habitat in the macroworld would be under threat, not merely of major disruption, but of total destruction.

"All in all," I murmured, "I'd rather be in Skychain City." All the systems in Skychain City had been installed by the Tetrax. The power-supply from the starlet had been switched off in levels one to four for a *very* long time.

"Why are they so determined to get us?" asked Susarma Lear harshly. "What makes *us* so interesting that someone would send something like that electric stick insect after us?"

Myrlin looked over his shoulder at her. "I don't know," he said soberly. "I'm not sure it's anything personal. It looks to me like a chain reaction. Something down below was aroused from inaction by the attempt the Nine made to explore the information-systems in the Centre. At first it probably acted reflexively, but now it seems to be organising a strategy of destruction. The entity that contacted Mike while he was interfaced with the Isthomi is probably something different—if it really was appealing for help, it may have brought us to the attention of its enemies."

"If your computerized buddies hadn't gone prying," she said, "we wouldn't be in this mess." She was still nursing aggressive feelings towards poor Myrlin.

"They wouldn't have embarked upon that kind of exploration if it hadn't been for what they learned from us," he answered mildly. "And I wouldn't have attracted their attention by buggering up one of their systems if *you* hadn't been chasing *me* with murderous intent."

"So it's all my fault?" she said. Her voice was still cutting, but I thought that she had some appreciation of the irony of the situation.

"No," I said. "You explained it to me before, remember? It's all my fault, for not taking Myrlin in and keeping him safe until your assassination squad arrived. I suffered a momentary lapse of generosity, and the consequences of my churlishness have imperiled the whole bloody universe. Lack of charity is a terrible thing, don't you think?"

"Well," she said, "I'll say one thing for you, Rousseau. Things are never dull when you're around."

"Not my fault," I assured her. "Just lucky enough to be living in interesting times."

The wall behind her suddenly lit up, presenting the appearance of another room, with that same silly chair and that same impeccable goddess. She was back in her thin dress, but I didn't ask her to change it. One Star Force colonel at a time was quite enough for me.

Her face was not shaped to show anxiety or stress. Indeed, it radiated imperturbability. I wasn't sure whether that meant that everything was under control, or whether things were so awful that the Nine didn't dare to let on.

"I will try to get a vehicle to you in a short time," she said. "I am sorry that it has taken so long."

"Have you zapped all the mantises?" I asked.

"The robot invaders have all been disabled or sealed in," she said. "Many systems are still non-functional, and the damage is severe, but the situation is now stable."

"We can't rely on it remaining stable," I said. "We've got to get ready to make our bid for the Centre as soon as possible. We can't just hang around, getting battered by one attack after another."

"I agree, Mr. Rousseau," she said, with a little smile that I didn't entirely like. "We must waste no more time before making a serious attempt to find out precisely what is going on in the deeper levels, and how we can rectify the situation. The power-supply must be restored, and the hostile force which is attempting to destroy us must be neutralised."

"Is the robot transporter safe?" asked Myrlin. He meant the one that the Nine had been building for our journey to the Centre. If we'd lost that, we might not have any alternative but to sit tight and wait for the next attack.

"It is safe," replied the Nine, "but it may be irrelevant. There is another way to make the attempt to reach the Centre, and this attack leads us to believe that we must attempt both, as soon as we possibly can."

My first thought was that they meant the deep elevator shaft which had brought us down from level fifty-two. It wasn't much use for our purposes, partly because it didn't go down much further, and partly because it wasn't big enough to carry a heavy armoured vehicle. But then I realised that without the central power-supply, the elevator wouldn't work. I also realised that without the central power-supply to open doors and activate other elevators, it was going to be a very tough job getting a truck down into the bowels of the macroworld—even if we could discover a route.

"What better way?" Myrlin had asked, while I was realising all that.

"Through software space," she replied.

"You already tried that," I pointed out, "and were nearly destroyed. Besides, *we* can't go through software space, can we?" It occurred to me even as I was saying it that it might be an unwise remark.

"Yes you can, Mr. Rousseau," she told me. "And if our present understanding of the situation is correct, we think that the entity which has made contact with you intends that you should."

Ever since humans first began building so-called artificial intelligences, people had looked forward to the day when it would be possible to duplicate a human mind in machine-based software. In the home system, our software scientists had not yet come close to the skill and sophistication that would be necessary to carry out such a task, but other races in the galactic community had got closer—the manufacture of Myrlin's personality by the relatively unsophisticated Salamandrans was a pointer to the possibility that such play with artificial minds was only just over the conceptual horizon. The Nine had begun their own existence as simulations of the personalities of another kind of Isthomi, incarnate in flesh very little different from mine. The entity which had contacted me while I was interfaced with the Isthomi had, it seemed, made some kind of biocopy of its own programming to colonise the software space inside my brain. The Isthomi had made similar biocopies of themselves in order to equip the fleshly scions which they had made. If that could be done, so could the reverse process: the Isthomi could make a machine-code copy of my personality within their own systems, including the extra software that the contact had foisted on me.

It was only natural, I realised, that the Nine had jumped to a conclusion which hadn't even occurred to me—that when my mysterious contactees had cried for help, they had expected that help to come through software space, not through the cracks and crevices of Asgard's massive macroarchitecture.

I was by no means convinced that it was a good idea.

"You want to make a copy of me," I said. "And send that copy out into software space to run the gauntlet of whatever it was that blasted you when *you* tried to reach the Centre."

"We have reasons for thinking that you might be able to succeed," she assured me.

"Maybe so," I said. "But I'm not so sure that I want to send a software copy of myself to the Centre. In fact, I'm not so sure that I want any software copies of me hanging about *anywhere*. You might have got used to being nine persons in one, but I'm accustomed to there being just *one* of me. I think I told you that I'm an essentially solitary person. I really wouldn't like to have to use numbers to distinguish each of my particular selves from all the other ones. It just isn't my style."

"Why do you think that Rousseau might succeed where you failed?" asked Susarma Lear, cutting through my objections as though they didn't much matter. I had a nasty suspicion that they didn't.

"We are now forewarned of the dangers and difficulties," replied the image in the wall. "We believe that we can now make software *personas* far less vulnerable to destruction than the exploratory probes which we have previously sent out. Such *personas* can be encrypted, written in an arcane language."

"What's an arcane language?" I asked, feeling slightly foolish.

But Susarma Lear was nodding, as though she understood. "It's what the Star Force—and everyone else—uses to protect its systems from hostile software," she said, airily. You can never be absolutely certain that you can keep tapeworms out of your machinery, so you have to make sure that the damage they do to your software once they're there is strictly limited. What you do is to keep your own information in a special code—an arcane language—which is immune to the spoiling that the tapeworm tries to do. If you're clever enough, the invader programme is unable to crash your system or bugger up your data. Right?"

She had turned to look at me, but now she turned back to face the avatar of Athene who looked, in some ways, uncannily like her. I had never thought of Susarma Lear as a dead ringer for Athene; personally, I thought that she was infinitely more convincing as a valkyrie.

"That is substantially correct," admitted the woman in the wall.

"Why can't you just make copies of yourselves in your arcane languages?" I asked. "You know how to operate in software space, and I don't. I'd be no use to you at all."

"There are two reasons why that may not be so," she answered calmly. "First of all, we are very much creatures of Asgard. Even though we have spent an unspecifiable span of time in a state that we now recognise as virtual imprisonment, cut off from the other native systems of the macroworld, we are nevertheless adapted by our nature and evolution for interaction with those systems. That gives us a certain amount of power, but it also makes us vulnerable. It would be very difficult for us to translate ourselves into a form in which we could protect ourselves from attempts by other native systems to attack and injure us.

"Your *persona*, on the other hand, has evolved in very different circumstances, and is quite alien to the native systems. If the analogy will help you, you might think of yourself as a virus to which Asgard has no inbuilt immunity, whereas we—even in mutated form—are viruses to which there is already a great deal of inbuilt resistance."

It wasn't particularly flattering to be compared to a virus, but I could live with it.

"And the second reason?" I queried.

"Medusa's head," she replied succinctly. I was glad to see that Susarma Lear now looked completely at a loss.

"You think I've got a weapon," I said, uneasily. "You think that whoever called for help gave me something I could use to answer the call: the biocopy."

"If it is a weapon," she told me, "it is probably a weapon which can only be used in software space. The biocopy itself is probably useless, save perhaps as a source of information. But if we can re-copy it along with the rest of your *persona*, encrypted to the best of our ability, then it may become a powerful instrument—perhaps as potent as Medusa's head."

As a source of information, whatever the entity had put into my head was certainly lacking in clarity. As messages from the world beyond go, my remarkable dreams were themselves pretty heavily encrypted. But I wasn't about to accept too readily the theory that I could be a hotshot superhero, if only I were rid of my body.

"What about you?" I said to Myrlin. "What have *you* been dreaming about lately?"

He looked at me in a way that told me he had already been interrogated on that point. He also looked slightly sad. "Nothing," he told me. "If whatever was out there tried to transcribe a biocopy into my brain, it seems that it didn't take. We're not certain about 994-Tulyar, but you were the only one who made any kind of conscious contact, and it looks as though you were the only one able to take what they tried to give us."

"Oh *merde*," I said, with a kind of sigh I didn't even know I could produce.

I had the distinct impression that I had once again been drafted into a war which I wasn't entirely enthusiastic to fight. As usual, though, it seemed that I might find it very difficult to say no.

ᐱ**8**ᐟ

When we got back to the place which the Nine had fixed up to provide living quarters for their guests and their scions, we were able to see the real extent of the carnage.

The village that they'd fitted out for us consisted of forty dome-shaped constructions, which were arranged in neat rows in one of the few open areas that this worldlet had, under a twenty-metre sky lit by electricity. The sky was still lit, but dimly, and there was a suggestion of twilight about it. At least half of the forty domes had been damaged by explosive blasts, and the streets were littered with debris. It wasn't easy to tell how many robot invaders had run riot in the village, but I counted eight carcasses made of assorted plastics and metals. Five seemed physically undamaged, and I could only assume that the Isthomi's scions had wiped out their internal programming with weapons like the one they had given Myrlin.

Nobody paid any immediate attention to our arrival. A few scions were still busy picking up dead and wounded humanoids on stretchers, ferrying them to doorways in the grey walls. Inside the labyrinth of tunnels the Nine would have set out a whole series of egg-shaped flotation tanks, where the wounded could be placed until they could do whatever was possible to mend the broken bodies. I knew they were clever, and could sometimes resuscitate people who would have been deemed dead by human or Tetron doctors, but the miracles they could work were limited, and most of the injured were in a very bad way. I looked at a

63

couple of Tetron scientists—only recently arrived on this level—who were being hustled away by the scions. I was morally certain that nothing could be done for them. They were dead, and far beyond recall to the land of the living.

There were several Scarid soldiers making a show of patrolling the streets, carrying the weapons they'd brought down with them when they came to negotiate a treaty with 994-Tulyar. They looked a little glazed, as one might expect of men who'd just come through an unexpected battle, but they also looked a little bit pleased with themselves. It wasn't hard to guess why. They were fighting men who'd recently been humiliated by the cunning of the Tetrax, forced to accept that their glorious empire was impotent to deal with the *real* universe. They'd come down here to learn their lesson from the all-wise and non-violent conquerors, but when the attack had come, it had been they and not the Tetrax who'd known how to react. They'd been able to put up something of a fight, and were proud of that.

As I looked around at the shards of the robots which had served as the assault force, I quickly realised that the Scarid soldiers couldn't have contributed much to their actual defeat—those which had been stopped by firepower had been hit by missiles much bigger than the ones the Scarida had in their popguns. Some looked as if they had blown themselves to smithereens, probably because something had been done to their internal software that had fatally disrupted their power-plants. It was the Nine who'd done all the hard work, despite their peaceful inclinations.

We tried to find some task with which we could usefully occupy ourselves, but the urgent work was virtually complete, and the less vital clearing up could safely be left to the Nine's robot servitors. I looked around for someone I knew, but the only person I recognised was an ashen-faced

Jacinthe Siani. I didn't particularly want to talk to her, but she obviously thought that it was a time for old grudges to be set aside. She came over.

"What happened?" she said. "I thought the war was over."

"That was the war between the Scarida and the inhabitants of Skychain City," I told her, drily. "This seems to be a war of much greater magnitude, fought by armies more peculiar than the ones we galactic innocents are used to. I doubt that there'll be any further call for your services as a traitor."

She didn't seem inclined to trade insults. She was frightened, and she seemed rather forlorn. She was human enough, and beautiful enough, to have made weaker men than me feel sorry for her, but I had no difficulty in resisting the urge to put my arm around her shoulder. She'd done me too many bad turns, and no favours at all.

"The sooner I can get back to the surface the better," she said. "I don't like it down here."

"It's a long, long way to the surface," said Susarma Lear, who had even less sympathy for the Kythnan woman than I did. "And the elevators are out. I don't think any of us will be going home for quite a while."

Jacinthe clearly hadn't thought of that. She looked at me forlornly with her big dark eyes, genuinely pathetic.

"It's a disappointing universe, isn't it?" I said. The words didn't come out quite as cruelly as I intended them. When it came to it, I just hadn't got the heart to turn the knife in the wound.

Jacinthe turned disconsolately away, and wandered off in the direction of the battered dome that was all the home she had left.

I went to look more carefully at one of the disabled robots.

It didn't much resemble the giant mantis that had come after me—it was more like a bipedal armadillo, with guns instead of arms. It seemed to me to be rather crudely-designed, as killing-machines went. This hadn't been a subtle attack, or a particularly well-prepared one. I inferred that the sudden hotting up of the war had taken the opposing forces somewhat by surprise. No doubt they were improvising as best they could, but they didn't seem to have had much time to prepare for the battle they'd just fought.

I asked one of the scions about the casualty figures. She didn't have an exact count, but she told me that more than three-quarters of the Scarid contingent had been killed or seriously injured, and that half of the Tetrax were dead. I asked about 994-Tulyar, but all she could say was that he wasn't among the casualties they'd collected.

"Did they get Finn?" asked Susarma Lear, and when the scion told her that Finn was still unhurt she said: "Pity." I knew how she felt.

Someone else had seen us, and came over to talk; the scion went on her way. I didn't recognise the newcomer immediately—it's not that all Tetrax look alike, but it does take an effort of mind to pay attention to their distinguishing characteristics instead of the mere fact of their obvious alienness.

"Mr. Rousseau?" he said, uncertainly. He obviously had the same difficulty with human faces.

I realised belatedly who he was. "673-Nisreen?" I countered. For the first time, I felt a small thrill of relief. Here was one survivor I could be glad to greet.

He gave me a slight bow. "I arrived here only a few hours ago," he said. "I know almost nothing of the situation. But I am unable to locate 994-Tulyar, and if he is not found—or if he is found to be dead—I shall be in effective authority over the remaining Tetrax here. I have spoken to the entities that you call the Nine, and they have told me that it may be some time before they can restore communication with the upper levels. I am, as you know, a biologist, and although I have been an ambassador of sorts to your own species, I am not at all sure where my responsibility now lies. I cannot tell what ends we might work toward, or what means we might employ in the hope of their attainment. It is said that you have a special intimacy with the curious intelligences that are native to this level, and you have been here longer than anyone else that I might consult. Will you advise me, Mr. Rousseau, as to what you think will happen now, and what we should do?"

I'd never been asked for advice by a Tetron, and had never expected to be. 994-Tulyar would never have condescended to ask me the time of day. In the one substantial conversation I'd previously had with Nisreen he'd seemed as patronising as any of his race, but I'd obviously made a favourable impression on him. The only problem was that I didn't know what advice I could give him. I thought fast, trying to come up with something that might justify his trust.

"The first thing the Isthomi will need to do," I improvised, "is to organise some kind of defensive strategy in case this happens again. I don't know who it was that sent those murder-machines against us, but we'd be foolish to assume that they've shot their bolt. The Nine know relatively little about weaponry. Scarid weapons are fairly crude, and your scientists may have more useful expertise—you'd better find out what help you can offer to the Isthomi in that regard."

Nisreen nodded. "I see," he said. Then he waited— obviously I'd only whetted his appetite for more.

"The Nine already have a lot of problems on their

plate," I said. "As you probably know, they've suffered a couple of disasters of a less crude nature. Now the attackers have switched off the power supply to the entire macroworld, the Nine will want to find out very quickly who they are and how they can be stopped. The people who stand to suffer most in the short term are the Scarida— you'll have to talk to whoever's left in charge of their team, to impress upon him that their interests and ours are identical. We don't want them deciding to do something silly, and we'll certainly need their fighting men if there's another attack."

He nodded again, but didn't even bother to provide a verbal prompt. He just waited for more. He was certainly expecting a lot from a mere barbarian. I decided, albeit a little reluctantly, to tell him about my plans.

"The Nine have been building a robot vehicle for me," I told him. "It's designed to cross more or less any terrain, even through a reducing atmosphere. I intend to take it down through the levels, relying on the Nine to find me a route. We need to find out what's happening down there— and whether we can do anything about it. If turning the power off was as simple as throwing a switch, then it can probably be turned on again with equal ease, and if one side in this war had a pressing reason for wanting it switched off, the other side will presumably want to switch it back on again. If the people fighting this war thought that the Isthomi were impotent to intervene, they probably wouldn't have tried to destroy them—which implies that there's something we can do, even if we can't quite figure out what it is."

I could tell from his expression that this wasn't quite the kind of advice which he had in mind, so I stopped. There really didn't seem to be anything else I could say. I decided that there was no point in bringing up the Nine's other bright idea about sending a task-force of personality-copies through software space. I still didn't like the idea very much, and I wasn't at all sure that I was prepared to volunteer.

"I'm sorry, Nisreen," I finished, "but I can't tell you what you ought to do. If there's a role for you to play in all this, you'll have to work it out for yourself."

Nisreen studied me carefully, his face quite inscrutable. "I am indebted to you, Mr. Rousseau," he said. "We all face a difficult time now, and I must undertake to make what contribution I can, as my duty demands. I will talk with you again, if I may. But may I ask one more question?"

"Go ahead," I said, generously.

"We once discussed, very briefly, various hypotheses regarding the possible nature of Asgard and its relation to the many star-worlds which support humanoid life. Can you tell me which hypothesis you now consider to be the most likely?"

It was a very good question.

"When I talked to you last," I said, hesitantly, "I suggested that Asgard, or something like it, might have been the common point of origin of the gene-systems which are scattered around the galactic arm—that the builders of Asgard had been behind the seeding of the star-worlds which produced the galactic community. The other hypothesis which I had in mind was that its task might be to gather genes from star-worlds, using the habitats in the levels to store and transport them. I can't say that I'm any nearer to deciding whether either or both of those speculations is true—but I have to admit that every day that passes seems to lend more credence to an idea that Colonel Lear favours: that Asgard is some kind of fortress, heavily armed and armoured to protect the life-systems to which it plays host against some hostile and destructive agency. If that's true, it seems to have already come near to failure in that purpose, and to be getting nearer all the time.

"In fact, if Asgard is a fortress, it looks very much as if the fortress has been breached, and that the entire macroworld is in danger—and not just from the slow death that will follow the power failure. We must at least consider the possibility that if this war is being waged by invaders of Asgard against its defenders, their objective might be its total destruction."

I could tell that I'd impressed him. He looked very serious indeed—as well he might, considering that I'd just suggested to him that if the mysterious battle raging around us were to be won by the wrong side, ten thousand life-systems might be blown to atoms.

The Tetrax had always posed as great believers in the brotherhood of humanoid races, and were never slow to preach to others the doctrine that truly civilized people outgrew the folly of war. I had always had my doubts as to whether the likes of 994-Tulyar really believed that, but 673-Nisreen seemed less of a hypocrite. For him, the thought that the godlike beings who had built Asgard were involved in the kind of war where multiple genocide might qualify as a minor incident must be a very shocking one.

As I had said to Jacinthe Siani, it was beginning to look as if we were inhabitants of a rather disappointing universe.

❦ 9 ❦

My own room was mercifully undamaged, and I was glad to be able to retreat into it at last. I removed my bloodstained shirt as carefully as I could, and inspected the damage with the aid of a couple of mirrors. The cuts seemed superficial, and were already on the mend—I obviously healed quickly now that the Isthomi had tuned up my body. I knew, though, that it was no good being potentially immortal if I persisted in such hazardous activities as standing next to explosions and playing hunt-the-human with fire-spitting dragons. What it would take to kill me, I didn't know, but I didn't particularly want to test myself to the limit.

I asked the dispenser to give me something for my headache, and was pleased that it was still capable of obliging me, even though the something was only aspirin.

Then I sat down on my bed, and relaxed for a little while.

A little chime sounded, but it wasn't the door or the phone. It was the Nine's discreet request for permission to ennoble my walls with their active presence.

"Okay," I said, tiredly. "I'm decent." It was a slight exaggeration, but I knew that the Nine didn't care.

They presented me with the customary female image, but she was standing, and she was wearing the Star Force uniform. It would have been in keeping with the propriety of the moment if she'd had a regulation flame-pistol in her belt, but even the Nine weren't prepared to go that far for the sake of mere appearances.

"I haven't made up my mind yet," I told her. "And

71

although it probably testifies to the limitations of my imagination, I actually care far more about what's going to happen to this sad bundle of meaty bones than the heroic exploits of any non-carbon copy of its animating spirit."

"I would like you to tell me about the dream," she said calmly.

"The dream?"

"When you were unconscious in the aftermath of the incident in the garden you had a dream."

"Is it important?"

"I believe so. It is the means by which the biocopy in your brain is making itself known to you. The imagery is undoubtedly borrowed—much as the image which I present to you now is borrowed—but there seems to be a serious attempt at communication going on . . . perhaps a desperate one."

I told her as much as I could remember. She winkled out a few extra details by shrewd cross-examination. I was glad I'd had the aspirin.

"The core of the dream," she assured me, "is the series of images which you saw in approaching its climax. The wolf-pack; the diseased world-tree; the ship of the dead; the traitor; the fiery army; the bridge; the face of a god."

"I don't think it means anything in particular," I told her. "I know where it comes from. It's part of another myth-set from my homeworld—the set from which we borrowed the name Asgard. The things I saw were all part of the build-up to *Gotterdammerung* . . . the twilight of the gods. It's not unnatural that I should try to represent a war inside Asgard in those terms: the gods versus the giants in the ultimate conflict. How else could I try to get to grips with what's happening here? It all comes out of something I read once, just like Medusa."

"There is no way that the biocopy can make itself known

to you save by exploiting the meaning of your own ideas," she told me. "It must speak to you by means of an imagistic vocabulary which you already know. It cannot invent—it can only select, and inform by selection. This notion of an ultimate war between humanoid gods and giants might be an invention of your own mind, but it must also be information given to you by the new programme that has colonised your brain. We must treat it as a message, and try to understand what it is trying to tell us."

I shrugged. "Okay," I said. "There's a war going on. How does it help us to characterise the sides as gods and giants? Does it tell us which side is which? Does it tell us who's trying to destroy us, and why? And does it tell us what we're supposed to be doing about it?"

"Perhaps it does," she replied with infuriating persistence, "if we can read the imagery correctly."

"Read on, then," I said impatiently.

"The primary personalities involved in this conflict are not humanoids," she said. "In fact, they are not organic beings at all. They are artificial machine-intelligences—akin to ourselves, but more complex and more powerful. The organic beings which created the Nine were making machine-minds in the image of their own personalities. The machine-intelligences engaged in this war were designed for different and more ambitious purposes. Some, we must presume, were designed to operate and control the macroworld—these are the entities that are represented in your dream as the gods of Asgard. The others, we suspect, must have been created for the specific purpose of attacking the macroworld and destroying its gods—these are the beings that are represented in your dream by the giants. They may not actually be intelligent—perhaps they are destructive automata akin to the things you call tapeworms—but they seem to be capable of wreaking considerable havoc.

"If we are to take the imagery seriously, the plight of the gods is desperate—the forces which are attempting to destroy them are pressing forward their attack. That attack threatens all the organic life in Asgard—represented by the world-tree of your dream—but some organic life-forms may have become instruments of the attackers—that is what is signified by the image of the traitor. Somehow, there is a vital function to be served by organic entities, although we cannot be sure whether that function is to be served by actual organic entities or by software *personas* which mimic them. That there is a heroic role to be played we are convinced, but where and how it must be acted out, we are not certain."

It was one hell of a story, but it seemed to me to be reading an awful lot into a dream. I had the uncomfortable suspicion that whatever I'd dreamed, the Nine would have been able to find a similar story in it.

"I don't know," I said, dubiously. "It would be more convincing if the supposed gods had managed to leave their message in Myrlin's brain as well as mine—or Tulyar's. Has Tulyar turned up, by the way?"

"No," replied the avatar of Athene. "We are unable to locate him."

All of a sudden, that sounded rather ominous. Even with most of their peripheral systems switched off, the Nine should have been able to locate a Tetron, living or dead, if he were somewhere in their worldlet. I remembered that although the Nine had been unable to find any evidence that any alien software had been rudely injected into Myrlin's brain, they had been more cautious in passing judgment on Tulyar.

"What do you deduce from that?" I asked, anxiously.

"It is difficult to know what to deduce," she said, hesitantly, "but it is possible that some kind of programming was transmitted into Tulyar's brain, and that it was not the same programme that was biocopied into you."

"By 'not the same' you mean to imply that it wasn't put there by the same side, don't you?" I said.

"It is a possibility," she admitted.

"You think Tulyar might have had something to do with the attack?"

"It is a possibility," she said again. There were, alas, far too many possibilities.

"Why has the war suddenly heated up?" I asked. "The macroworld must have been in trouble for a long time, to judge by the condition of the upper levels. Hundreds of thousands of years—maybe millions. How come the power got switched off *now?*"

"The balance of power between the beleaguered masters of the macroworld and the destructive entities must have been in a state of equilibrium," she said. "Perhaps there had been a stalemate, lasting for what you would consider to be vast reaches of time. Perhaps, on the other hand, there has been ceaseless conflict in the regions below, with the balance of power constantly changing. We suspect that this worldlet, and others like it, may have been sealed off at some time in the distant past, and that we were deliberately hidden away, for our own protection. When we were provoked by what we learned about the existence of the greater universe to begin more adventurous exploration of the deep levels, we may have unwittingly exposed ourselves to the hostile attention of the destroyers. Our first encounter with them did, indeed, come near to accomplishing our destruction.

"The second contact, in which you played a crucial role, probably began as an attack by the 'giants,' but this time there was an intervention by the masters of the macroworld, possibly undertaken at considerable risk to themselves. They may well have saved us from destruction, but they could not establish any direct communication. Only you managed to make any kind of sense out of the contact, and I believe that you were quite correct to construe what happened to you as a desperate plea for help.

"Perhaps as a result of their foray in our support, the masters of the macroworld have lost further ground to their enemies, and that is why the power-supply has been interrupted. We erected what defences we could against attacks in software space, but—perhaps foolishly—had not expected anything so crude as a straightforward physical assault. The surprise factor gave the destroyers a temporary advantage that they should never have been allowed, and we have all suffered in consequence. We have now sealed our boundaries against further attacks of either kind, but we do not think that we are sufficiently powerful to resist indefinitely the assaults of a superior power. Steadfast defence may not be adequate to the demands of the situation. That is why it seems imperative that we make contact with the masters of the macroworld, and why you must give us what aid you can."

It was a pretty fine speech, and a good story too. With the fate of the macroworld hanging in the balance, how could I possibly be so churlish as to refuse to have myself copied? On the other hand, if the battle was taking place on such a monumental scale, how could an insignificant little entity like me possibly make any difference?

I didn't ask. I already knew what the Nine had elected to believe. Supposedly, I had a weapon: Medusa's head. There were, of course, little problems like not knowing what it was, how to use it, or what it was supposed to do, but I had it. At any rate, the Nine *believed* that I had it.

"You live in software space," I said, rather feebly. "It's your universe. I can't even imagine what it would feel like to be a ghost in your kind of machine, or what the space I'd be in would look like—if look's the right word, given that I'd presumably have an entirely different set of senses."

"That would depend entirely on the kind of copy which was constructed," she said, eager to reassure me. "Any copy would, of course, have to retain the essential features of your personality. Let us say that it would need to be topographically identical, but that there would still be a great deal of flexibility in regards to its folding. The manner in which you would perceive your environment would depend very much on the pattern of your own encryption. Just as the world that you presently inhabit is to some extent contained within the language that your culture has invented to describe it, so the constitution of the software universe depends on certain features of the language that allows you to operate there—but with a much greater degree of freedom.

"Humanoid languages are easily translated into one another because the preconditions of the physical world exert such strong constraint on the descriptions you construct. Software languages are much less easy to translate one into another because the physical attributes of software space are not so rigidly pre-defined. That will be to our advantage in two ways. We desire to encode the copy of your personality in a language as esoteric as possible—one which will superimpose upon the perception of software space a way of 'seeing' radically different from that of the entities which would try to destroy you. It will also enable us to equip your software *persona* with perceptions that will make some kind of sense to you in terms of your present sensorium. Do you understand that?"

The easy answer to that question was a simple "no." No doubt the Nine could have given me a much more elaborate and painstaking explanation, given time, but I was sure that they were hurrying for a reason, and I felt that I had to do the best I could.

"What you mean," I said, carefully, "is that software space hasn't much in the way of properties of its own. Its properties are largely imposed by the programmes that operate in it, which can define it more or less as they like. So, if you turn me into a computer programme, the way I'll experience myself—and the world which I seem to inhabit—will depend very heavily on what kind of programme I am. Whatever arcane language I'm written in will determine the kind of being I seem to myself to be, and the kinds of beings which other programmes will appear to be."

She nodded enthusiastically, and smiled, having slipped back into her silent-movie mode again. "That's correct," she said.

"Do I get a choice?" I asked. "Can I be whatever I want to be?"

"That's not possible," she replied, amiably. "There are powerful constraints on what we can do. But we must produce a copy which will be able to operate effectively; there is no need to fear that your copy will perceive itself in fashion which is radically alien."

"That's a relief," I muttered, not entirely reassured. The word "radically" might conceal a multitude of complications. I noticed that we were now operating on the assumption that I was going to go ahead with the scheme.

"Trust us, Mr. Rousseau," she said. "Please."

There was something about the way she said it which implied that any trust I pledged was going to be severely tested in time to come. She had already admitted that she was by no means certain that her conjectural account of the situation was correct, and I had the feeling that there might be more in her speculations than she had yet cared to reveal.

I stared into her beautiful face, which seemed to have softened slightly around the jawline. Her eyes were big and dark and pleading, and she was putting on a more convincing show than Jacinthe Siani had. She was doing her level best to present me with a sight to melt any human's heart. I'd never had much to do with women, and the specimens with which I'd lately come into contact were the kind that help one to build up a fair immunity to feminine charms, but I am only human.

At least, I was *then*.

"But what happens to me?" I asked stubbornly. "This flesh and blood thing with a sore back and a growing anxiety about the dangers of going to sleep?"

It is possible," she said, "that the ultimate fate of your fleshly self might depend on the success of your copy in making contact with the masters of the macroworld. But in any case, the plans which you have made may proceed as you wish."

I had already guessed that she was going to say something like that. *Think of it not as losing a body, but gaining a soul.*

I felt a pressing need to stall her, and perhaps to be on my own for a few minutes, to give the matter further thought, though I could see no alternative but to bow to the pressure of inevitability. I could have told her to switch herself off, but for some reason I didn't want to have to stare at the blank wall where she'd recently been.

"Are you sure you can make me tough enough to get by?" I asked her. "To judge by what I've just seen, software is very easy to kill."

"The weapon which you saw Myrlin use is one which can only be fired from real space," she said. "The entities which inhabit software space are by no means toothless, but they will not be able to project disruptive programming into you quite as easily as that."

Which didn't mean, I noted, that they couldn't shoot de-structive programming into my software self—only that they'd find it difficult.

"Is there a constructive version of the weapon?" I asked her—on the spur of the moment, because the thought had only just occurred to me. "Can you transmit programmes through the air with a magic bazooka, instead of having to use wires the way our mysterious friends did when they in-jected Medusa into my brain?"

"In theory, yes," she said. "But it is difficult in the ex-treme. The receiving matrix, whether organic or inorganic, would have to be *very* hospitable to the incoming programme—otherwise the effect would be purely disrup-tive. An alien programme really needs a physical bridge of some kind, like the artificial synapses that were in place during your contact, if it is to be efficiently intruded."

It was interesting as a hypothetical question, but it didn't really connect up with the immediate problem, which was to reconcile my reluctant mind to the prospect of a peculiar duplication.

"I need some fresh air," I told her. It was a stupid thing to say, because the air outside my igloo was not in any way fresher than the air within—I just felt that I needed to get outside.

It turned out to be a stupid thing to do, too, because no sooner had I opened the door than John Finn stuck the business end of a needler into my windpipe and told me that if I didn't do exactly as he said various vital parts of my fleshy self would be scattered hither and yon amidst all the unpleasant debris which already littered the area.

"Look, John," I said, patiently. "I'm aware of the fact that you have a little learning difficulty, but even you must remember that we've been through all this before. If you wanted to exercise your death-wish, you could have done it this morning."

"Personally," he said, "I'd just as soon kill you, but I'm assured that for some stupid reason you're considered to be quite valuable. No other hostage will do as well. Just behave yourself, and your freaky friends in the walls will make sure that no harm will come to you. No mindscramblers, no clever tricks at all—they'll just give us what we want, rather than risk any harm coming to you. See?"

"What do you want?" I asked, flatly.

"We want to get the hell out of here before those killing machines come back. We want that armoured truck the magic Muses have been building for you."

While he talked he urged me into action. He came round behind me but he kept the needler jammed into my neck, so that if anything unexpected happened he could blow my brains out without any delay at all. I allowed him to shove me where he wanted me to go.

"Whose bright idea was this?" I asked.

"Just keep walking," he told me. The light was still gloomy, and there appeared to be nobody else about, but once we were away from the domes a couple of other armed men fell into step with us. I wasn't in the least surprised to see that they were Scarid soldiers. They were the only people around who were stupid enough not to realise that they were safer behind the Isthomi's defences, and that once outside them there'd be no way of getting all the way back up to level fifty-two.

"You were bloody lucky to get away last time," I told him in a low voice. "The colonel's been regretting that she didn't shoot you ever since. She'll be ever so grateful for a second chance."

"She isn't going to get it," he said optimistically.

There was a car waiting for us in one of the Nine's labyrinthine tunnel-systems, and I gathered that one of Finn's friends had already made it clear to the Nine exactly what they wanted done. The Nine had apparently decided to play ball. I could only assume that they really did consider me a uniquely valuable asset, and were prepared to hand over the robot transporter rather than risk my being damaged. It also occurred to me, though, that the Nine seemed to have lost interest in the transporter and in the possibility of getting my fleshly self to the Centre by conventional means. So much for my plans going forward as I had intended.

"I suppose I should have asked the Nine to take care of that bug you planted," I remarked, as I took my place in the front seat of the car. "You'd never have figured out that I was so important to the Nine if you hadn't listened in."

He sat directly behind me, never relaxing the pressure of the gun on my skin. It reminded me very strongly of the first time I had visited this level, when Amara Guur had treated me in exactly the same fashion. The Nine had supplied Guur with a weapon that wouldn't fire, looking after me even though I wasn't nearly as valuable then as I seemed to be now. It would be too much to hope, though, that the weapon which Finn had now was useless. Someone had probably tried it out during the morning's skirmish.

Another Scarid came out of the shadows to join us in the

car, making three in all; they seemed desperately morose. They were all officers, but none of them seemed to be assuming command. I was puzzled, because I couldn't see why they'd consent to taking orders from a jerk like Finn. I could understand how they might feel very much out of their depth, and how eager they must be to get home. I also knew how this kind of strong-arm tactic was very much their way of doing things—but it still didn't add up that they would turn in their hour of need to a no-hoper like Finn.

My puzzlement increased when a fourth figure came towards us from the direction of the village. It was Jacinthe Siani. She, of all people, should have known better than to get involved in this, but she was under Scarid orders now, and they probably hadn't given her a choice. She took her place behind me.

"If you try to take the transporter out," I said, speaking in parole rather than English so that the Scarids could understand, "you'll very likely run into more of those things that attacked us. The Nine have defences now—here you're safe. You could be going to your deaths if you try to go up through the levels, even if you can figure out a route."

"Shut up, Rousseau," said Finn, also in parole. "We know what we're doing."

I shut up. After all, I told myself, why the hell should I care if John Finn and a bunch of Scarids wanted to get themselves killed? There was no reason at all—except that I didn't want them to take my transporter. If I was ever going to get to the Centre, I'd need it.

It didn't take long to get to the manufactory where the Nine had been putting the robot together. It was even less well-lit than the residential area, and it seemed unnaturally still and silent. All the mechanical arms projecting from the walls were idle, mostly drawn back and folded. The transporter stood in lonely isolation in the middle of an open space. It seemed to be finished, and it had the special gleam of something brand new and never used. It was much bigger than the truck I'd used for work on the surface, but it didn't look so very different. Most of its elaborations were internal—although it did have a turret on top with three different guns mounted on it.

"We're going to drive to a certain place," Finn told me, "where we have a couple of friends waiting. Then we're going to give you something to hold—it'll be a bomb, but don't worry about it going off, because I'll have the detonator safe about my person. Once we're out of the habitat, with Asgard's nice thick walls separating us, we'll be safe, and so will the bomb. We'll never see one another again."

I reflected that it wasn't all bad news.

Finn and I climbed into the front seat of the transporter, while the Scarids got into the cab behind us. There was a set of manual controls, although the robot was really intended to drive itself, or to interface with another silicon-based intelligence. The manual controls had been designed with a human driver in mind, though, and followed a common stereotype. I had no difficulty in starting up and driving off into the tunnel ahead. It was only just wide enough to accommodate us, but there was no problem in following it. I didn't have to make any turnings—the Nine had obviously been apprised already of the destination that Finn had in mind, and they were happy to open up a route that would take us directly there.

There didn't seem to be any point in further exercising my limited powers of persuasion, so I did exactly what Finn wanted me to do, taking comfort from the fact that I was probably driving him to the doorstep of his appointment with death.

When we stopped, I couldn't see anything much outside

except for a circular space with an empty shaft above it. I assumed that it was a platform that could lift the truck up to the next level—maybe several levels.

We remained in the cab while Finn carefully taped a cylindrical object to the part of my back that was most difficult for my hands to reach. It was no bigger than Myrlin's thumb, but if it really was an explosive device—and I was quite prepared to believe that it was—it could do a lot of damage.

Finally, Finn ordered me to step out on to the platform. It wasn't until I got down that I saw the other waiting figures, away to the rear. They came slowly forward, and I got two shocks, the bigger one hard on the heels of the smaller.

The first shock was that they weren't the Scarid soldiers I had been expecting—they were Tetrax. The second shock was that the one who led them out was 994-Tulyar. I knew him well enough to be sure that I could recognise his features, even though he had an expression on his face that I had never seen before. He looked at me with glittering eyes that somehow caught the light shining from the walls. With the empty, unlit shaft above me, I felt as though I were standing in a pool of darkness.

"They told me you were missing," I said to him. When he made no reply, I realised that something was very wrong. I wondered briefly whether I could possibly have made a mistake in identification, but I knew in my heart that I hadn't. This was Tulyar—or, perhaps, *had been* Tulyar. I wondered whether the folklore of the Tetrax featured such beings as zombies.

He still didn't say anything. He just stared at me, with what seemed to be an animosity beyond my understanding. But then he glanced sideways, quickly and furtively, and I felt a sudden flood of relief. I was sure that he wanted to kill me, but he knew that if he did, the Nine would strike back at him.

I realised that there was more to this crazy affair than the feeble-minded desire of a handful of Scarid bully-boys to get back home. Finn wasn't just trying to escape. He was playing the mercenary again, figuring that he might get a greater reward from a grateful Tetron high-number man than he could expect from Star Force justice or the hospitality of the Isthomi.

I looked sideways at one of the Scarid officers. "You think this guy is going to take you to meet your ancestors, don't you?" I said, with faint disgust. "You don't intend to go up—you're going down."

"Shut up, Rousseau," said Finn, unceremoniously. He took the gun-barrel away from my neck for the first time. "Get over there, out of the way."

"John," I said, feeling at least a quantum of genuine concern for him. "It's not Tulyar. I know it looks like Tulyar, but he wouldn't pull a stunt like this. Something else has colonised his brain—it got into him when he tried to interface with the Nine and got caught up in their close encounter with something dangerous. He's been taken over—possessed by some software demon."

It was no good. Finn and the Scarids wouldn't believe me, and I couldn't really blame them. They didn't know about Medusa's head, and they couldn't begin to understand what kind of war was being waged inside Asgard. 994-Tulyar didn't move or speak. He just waited. I wondered if I could appeal to his better nature, thinking that perhaps the real Tulyar was still in there somewhere, still potentially able to speak or think or act if only he could figure out the way.

"Tulyar?" I said. "Do you know what's happening to you?"

It was a stupid question. This wasn't just a misguided Tetron following some suggestion that had come to him in a dream; it was another kind of person entirely. Whatever had intruded upon the Tetron's mind had done a far more comprehensive wrecking job than the thing that had got into mine. Assuming that what was in me wasn't just a delayed-action seed of destruction, I was a lucky man. Looking at Tulyar, or what had once been Tuylar, gave me a little more confidence in the supposition that I had been drafted to the side of the angels.

"Do as you're told, Rousseau," said Finn coldly, his voice grating with evident strain. "Just get out of the way, and everybody will be safe and sound."

Uncomfortably aware of the thing taped to my back, I moved away from the circular platform and into the mouth of the tunnel through which I'd brought the truck. My gaze flicked over the three Scarids and the two other Tetrax— neither of whom, I was oddly glad to see, was 673-Nisreen. They were all showing signs of anxiety, but they all seemed committed. I knew how sensitive the Scarida were about the question of their hypothetical ancestors, who had suppos- edly laid on the power that had recently been switched off, for the benefits and greater glory of the Scarid empire. I knew, too, how strong the Tetrax were on matters of obliga- tion, and how nearly impossible it would be for men placed under Tulyar's orders to defy him, even though they could plainly see that there was something very weird about him.

"Let them go, John," I said to my fellow human, figuring that the brotherhood of man ought to count for *something*. "Stay here."

His reply was brief and obscene. He'd never liked me, and that dislike had got in the way of his common sense on more than one occasion.

"You don't know what you're doing," I said, looking now at Jacinthe Siani.

"Do you?" she countered. "Does any of us?"

There wasn't time to have a debate about it. The Scarids were already loading themselves into the rear part of the cab, and whatever it was that was wearing Tulyar's body followed them. The remaining Tetrax got into the front seat, while Finn went last of all. The door shut behind them.

As the platform began to sink into the depths, carrying the truck away into abyssal darkness, I put out a hand to steady myself against the wall, feeling suddenly very weak.

Eventually, the wall lit up, and there she was, looking as sprightly as ever.

"You can remove the explosive charge now, Mr. Rousseau," she said. "It's quite safe."

"Considering that your power is supposed to be not far short of godlike," I told her, "you're pretty damn useless every time it comes to the crunch." I figured I was entitled to feel a little resentful.

"I must apologise for not warning you that it was about to happen," she said, "but as you know, they were able to listen in on our conversation."

"You knew what they intended to do?" I said.

"Certainly."

"And you deliberately let them get away?" I was annoyed, having jumped to the conclusion that the Nine were really quite glad to wave goodbye to my transporter, on the grounds that it would narrow my options to the point where I'd have no choice but to go along with their plans. But I'd misjudged them, as usual.

"When we realised that something had been implanted in the Tetron's brain—and that it was not akin to the programme sent to colonise your own brain," she said, equably, "we could only conclude that it had been intruded by the enemy. We had then to consider what the best thing was to do with a possible enemy in our midst. Had it shown any hostile intention, we would of course have destroyed it, but in fact it seemed to want only to escape. It seemed to us to be an opportunity not to be missed, though of course we were concerned to conceal that judgment."

"Opportunity?" I echoed. "Opportunity to do what?"

"As you guessed yourself," she said, "the biocopy which has apparently taken over Tulyar's body knows how to get into the deeper levels, despite the apparent difficulties of so doing. We must assume that it knows how to reach its destination."

"How the hell does that help us? He's got the only transport!"

I have to admit that she was very patient with me. "The reason that it took time to construct the vehicle," she pointed out, "was that it was very difficult to programme the machines which built it. Now that they know how to do it, they can construct a duplicate in a matter of hours. We had quite sufficient time to equip the vehicle which they have stolen with a device whose model I'm sure you remember."

Enlightenment dawned.

When the Tetrax had sent us into the levels to carry plague into the Scarid empire, they had thoughtfully equipped our boots with a device which leaked an organic trace, easily followed by an artificial olfactory sensor. That device, detected by John Finn, had led the Scarida down to the world of the Isthomi just in time to throw me in at the deep end of the crucial moment of contact. I had always assumed that it was 994-Tulyar who had been responsible for the trace.

Now, it seemed, the tables had been turned. Finn, Tulyar, and their allies were laying a trail which might lead the corporeal me—and a few friends—all the way to the Centre.

The boot, for once, was on the other foot.

⌁ 11 ⌁

At this point in my story, I fear, the narrative flow becomes slightly confusing, for reasons which the reader may already have figured out.

I must admit that I did not anticipate any considerable confusion myself, even when I realised that I had tacitly given way to the Nine's demand that I be copied. I had interfaced with the Nine on several previous occasions, and I supposed that this special interfacing would not feel significantly different. At the end of it, I knew, that creature of flesh and blood which I thought of as the real me would simply get out of the chair and continue with my real life. The fact that there would be a ghostly entity drifting through the vast labyrinth of silicon neurons and optical fibre sinews that was Asgard's diffuse "brain" which would also think of itself as Mike Rousseau, sharing all my knowledge, all my memories, and all my hang-ups, did not strike me as an item of any great relevance to the flesh-and-blood Rousseau's future experience of self.

It turned out that I was wrong.

Exactly how and why I was wrong will become clear in due time, when my story—perhaps it would now be more appropriate to say *stories*—approaches its—or *their*—climax. For the moment, I need only say that the person who is recording this story has two sets of memories to draw upon, and must—if the story is to make sense—describe two independent series of events.

It might perhaps be easier for the reader if I were simply

to shift one of the continuing narrative threads into the third person, possibly referring to the software copy as "the other Rousseau" while retaining "I" for the flesh-and-blood appellant which held the sole entitlement to it until the crisis in my affairs made division essential. But that would misrepresent to you the nature of the entity that is now telling the tale, and I cannot help but feel that such a move would be misleading, if not tantamount to self-betrayal.

I must, therefore, ask my readers to forgive me for exposing them to the possibility of mild disorientation. From this moment on, the perpendicular pronoun will be applied without discrimination to two very different entities—but given the fact that those two persons embarked upon very different adventures in what appeared to them to be very different worlds, I do not think it likely that the reader will ever be in doubt as to which of the two is the referent of any specific passage of prose. In the interests of simplicity, I shall present the two narratives in two series of alternating chapters, although there is a certain arbitrariness about the parallels thus produced. Software time is no more like clockwork time than software space is like the kind of space that is to be found in a cupboard or a cosmos.

✦ 12 ✦

There seemed to be a sky, which was grey and overcast, heavy with roiling clouds racing before an erratic wind. The clouds seemed so low as to be barely out of reach, as though I might reach up my hand and feel the cool, moist breath of their passage.

The sea was a duller grey, the colour of lead, and although it was no less troubled, its waves trod the paces of a dance that was far more leisurely than the light fantastic of the clouds. There was very little spray, and it seemed as though the ocean were made of some more glutinous compound than mere water, as if it were thickened by dissolved slime.

The ship on whose deck I found myself standing was a curious vessel, more like a sketch of a ship than a real entity of wood and iron. It seemed to me to have been modeled on a poorly-remembered image of a Viking longboat, with a red-and-gold patterned sail billowing upon its single mast, and forty pairs of oars moving in an uncannily-precise rhythm, quite unperturbed by the wayward rise and fall of the waves.

There were no visible oarsmen; the oars projecting from the flank of the vessel seemed to work entirely by them-selves, growing organically from the hull. The deck, which extended most of the length of the ship, was lined with silent warriors, huge and blonde, with horned helmets and armour of gleaming bronze. They carried spears and broad-swords, but the swords were sheathed. They stood immobile, like carved chessmen waiting for a game to begin. There was no possibility of mistaking them for real people; like the boat, they seemed to me more like entities in an animated cartoon.

The prow of the ship was shaped into a curious figurehead with anchored snakes instead of hair, and the snakes moved sluggishly as the bows dipped and rose with the swell. Beneath this image of Medusa, carried high above the waves, there was a sharp spur, which gleamed as if it were made of steel. Had the gorgon's head been attached to a body, it might have been riding upon the spur as if on a broomstick, and the implication of that absent form gave the spur a gloss of phallic potency.

The bridge at the hind end of the ship was a paltry affair, consisting of a raised deck protected only by an ornately-carved railing. There was a wheel controlling the rudder (though that seemed to me to be as anachronistic as Medusa or the ramming-spur), but no substantial wheelhouse.

I found myself gripping the rail very tightly, bracing myself against the rolling and yawing of the ship.

I had never been on a ship before—the closest I had ever come to an ocean was driving along the shore of one of the icebound seas on the surface of Asgard. That had certainly been grey, but the way the bergs floated in the shallow water had made it seem utterly serene, while this water, in spite of its apparent viscosity, had an obvious inclination to the tempestuous.

I felt, paradoxically, that I should have been seasick, or at the very least uneasy and uncomfortable. In fact, I did not. The best attempt I can make to describe what I felt like is to say that I felt mildly drunk—at precisely that pitch of intoxication where the befuddled brain seems disconnected from the body, anaesthetised and incipiently dizzy. I felt unreal, and that seemed to me to be an utter absurdity, because I knew full well that from the viewpoint of my parent self I was unreal. I had been copied into a dreamworld, but there was surely a ludicrous impropriety in the fact that I felt like a dream-entity.

Had I, I wondered, any instinct to survive in my present form? Had I sufficient strength of will to continue to exist from one moment to the next?

Oddly enough, that was a frightening thought. I did not feel like myself—and knew, indeed, that in a sense I *was not* myself, and that there was another, very different self walking away from the interface in the solid world of Asgard's physical mass. And yet, I was all the self I had, and I knew that this splinter-consciousness, however drunk with its own absurdity it might be, was an entity capable of being destroyed, and that such destruction would be no less a death than would one day overcome my fleshy *doppelganger*.

I looked around, and found that I was not alone. Mercifully, I was not the only volunteer who had come forward to undertake the high road to the Centre while his solid self attempted the low. Myrlin was watching me. He needed no rail to assist in his support, but seemed quite steady on the deck, riding its movements with casual ease. He seemed no bigger here than he had in the flesh, but that had always been quite big enough—in the flesh he was a two-metre man with a lot to spare, and his ghost-self here retained the same appearance of hugeness. But he did not look real. As I met his gaze, which was as curious and as puzzled as my own, I had to admit that he looked no more authentic than the silly ship on whose deck we stood. He too was more like a cartoon image than a real man.

He was dressed in armour, which was black and shiny, as if lacquered or highly polished. Its sections were moulded so accurately to his body that it looked like an exoskeleton.

He was bare-headed, though, and his colouring was subtly altered. His hair was lighter, although it tended more to auburn than blonde, and his eyes were so bright in their greyness as to seem almost silver.

In his right hand he was carrying a huge sledgehammer, whose head must have weighed at least a hundred kilos, although he seemed to feel not the slightest discomfort in bearing it. He had a large sword in a scabbard at his belt. Despite his seeming inauthenticity, I could not help but feel that this was the role for which fate (as opposed to the cunning Salamandrans) had shaped him. As a barbarian warrior he was somehow convincing, whereas the real android, set against the backcloth of Skychain City and the deeper levels of Asgard, had always seemed awkwardly out of place.

I looked down at my own body, to see what I might be wearing, and found that I was armoured too, though in a slightly different fashion. It was as though I had garments knitted from fine steel thread, which seemed both very strong and very light. Like Myrlin's, my armour was lacquer-bright, but my colour was a dark red, the colour of burgundy wine.

I hoped that I wouldn't present too tempting a target, if and when things warmed up.

Looking down, I could see the backs of the hands that gripped the rails. I felt a slight rush of amused relief as I realised that I knew them. I knew them like the backs of my hands . . . although I was not aware that I had ever paid particularly scrupulous attention to them in my former life. Perhaps it was only in my mind—a reassurance, which I needed, that I was still who I was, really and truly.

I had a sword and a scabbard of my own. The weapon looked big and cumbersome, but it didn't feel that way. It wasn't only that it felt light—it felt as if it had a strength of its own, and perhaps an innate skill, which I only had to liberate. This was a magical sword, and that status seemed no more absurd than the fact of my existence here, for this was a world where all was magical, where the laws which regulated other spaces and times could be modified at will, if one only knew how and had the faith that one could do it.

I had another weapon too—a big longbow, leaning upon the rail beside my hand. It didn't fall or bounce around when the ship lurched, and I guessed that it, too, had a competence of its own. There was a quiver of arrows behind my shoulder, Robin Hood style.

Bring me my bow of burning gold, I quoted silently, with drunken eloquence. *Bring me my arrows of desire!* And then, in more sombre mood: *Things fall apart; the centre cannot hold; mere anarchy is loosed upon the world. . . . The blood-dimmed tide is loosed, and everywhere the ceremony of innocence is drowned. . . .*

I turned again to look at the third person who was standing on the small raised section of deck. She had moved to stand by Myrlin, and was watching me studiously. It wasn't Susarma Lear, though she had some of Susarma's features. I had seen her many times before, looking out at me from her crazy looking-glass world, always behind an invisible but solid barrier—not really there at all.

Now, she was really here. Or, to be strictly accurate, I was "really" there.

Her dark hair was still worn long. It hung, straight and sheer, almost to the middle of her back. She was all Amazon now, though, in armour like mine in style, but burnished dark gold. Her eyes were brown, but like Myrlin's eyes they had an inner glow that made them seem bright, as though they were radiant with heat. She was carrying her own bow,

as tall as she was, and her own quiver of arrows. She had a
sword, too, but she didn't seem unduly burdened. She did
look real—though that was undoubtedly a consequence of
my knowing that she really belonged here. She was the
Nine, and she didn't need to become a caricature to take
the appearance of Pallas Athene, warrior goddess—the role
was already hers, custom-made.

I took my hands off the rail, and stood upright, slightly
surprised to find that I could do it.

"You chose this," I accused her. "We could experience
this according to any scheme of interpretation—any framework of appearances that we cared to import. Why didn't
you give us Star Force uniforms and flame pistols? Why not
an armoured car and a road to drive it on? We could have
felt at home there. Why this fantasy . . . this fairyland?"

"Do you remember what happened to Amara Guur when
you fought him in the flower garden?" she countered. "Do
you remember why he couldn't fight effectively?"

I remembered. Unlike me, he'd never been in low-gee
before. When the fight started, his instincts took over, and
all his reflexes were wrong. He was betrayed by his own
skills.

She saw that I understood. "This isn't the world you've
always known," she said. "If I were to make it look like that
world, you'd be forever trying to act as if it were. Here, you
must act on this world's terms. We have a great deal of
latitude in converting our experience into pseudo-sensory
interpretations, but we don't have complete freedom. The
constraints this world exercises on the way you can see and
manipulate it are weaker than the constraints of the world
where your other self lives, but there are constraints. There
is an actuality here, which must be accepted in order to be
dealt with."

"Yes," I said, "but this is silly."

"On the contrary," she assured me, gravely. "It may seem to you to be absurd to build a world of experience out of bits of ancient mythologies and literary fantasies with which you had contact in your youth, but it is the perfect strategy for the circumstances. Those fantasies had real meaning for you once, and still do, although you have put them away as childish things. There has always been a private world within your mind—a refuge which offered relief from the oppressive solidity of the world of material objects. That world reproduces the kind of dominion that your personality has within your corporeal body—a power which still has limitations, but lesser ones. The magical world of your ancient myths and folklore fantasies arises out of an attempt to map the properties of the mind onto the properties of the spatial universe. Software space really is that kind of universe, where the personality holds that kind of dominion.

"You are now in a world which can best be understood—which can only be understood—in terms recalling the ideative framework of myths and fantasies. My borrowing may seem unduly confused, but the confusion is inherent in your own memories and your own mind, which can draw with careless abandon on all kinds of source-materials. The point is that these experiences can and do make a kind of sense to you—you are *at home* here, and when the time comes to act, you will be able to draw on resources other than the reflexes which you learned in order to operate in the material world—resources which are far less likely to let you down."

"Less likely?" I queried.

"There are no guarantees, Mr. Rousseau. You still have to learn to draw upon those resources, and make the most of them. We are embarked upon a journey into great danger, and we will surely meet enemies. I cannot tell how powerful they may be, or how clever, but they will certainly oppose us with all the strength and cunning they can bring to bear."

I put my hand on the hilt of my sword, gingerly, not knowing what it would feel like. It felt solid enough, but I knew too much to find that feeling of solidity reassuring. I reminded myself that it wasn't really solid. Nor was the ship. Nor was I. Nor was the whole vast world in which I was adrift.

"I thought you copied us into an arcane language, so that the hostile software couldn't get at us," I remarked. "Come to think of it, I thought there were good reasons why you couldn't copy yourself, so how come you're here?" The horrible suspicion began to dawn on me as I spoke that I might have been lured into volunteering for this mission on false pretences.

"What you see before you," she said, with a disarming smile, "has more in common with one of my scions than with the ninefold being which formerly employed this appearance to speak to you. I am not so much a copy as a redaction. I have no more power here than you or Myrlin, and I strongly suspect that I may have less. I still believe that you have weapons other than the ones with which I have provided you, and that when the time comes you may find a way to import extra power into the appearance of the gorgon's head which I have added to our arsenal. It is important that you understand this; you may look to me for explanations, but when the battle begins, I am no more powerful than you, and probably less."

"You'd better give us those explanations," I said, with a hint of bitterness. "Now I'm here, I have the feeling that we haven't gone into this deeply enough in our hurried conversations of the past few days."

"We are encoded in an arcane language," she said. "It will not be easy for destructive programmes of any kind to attack us—especially if, as I hope, the invaders of Asgard are unintelligent automata. But we must assume that whatever forces are arrayed against us will have some power to react to our presence and adapt to it, with a view to destroying us. I think that we must expect our enemies to break into the frame of meaning that we are imposing upon software space. They will appear as monstrous irruptions of various kinds—I cannot tell what precise forms they will take, but in order to attack us they will have to formulate themselves according to the patterns that we have preset. They will, in effect, have to translate themselves into the symbolic language which we have adopted—a language based in your imagination."

"I have a depressing feeling," I said, "that you're telling me that the things which are trying to kill me are going to do it by turning themselves into the stuff of my worst nightmares."

"That is a neat way of putting it," she conceded with irritating equanimity.

"And our friends, if we have any?" Myrlin put in. "They too will have to intrude themselves, in much the same way?"

"If we receive any help," she agreed, "it will follow a similar pattern of manifestation."

I looked at the deck where the silent soldiers were arrayed, preternaturally still.

"What about those guys?" I asked.

"Automata," she said. "Non-sentient programmes, very limited in what they can do. But they will help to defend us when the time comes, and if we are fortunate we may not have to face anything more adept than they are. The enemy may not find it easy to dispose of them."

I had the suspicion that she was being deliberately optimistic. While we were talking I had grown more accustomed to my bizarre surroundings. I was beginning to acquire a feeling of belonging here. It was as though that peculiar fellow who had elected to make his living as a snapper-up of unconsidered technological trifles in the desolate caves of upper Asgard had all the while been nursing an *alter ego* compounded out of the fascinations of his infancy: an all-purpose hero equipped to fend off nightmares and confront the gods on their own terms.

It's sad, in a way, to be forced to acknowledge the desperate lengths to which the human condition forces us to go, within the secret confines of our inmost souls, in search of solace and wish-fulfilment. But I guess our private fantasies are no more unique than our faces, and partake of no more artistry.

In another way, though, our capacity for fantasy is a hopeful thing, because it reassures us that whatever the cold and empty universe does in its mindless attempt to crush our vaulting ambition and make us see how small and stupid we really are, we can mould something better out of our common clay, and rise from our galactic gutter to contemplate the stars.

I stood up straight, staring past the gorgon's head at the empty sea ahead of us, and wondered what kind of fabulous shore it was that we were trying to reach.

⋏ 13 ⋎

I came out of the interface with the sensation of waking from a dreamless sleep. The filaments had already withdrawn from my flesh, and I was slumped in the chair.

Susarma Lear bent over me as soon as I opened my eyes, and for once her own eyes were warmed with faint concern. It seemed that she was getting to like me just a little, despite the fact that I was not cast in the Star Force's best heroic mould.

"You okay, Rousseau?" she asked.

I breathed out, and felt the inside of my mouth with my tongue. It was a bit fuzzy, with the merest hint of an unpleasant taste.

"Sure I'm okay," I told her. "You ever hear a document complain about being put through a photocopier?"

Her eyes hardened again. "You're a real wit, Rousseau," she said. "You know that?" I knew it, but it didn't seem polite to agree, given that she sounded so unenthusiastic about it.

"How's Myrlin?" I asked, peering round the edge of my hood at the other occupied chair. He was coming round too, and he put up a hand to signal that he was adequate to the task of getting up and getting ready for the next step in our campaign.

There was no rush; now that the Nine's robot arms were programmed, they could put a new truck together more quickly than would have been humanly possible, but that still wasn't quite the same as waving a magic wand and saying the word of power. In the real world, these things take time.

I got out of the chair and left the room, heading back home. I intended to use up a precious hour or so doing absolutely nothing—not even thinking, if I could possibly avoid it. I thought I could. I wasn't keen on having company, but the colonel came with me. There were obviously things on her mind.

"I still don't understand," she said, "why the bastards didn't call on me. They must have known what was happening, even if they couldn't stop it themselves. I could have plugged Finn."

I hadn't had the time or the inclination to fill her in on the whole thing. Clearly, the Nine hadn't taken pains to explain it to her either.

"It was a set-up," I told her, tersely. "The Nine wanted them to take the truck. We think they might be able to lead us to the Centre. Whatever got into Tulyar's brain during the software skirmishing seems to have sole tenancy now, and I guess it has a mission of its own to complete. It may not be entirely *compos mentis,* and there's a chance that it isn't very intelligent, but it does want to go somewhere. We're going to follow it."

"We?"

"You said you wanted to come. Changed your mind?"

"Hell, no. Anywhere out of here will look pretty good to me. But are you sure that you know what you're doing?"

"No," I said, succinctly. "But there's nothing much to be gained by staying put, is there? I'd catch some sleep if I were you—in fact, if I were you, I'd consider myself very lucky to be able to catch some sleep without wondering if some clever nightmare might gobble me up and wake up in my place."

She looked at me suspiciously. "You think you might end up like Tulyar? You're afraid that something got into your head, too, and might be planning to take over?"

"So far," I told her, "I feel as though I'm in sole charge. The Isthomi figure that I got some kind of donation—a weapon for my software self to use—but they think that its only function as far as I'm concerned is to feed information into my dreams. We're hoping that the software which got to me was sent by the good guys, and that they're gentlemanly enough not to do me any permanent damage—but there's no way to be sure just yet."

"If you turn into somebody else," she said, with a less-than-wholehearted attempt at levity, "what would you like me to do about it? Should I shoot him?"

"Well," I said, "I guess it all depends whether you like him better than me. But if you can stand him, I'd like you to look after him for me. Someday he might want to give my body back, and I'd rather it wasn't all shot up."

It says something for my state of mind that this faintly surreal conversation sounded perfectly normal. I wondered if I might already be losing my grip, and suppressed a small shudder as I remembered the bleak stare in 994-Tulyar's eyes. If I ever looked like that, I'd try to avoid mirrors.

"Why do you think Tulyar—the thing that's in Tulyar's body—is heading for the Centre?" she asked. "If the easiest way to get there is the way your *alter ego* is going, through software space, why are the enemy trying to do things the other way about, sending their copy through real space?"

That was a good question, and I'd already asked it of the Nine. "We probably won't know until we get there," I said. "But the way the Isthomi have it figured, the builders were humanoid—pretty much like you and me, now that the Isthomi have massaged our quiet DNA into toughening up

104

our bodies. They created artificial intelligences to control Asgard: man-made gods, much more powerful than themselves. Maybe they didn't entirely trust the gods they made, or maybe they were fearful of exactly the kind of invasion they seem to have suffered, but for one reason or the other they may have reserved some key controls for purely mechanical operation. The Isthomi believe that there are some switches down there which can only be thrown by hand. Their guess is that when the invaders got the upper hand, the builders sealed off the Centre to protect those switches, and that it wasn't until the moment of contact, when they made a biocopy of one of themselves in Tulyar's brain, that the invaders finally got themselves a pair of hands—or, given Tulyar's authority and the gullibility of the Scarida, several pairs of hands."

She thought about it for a moment or two, and I could see that she didn't like it. I could hardly blame her. It had far too many wild guesses in it to suit me.

"These hypothetical systems which need mechanical operation," she said, testily. "What exactly would they be?"

I shrugged.

"Well," she said, "they obviously don't include the light-switch, do they?"

"Apparently not," I said. "Unless Tulyar isn't their only pair of hands. Maybe he's got cleverer hands than the guys who switched off the lights. On the other hand. . . ."

I stopped, wondering whether it was really worth going on with the game of make-believe.

"Go on," she said, tiredly. She was obviously wondering the same thing, but she wasn't about to leave the sentence dangling.

"On the other hand," I went on, "It might have been the other side which switched out the lights. Maybe Tulyar's gone to switch them back on."

She studied my face carefully. We were out in the open again now, almost back on my own doorstep, and unless I invited her in the question-and-answer session was reaching its end. She had one last play to make.

"What you're telling me," she said, "is that you don't really know which side we're on. We don't know who the invaders are, or what their purpose is, any more than we know who the builders are. And we have no way of knowing for sure which are the good guys and which are the bad guys."

"That's about the size of it," I said. "We have to go after Tulyar with an open mind. The only problem is, I opened mine a bit too wide. I don't know what the hell is happening in this goddamn war—but I'm no longer in a position to dodge the draft."

She decided to let me go, and left me standing on my doorstep while she went on to her own little igloo, presumably intending to follow my advice and get some rest. But my plans to put in a little quiet time were not to be allowed to run smoothly. 673-Nisreen had been waiting for my return, and I could hardly shut the door in his face.

"Mr. Rousseau," he said, in that scrupulously polite manner which brooked no opposition, "may I talk to you?"

"Sure," I said, wearily. "What is it?" I didn't invite him in, because I had a sneaking suspicion that it might be difficult to get rid of him. While we stood outside, I figured, it should be obvious to him that ours was to be just a passing encounter, not to be too long extended.

He was pretty quick on the uptake, and came straight to the point.

"I have received orders from 994-Tulyar," he said. "They were delivered to me after he quit this level."

"And what do the orders say?" I asked.

"That I am to do everything possible to detain you here, and to sabotage the Isthomi systems if I can."

I raised my eyebrows. "I infer from the fact that you're telling me this that you have no intention of carrying out the orders," I said.

"The Isthomi have told me that 994-Tulyar has been taken over in some way by an alien personality. They say that you can confirm this."

I nodded, slowly. "I think it's true," I said cautiously.

"In that case," he said, "I would like to accompany you when you go in pursuit."

I was astonished. High adventure wasn't the Tetron style, and the Nine must have told him that he would probably be a lot safer here than down below.

"Why?" I asked.

"It is a matter of duty," he said.

"I would have thought that your duty was here, looking after the rest of your people."

His small dark eyes glistened in the faint light as he blinked. His wizened monkey-like face seemed strangely forlorn for a brief moment.

"I can do no 'looking after,' Mr. Rousseau, as I think you know. In other circumstances, it is true, the obligation placed upon me would be to learn everything I can from the Isthomi, which might be of value to my people, but I have thought about the way things stand, and I believe that a different course of action is demanded."

"So you want to come with me—to the Centre." I was still having difficulty believing it.

"If things remain as they are, Mr. Rousseau, I will never regain contact with my people. We are in the depths of the macroworld, surrounded by enemies. The only hope there seems to be for our salvation is that you, your brave colonel, and your giant friend will somehow find a way to rectify the power-loss. 994-Tulyar, or whatever alien entity now uses his body, may try to prevent you. It would not be honourable for me to stay here while you undertake such a mission. I must go with you."

"673-Nisreen," I said, hesitantly, "you're a scientist, not a fighting man—not even a peace officer."

"Are *you* a fighting man, Mr. Rousseau?"

It is sometimes necessary to come face-to-face with unpalatable truths. "I am *now*, Dr. Nisreen," I said.

"We do not always have a choice in such matters," he said, with the air of one who has made his point. "Do we, Mr. Rousseau?"

He was probably right. "Okay," I said, with a shrug. "You're in the team. But you have to remember that the game is likely to be played by barbarian rules. You don't have any rank to pull just because you're a Tetron."

"I claim no debt from anyone," he told me. "I think we are now in the fifth phase of history, and must set aside the old ways."

He was talking about the theory of historical phases which the Tetrax had developed, in which Earth was stuck in the third phase, when power was based primarily in manufactured technology, while Tetra was in the fourth, where power was based in obligations of service—negotiated slavery, as humans tended to think of it. I nearly asked him what the basis of power was supposed to be in the new phase which he'd just invented, but as I opened my mouth to frame the question I realised that I didn't have to. The power-base in phase five was inside the machines—it resided with man-made gods like the combatants in the battle of Asgard. 673-Nisreen had seen a vision of the future, and had glimpsed the *deus ex machina* that would put an effective end to the humanoid story. Maybe that was the real lesson that Asgard had to teach the ambitious galactics of the Milky Way: in the greater scheme of things, we were pretty small beer.

Aborting the question, I said instead: "You'd better get some sleep. We start as soon as we can, and if we have to run a gauntlet of killer machines like the ones which nearly wiped us out today, we aren't going to have a very restful journey."

He nodded, politely. "I fear that you are right, Mr. Rousseau," he said. "I will bid you goodnight."

I wasn't so sure that Susarma Lear was going to thank me for adding a Tetron to the strength—even a Tetron who seemed infinitely less devious and dangerous than the late but not-yet-lamented 994-Tulyar. She didn't like or trust the Tetrax, and she had every reason not to. *But what the hell,* I thought, *it's their universe too, and I guess he's just as entitled to do his bit in the attempt to save it as anyone else.*

⤢ 14 ⤣

Freezing fog closed in around the ship, so thick that I could hardly see the sluggish waters lapping against the timbers of the hull. I had acquired a cloak to fold about myself, black as night in colour, and when I pulled it tight it secured such warmth within that the wind seemed to bite all the more fiercely into the skin of my face.

"This is none of our doing," I said to the woman who waited by my side, still nameless while I hesitated to think of her as Athene. "What's happening?"

"It is the beginning," she said. "Whatever forces are arrayed against us know that we have set forth. They are trying to make themselves felt in the order which we are imposing on the software space through which we move; they will soon begin their attempts to disrupt our course."

I looked out into the grey mists, which swirled eerily. It was as if the clouds which once had raced above our heads had slowed in their paces, falling as they slowed. If we had tried to shape this world as Midgard, home of men, then our enemies were trying now to draw us into Niflheim, domain of the goddess Hel, for whom we name the place where the dead must go to be punished for their sins. There were demons in those mists, and I could see their faces, skull-faced and hollow-eyed as they struggled—fruitlessly as yet—to make themselves coherent, to find the power to reach out and rake us with their angry claws.

I knew that the creation-myths of the Norsemen imagined that Niflheim had existed even before the earth—a world of fog and shadows on the lip of the great abysm of space. But I could not remember how the world which men would inhabit had been born from that formless chaos. I was disturbingly aware of the fact that if that lesion in my memory was real, and not merely a matter of my being temporarily unable to bring the matter to mind, then this world might not know how its birth and maturation must proceed.

I played with the proposition that perhaps the god who shaped the earth from which the human race emerged had only been attempting to recall a dimly-remembered story, and that all the troubles which had plagued mankind were the faults of his forgetfulness. I toyed with the notion that the universe of infinite space from which I had come was itself only software space within a machine of greater magnitude, its hard and unbreakable laws merely the certainty of some finely-tuned intelligence which did not doubt the propriety of its designs.

Here, though, playing with ideas might be dangerous, and it was foolish of me to add to the unease I already felt.

I drew the collar of my cloak upwards, using its warmth and softness to soothe my stinging cheeks and ears. Time passed, but its passing seemed to leave little trace upon my memory, and I felt that I could not reliably tell whether we had been sailing for hours or days. This was dream-time, immune to measurement by clocks or by the beating of my silent heart.

I had removed the quiver of arrows from my back, and placed them beside the bow that rested on the wooden rail. The figures which were carved in the wood of the balustrade were not pictures, nor the letters of any alphabet which I knew, but I fancied them to be runes laying out some powerful protective spell, so that this ill-fortressed deck might not easily be stormed.

A more substantial shadow drifted from the mist high above us, and swooped down, taking shape as a huge predatory bird, but it was only a ghost—as I ducked beneath its course I felt no breeze as of a body passing, and knew that there was as yet no danger in it. But from that moment on, the higher fog seemed to fill with such raptorial shadows, which soared in patient circles as if waiting for a solidity which they knew they must ultimately discover. They seemed to suck the darkness from the swirling mists, so that the background against which they moved grew gradually lighter, as though there were a bright white sky behind the vaporous haze, struggling to shine through.

Dare I wish for the glare of a bright sun to melt these mists? I thought. *Should I chant some magical verse to bid the fog begone?*

I did not try it; not because I was certain that it would not work, but rather that I was afraid that it would not work to our advantage. We had set out beneath a dull and sullen sky, perhaps for adequate reason, and I knew enough of the perils of magic to know that a foolish spell must always rebound upon its user.

The plash of the invisible oars could still be heard as they dipped into the water to haul us across its surface. I wondered whether there were fish in the sea which saw us as a marvelous many-legged insect scudding across the surface, but it was not a cheering thought.

Myrlin was standing at the wheel, holding it loosely, while the woman looked on. I did not know whether the wheel was such as to need a man to guard it, or whether the rudder moved with the same innate intelligence as the oars; I fancied, though, that Myrlin felt better having the semblance of a job to do. I went to stand beside him, taking my bow and arrows from the side of the ship to the bulwark's ledge that formed the front-facing wall of our platform.

"It seems that they are becoming more distinct," he said, glancing upward at the circling shadows. He sounded uneasy; no doubt he would rather postpone our first moment of real danger for as long as possible, though when it came it would immediately banish any sensation of having been delayed. I turned to our companion, goddess in mortal guise, to study her as she stared up into the sky, with an expression of considerable vexation.

"Too soon," she murmured, and seeing me looking in her direction, added: "Do not worry, I beg of you. If they begin to come through now, they will be very weak. Our world will not be breached so easily."

As if to contradict her, another shadow swooped at her, zooming from the heights like a black eagle, claws extended to tear and rend. She could not help but draw her face away, and put up a defending arm, while the folds of her dark cloak fell momentarily away from her golden armour.

Whether the hand made contact with the shadow-thing it was difficult to say, but she sustained no hurt from it and the bird-demon soared away again, impotent still.

It was obvious that the next swoop might not be so impotent, so dense were the shadows now becoming, so fast and furious in their flight. I drew my sword, and threw back the cloak, determined to hide from the cold no longer.

As if glad to meet my challenge, three of the shadows dived at once, hurtling towards me with wing-tips drawn back. I watched the heads of the creatures, and saw their bird-like faces dissolve, to be replaced by features far more humanoid, save for pointed teeth behind gaping lips. Their great claws thrust out before them seemed to grow as they drew near.

I slashed with the sword, finding it remarkably easy to

wield. For a moment, I had the sensation that the blade itself was only shadow, not substantial at all, and feared that
it could not disturb the attack of the harpies, but the lack of
apparent weight was no reflection of a lack of effective substance.

The single sweep of the sword cut through all three of
the bird-demons, and it was they who lacked the substance
to interrupt its passing. It cut through them as if they were
no less vaporous than the clammy mist, but as it did it tore
them savagely, so that their forms were shattered, dissolving
into blood-red clouds. They had no momentum to carry
through their thrust—the sword caught them and hurled
them away, scarlet-and-black shreds that had lost all semblance of what they had tried to be. They disappeared over
the parapet, on a downward-looping trajectory, but there
was no sound of any splash as they hit the waves.

There surged through me a feeling of such power that I
felt momentarily giddy. The casual ease of the victory im-
parted such a sense of exultation that I could revel in the
sensation of being a person of great substance . . . one who
would never need to yield to the monsters of the night.
Though reason told me that this was the merest of begin-
nings, and the most derisory of all the tests which were to
come, still I felt indomitable, as though I knew for the first
time in my existence what it might mean to be a hero. I still
felt as though I might be drunk, but this was the glorious intoxication of triumph and exultation.

Without meaning to, I followed the course of the shattered bird-things, moving over to the side of the ship and
placing my left hand on the parapet while I peered into the
thicker mists which hid the sea.

I could see no more than I could hear, and the broken
things were utterly gone in the confusion, but while my

hand rested on the parapet something long and black snaked out of the murk as though it came from beneath the belly of the ship, and wrapped itself around my wrist.

It had the texture of something very soft and slimy, and yet it tightened in a muscular fashion once it had me in its grip. It put me in mind of the head of a great leech, and I half-expected to feel the bite of something acid as it tried to draw my blood. My reaction was one of instinctive horror, and I tried to pull my hand away with a convulsive jerk— but that was exactly the wrong thing to do. It was as though the strength of my backward thrust was immediately reflected in the body of the thing itself, as though my action had added to its own capacity for elastic reaction. As my arm reached the full measure of my jerking pull, it was suddenly wrenched back again, with such force that I nearly overbalanced.

In that moment, I think, there was a real danger that our defences might be breached by the enemy's first hopeful foray. I could have tripped, felled by my own unreadiness and clumsiness, and if I had been dragged over the edge of the parapet and down into the turbulent waters, the shock of immersion would surely have driven all sense from my mind and left me at the mercy of whatever half-formed sea-monsters were nascent there.

But I did not fall; my reflexes, however untrained or doubtfully adapted, caught me up and steadied me, while the sword in my right hand cut downwards, almost of its own accord, and sheared through the black tentacle as though it were hardly there.

Again there was a stain as if of blood upon the mist, but then the loop which wound around my wrist dissolved into the icy air, and the rest of the thing was gone into the waters.

"Too soon it may be," I shouted to my companions,

though there was not sound enough to require me to raise my voice, "but it will not stop them. They are at us, and I do not believe that they will give us pause to rest."

She did not need the warning. Her slender sword was in her hand, and Myrlin came back from his senseless duty at the wheel, with his own weapons ready. He towered above me by a full head and more, and as he whirled his blade about his head, slashing at the demons of the air who came at him with many ugly faces and countless thrusting talons, he seemed closer kin to god or titan than to mankind.

More of the black things curled on to the deck, some climbing in sinuous fashion, others striking like whiplashes. I swung the sword back and forth, cutting through them as fast as they reached for me, and though one touched my ankle it had not the time to curl around it.

On the deck below us, the automata came to life at last, and with their own weapons drawn began to fight against shadows raised as though from the sea itself—vague things with dog-like heads and arms like huge apes, which reached for them in ponderous fashion.

The skirmish seemed to last for some while, but it quickly became obvious that these lumpish things had no more power to hurt our defenders than the bird-demons and the slimy ropes had to carry us away. When that fact became clear within my mind, it seemed that the knowledge itself was enough to put an end to the episode. One moment the demonic birds were crowding around us as thickly as they could; the next they were gone into the mists, flown away to leave the lowering sky much brighter than it had been before they filled it.

I took this as a good sign, until I saw the expression on my female companion's face, and knew that this was not the way she had hoped that things would go.

"They know we are here," she said, "and are prepared to test us. I had hoped to find less quickness of reaction, and I know now that we have more to fight than mere automata. There is a mind in this, and I cannot tell how clever it will prove. I fear that we may have underestimated their capacity to deal with such as we."

"Well then," I said, "we must hope that they in their turn will underestimate our capacity to deal with such as they."

As I said it, the mist seemed to darken again, and renew its iciness, making me shiver even within my cloak. Hero though I was, armed and aided by gods, I felt a chill course through me, which promised me an abundance of pain and anguish in time to come.

◄ 15 ►

There were five of us in the truck—or six, if we counted non-humanoids. That was one more than was specified in our original plans—but I thought we'd be able to cope, given that the truck we were chasing had eight aboard. As I had anticipated, the admission of 673-Nisreen to our company met with the unequivocal disapproval of Susarma Lear, who was still nursing an altogether reasonable suspicion of the probable perfidy of all members of the Tetron species, but by the time she realised he'd been added to our strength his position was a *fait accompli*. She had no opportunity to start an argument about it.

The scion who had been appointed to come with us was quite indistinguishable, in my eyes, from all her fellows. She suggested that we should address her as Urania-3, but there didn't seem to be any point in retaining the number, so I promptly abandoned it.

The sixth member of our expedition might also have been reckoned to be a scion, though it (or "she," as consistency demanded that I think of her) wasn't any kind of organic entity. At rest she looked not unlike a suitcase, but she was studded with connect-points for all kinds of leads: metal, glassfibre, and organic, and she could extrude pseudopods of all these kinds in order to hook herself up to virtually any kind of system she was likely to meet. If necessary, she could slide artificial neurons into humanoid flesh, just like the hoods of the chairs the Isthomi used for interfacing with us, but she was equally at home interfacing with the systems of the robot transporter.

Her main purpose, to my mind, would be to help us open the many doorways that must undoubtedly lie between ourselves and the lowest levels of the macroworld, at least some of which would presumably need external supplies of power because they had no stored potential of their own and could no longer draw upon the great network. I had no doubt, though, that she thought of herself as the real guide and leader of the expedition—a far more powerful and more versatile incarnation of the Nine than Urania. She had no voice of her own, but Urania told us that we could refer to her, if we wished, by the name Clio-14. Again, I promptly forgot the number, and I had some difficulty at first in thinking of her by name, given that she was so very different in form from the furry humanoid Clios I had known.

By the time we had loaded extra power cells and the various kinds of equipment which either the Nine or I considered potentially useful, the free space aboard the truck was getting very cluttered. Anyone who was not in the cab had only two choices—they could sit in the gun-turret or lie down in the narrow bunk-space. To begin with, the colonel took the turret while Myrlin, Urania, and Clio shared the front seat with me and Nisreen lurked in the rear.

"Are you sure you can handle the guns?" I asked Susarma, before she went up.

"They're guns, Rousseau," she informed me with vitriolic contempt. "Given that the original plan was that you should be able to shoot them, I don't think I'll have much difficulty, do you? Are you sure that you can drive the bloody truck?"

It wasn't quite like that. The original plan had been that the intelligent suitcase, hooked into the robot's systems, could do the driving and man the guns, both at the same time. Needless to say, the robot had external sensors that could function far better as eyes than our real eyes peering through windows. Both sets of manual controls had been intended as back-ups. Susarma Lear still hadn't cultivated the correct frame of mind for dealing with the Isthomi. I didn't try to explain, because Clio had been quite willing to share control of the guns with the colonel, on the grounds that reflexes trained by the Star Force might easily out-perform her own mechanical responses in a tough combat situation. Beyond the Nine's protective barriers, there might be all kinds of electronic highwaymen lying in wait for us—and our recent experiences suggested that it might not be so easy getting past them. A dozen mechanical mantises would be no mean opponents.

We were so certain that there would be an ambush waiting for us at the bottom of the shaft that the Nine had given us reinforcements to assist us in getting past square one of the game. Following us along the corridors through which we took the truck on the way to our departure point was a ragged army of robots. Not one of them had been de-signed for fighting, and many of them hadn't had any weapons grafted on, but their role wasn't really an offensive one. Their job was to intercept anything thrown in our di-rection which might otherwise do us damage. They were a suicide squadron.

The robots were as ill-assorted a gang as I could ever hope to see—half of them on wheels, half ambulatory; some small and round, others like crazy assemblies of girders. In terms of animal analogies they ranged all the way from grubs and wireworms through crabs and giant turtles to sur-real monstrosities which could only be described in terms of silly old jokes about what you'd get if you crossed a giraffe with a stick-insect or a peacock with a squid. What most of them had originally been designed for I could hardly begin to guess. Every spare mobile the Isthomi had was here, and though none of them qualified as an actual person in the way that Clio allegedly did, some of them were pretty smart machines. It was a terrible waste to use them as mere cannon fodder.

The Nine had initially sealed off the platform which Finn's party had used for their descent, but before we took the new robot truck out there, they had brought it back up from the depths and made sure that it was empty of would-be invaders. That circular section of chitinous concrete was the last safe place in Asgard, and once we drove off it into the mysterious spaces of whichever level it could take us to, we were on our own.

It wasn't until we crowded on to it that I saw the suicide army in its full strength. I knew that no more than one in five could even be credited with a sensible measure of artificial intelligence, let alone a suspicion of sentience, but I couldn't help but feel sorry for them as they shuffled dutifully around, cramping up their disfigured limbs in order to make room for one another.

We who are about to die salute you, I thought. *All hail to the Caesars of Asgard.*

The journey down was longer than I expected, given that the Nine had already told me that their explorations in a downward direction hadn't been too successful. I'd been expecting to go down ten or a dozen levels, but by my rough calculation we dropped nearly two thousand metres into the darkness—which was probably somewhere between seventy-five and eighty-five levels. While we descended I tried out a few equations in my head, wondering—as I'd often done before—how many levels there might be between the Nine's habitat and the bottom of the world. There were too many unknowns, most notably the size and mass of the starlet around which the macroworld was constructed, but if I fed in guesses which seemed to me to be halfway reasonable I kept getting answers of the order of magnitude which extended from five hundred to five thousand levels. That was a big margin of possible error, which became much larger if my assumptions about the starlet were cock-eyed, but for some reason it felt good to have figures in my mind, ready to be refined to reflect any new data which came in. I felt that my progress toward the Centre could be mapped by the increasing precision of my estimates regarding its proximity.

When the platform stopped, having reached the bottom of its shaft, I switched the truck's lights full on, and Urania promptly bent over her sister the suitcase. She wasn't controlling her—she was merely making ready to relay to us any messages or commands which Clio wanted passed on. I was sitting in front of the manual controls, ready to grab them if the circumstances should make it necessary, but I knew that no such situation was likely to arise and I felt uncomfortably impotent. I even envied Susarma Lear her control of the guns.

There was no time to think too hard about it, though, because the moment the platform ceased its descent our sacrificial army of tin gladiators was scattering into every space they could find, and the explosions were already beginning: one, two, three.

We could hear the blasts and see the splashes of fire, but they were not so very close at hand—the jury-rigged soldiers whose job it was to get in the way were playing hero and victim to the very best of their ability. I only hoped that those which had some elementary capacity for fighting back were sending forth their own missiles to wreak a measure of havoc among the enemy. Some pretty heavy stuff must have been fired at us, because we rocked slightly as we got underway, but we sustained no damage.

Susarma began returning fire as soon as she had space to fire at the bad guys without hitting our own troops. She sent streams of flame-bolts out in two directions. The flame-bolts, which became gaseous almost instantly once they were in flight, were much more difficult to stop than the solid missiles which were fired at us; although they couldn't penetrate armour as heavy as the stuff which was wrapped around us, they could do a lot of damage to anything that was slightly less robust—including the gun-barrels and firing mechanisms of the robots arrayed against us. Clio was firing too—she still had control of the magic bazookas: the software disrupters.

It would have been nice to know what kind of carnage we were creating in the enemy ranks, but I couldn't see a damn thing through the flickering glare except for a few shards from the bodies of our defenders which impacted with the bar of clear plastic which served as a window.

The truck was accelerating as fast as it could, and the momentum threw me backwards. The doorway through which we passed wasn't very tall or wide, and there was something in the open space beyond it which had fired at least one of the three biggest missiles which had come at us, but the only thing we could do was go like hell and try to break through the ambush.

I presumed that Clio was able to send signals of some kind to the suicide squadron, trying to make sure that they all got blown to bits usefully, but there was no way I could keep track of what was happening. I just held on tight while we rocketed away from the shaft, hoping that Susarma and the suitcase were equal to their task.

We had to swerve round something big and solid, and then had to run a gauntlet of things which came from either side, determined to blow us away if they could. A couple were essentially similar in design to the mantis which had chased me in the garden, while others were just cannons on legs, but as each one came up something zapped it—if none of our fast-diminishing army of supporters got it, Susarma or Clio did. These things were obviously operating a long way from home: they were geared to travel as well as to fight, and their firepower was correspondingly modest.

There was a sudden series of explosions in front of the truck, as the road seemed to rise up to attack us with tongues of flame. I winced, realising that it had been mined with explosive charges which could throw us up in the air and turn us over even if they couldn't crack our under-belly—but the suitcase had detected them early enough, and every one of them was exploding prematurely.

The battle lasted about two minutes and fifteen seconds, and when it ended our robot transporter was hurtling into the darkness at a hundred kilometres an hour, its steely carapace whole and essentially undamaged. The sound and the fury faded behind us, our automata and theirs still exchanging whatever shots they could. I think the battle continued, sporadically, for a few more minutes when we were out of it, as the two companies of machines made what efforts they could to mop up. There was no way to know how many survivors there might be, and whether any of them might be ours. We didn't intend that any pursuers should ever catch up with us.

The lights of the truck were now the only source of illumination in the neighbourhood. They showed us the way ahead clearly enough—in fact, I could see the tracks which the other truck had left in the soft earth. It was more difficult to see what lay to either side of the road, but we were out in the open, although we frequently passed hugely thick pillars connecting the floor to the ceiling. This had once been some kind of forest, but it had obviously been dead long before the lights were switched out. The trees were leafless, most of the branches broken away to leave the jagged boles jutting like rotten teeth. They showed up grey in the light, and gave the impression of being petrified, yet somehow still brittle.

Nothing moved. Even the dust kicked up by the truck we were chasing had settled back to the ground.

"Have the Nine explored this level?" asked Myrlin. "Do they know what happened here?"

"Our machines have been here," Urania replied, with a slight uncharacteristic hoarseness in her voice that suggested that the experience of conflict had not left her unaffected. "They found little here to interest us, and we already had a way down into lower levels than this one, so we made no attempt to search vigorously for new routes. We are not sure what manner of disaster destroyed the life-system."

"Could it be that the trees are simply the last evidential remains of an ecocatastrophe?" asked Myrlin, whose own voice was not completely steady. "It might have been something initially trivial—closed ecospheres must always be vulnerable to mutant viruses which break crucial food-chains by wiping out the members of a particular group of species."

"It is unlikely," said Urania, soberly. "The extending consequences of such an event might easily be disastrous for higher species, but it is difficult to believe that it could exterminate *all* life. It seems more probable that this habitat was deliberately sterilised."

"An act of war?" I ventured, knowing that she wouldn't be able to answer. If she had, she'd have told us already.

"Not necessarily," she replied with all due caution.

"How many levels further down did your explorer robots manage to penetrate?" I asked.

"The lowest level we have attained is one hundred and three below this one, although we did not gain access to all the intermediate ones."

"Any more dead ones?"

"Only one," she said. "But seven of the habitats have reducing atmospheres, and were difficult to explore. A further ten have ecosystems which are entirely thermosynthetic, and six of those are entirely dark, consisting of organisms which make no use of bioluminescence at all."

"How many of the remainder have indigenous humanoid life?"

"Four of the seventy-one about which we have information," she said. "We have not attempted to communicate with any of them, but have been content to observe. None of the four seemed aware of the fact that there are habitats other than their own; all were technologically primitive in our terms—even by galactic standards. Their use of the power available to them from the central network was very limited, although that will not insulate them from the ecocatastrophes which will occur as a result of the switching off of that power."

There wasn't much point in following up that line of conversation. It wouldn't matter much whether a habitat was humanoid-inhabited or not, whether its atmosphere was oxygen-rich or reducing, or whether its organisms were photosynthetic or thermosynthetic: the big switch-off had left them all to live on their energy-capital. Some of them would be able to support sophisticated organisms for hundreds of years, simpler ones for hundreds of thousands, and bacteria for hundreds of millions; but in the end, if the power never came back on, entropy would turn them all into so much sterile sewage.

"Anyhow," I said, "we could always cross our fingers and hope that some of the levels further down have intelligent inhabitants who do know their way around, far better than we do. For all we know, a hundred worldlets could have sent out teams of repair-men, every one of them so clever that bringing the power back will be just like mending a fuse."

"We can hope," said Susarma Lear, who had just climbed down from the turret, having concluded that there was nothing else out there to shoot. "But I've told you before, Rousseau—hope just isn't enough."

As mottos went it had its good points, but in a morale-boosting contest it could only be a hot contender for the booby prize.

"Well, if it's all down to us," I said, "we'd better look after that bloody suitcase, because everything I've seen of humanoid intercourse with machinery tells me that we're a hell of a lot better at smashing things than we are at fixing them."

"We may find scope for the exercise of both talents before we're through," said Myrlin, with the air of one who does not fear contradiction.

"We will do what we can," said Urania simply. "We can do no more."

The mist had faded into a light, silvery haze, and visibility on all sides of the ship had improved dramatically. A dead calm had fallen upon the sea. Where our oars disturbed the surface there was turbulence, and the ripples spread out slowly from each point of contact, but the viscous water damped them down and swallowed them. The wake which we left behind us was similarly impotent to disturb the waters for long; it too was calmed and soothed so that it stretched behind us for little more than a boat length, like gently-trailing tresses of weed.

I watched dark-haired Athene as she stared over the rail at the still and silent sea, clearly perturbed by what was happening, because it was so unexpected. I think she would have preferred a more recognisable menace, which could be opposed in straightforward fashion.

"What is happening?" asked Myrlin—not of her, though it was she who was surely best placed to answer—but of me.

"They appear to have made a temporary withdrawal," I said. "I suspect they're taking time out to think things over. A council of war, maybe. When they have another go at us, they'll have a better idea of what to do. I have a suspicion that they may have done this sort of thing before, and know one or two tricks that our side hasn't even thought of."

She turned to look at me while I spoke, and the bleak look in her eye suggested that she had reached similar conclusions.

"It is too soon to despair," she said, sharply. "While they withdraw, we make progress. Our weapons are still potent, and whatever monsters they may produce can only become solid enough to do us harm by rendering themselves vulnerable to our power of retaliation. You are more difficult to destroy now than ever you were as creatures of flesh and bone—remember that!"

While she instructed us to be brave, our surroundings began again to change. The mist began to thicken again, and draw about us, so that we could not see such great expanses of mirror-bright water to either side. The mist changed colour, too, so that it was no longer silvery-white but a roseate pink. At first I thought of this as if it were an infusion of something the colour of blood, which paled only because of its dilution in the mist, but there was too much yellow in the pink for that, and it was a colour I had only ever seen in the fragile petals of sweet-smelling flowers.

I had the strangest impression that this must be the most perfect of the colours which mist might have: a colour for sugar-sweet clouds in a child's vision of paradise. I looked upwards, to the top of the mast, where the stirring of the wind had not completely ceased, and I saw wreaths of the mist thickening like radiant tongues of pink flame. The sea, beneath this glowing coloured vapour, could not help but lose its greyness, but the light that it reflected was by no means so pale. It was a red deeper by far, but still not like the colour of blood, tending more to the orange part of the spectrum. It put me in mind of films I had seen—the films by which I had learned the landscapes and appearances of the homeworld which I had never visited—where the camera's eye had looked boldly into the face of the setting sun. It had stuck in my memory that the sun in such circumstances seemed hugely bloated by virtue of its proximity to the horizon, its image rippled by the hazy movement of the heated air.

I could easily imagine that the ocean upon which we floated was the surface of a dying sun, an infinite lake of quiet fire. Despite the redness, though, there was no heat at all. I no longer felt the need to draw my cloak tightly about me, but neither did I feel a need to discard it. There was still a hint of chill creeping in my bones.

"Look!" said Myrlin, pointing dead ahead. We could see very little beyond the figurehead which was carved to represent Medusa, whose serpentine tresses were themselves half-obscured by numinous tongues of rosy vapour, but we could see that the fog in direct line with the vessel's course was beginning to thicken and to move in a much more agitated fashion. Its colour was darkening too, though not consistently, and as I struggled to make sense of what was happening I formed the notion that some kind of great arch was forming in the mist, through which the ship must sail, and that this arch was made of a blazing redness.

The sea was disturbed now, but not in the chaotic fashion of a surface stirred by eddying winds. It was as though there were some kind of force flowing from the points where the fiery arch met the water, which was causing great ripples and surges. As the ship began to meet these ripples, the bow began to dip and rise.

There was a sound, then, like the moan of some desolate creature slowly dying—a faint, hollow, hopeless sound which echoed eerily across the face of the water.

I concentrated on the arms of the arch into which we were sailing, which were thickening all the time from the gathering cloud, and now seemed like huge rotating pillars, far thinner at the bottom than the top—great vortices which slipped sinuously from side to side as ripples of expansion passed up from the water, loosening their hold on verticality.

"They're sucking up the water!" I shouted as I realised what was happening. "Like a brace of tornadoes!"

The movement of the ship was increasing in its violence with every second that passed, and I moved in from the side, gripping the rail close to the position of the wheel, with which Myrlin was now trying to grapple.

They had sent no monster to fly at us or rise from the depths, but were raising against us the very elements of this world which we had made—they were attacking us with a storm, trying to upset the very fabric which we had imposed upon software space.

"Be calm!" commanded the gilt-clad goddess. "Hold hard, and we will ride it out. We are unsinkable!"

It was a promise which I longed to believe, but the sea boiled up beneath us as if it were a cauldron brought hurriedly to the boil, and there came into our faces a howling tempestuous wind like the voice of a wrathful god, while the mist fell all about us cloyingly, as though precipitated from solution in the air. There seemed little doubt that our ridiculous vessel would be smashed into matchwood, and our own bodies torn apart by the fury of the storm.

I could not stand before the forces that were beating and wrenching at me from all sides, and fell to my knees. But my hands gripped the rail all the tighter, and I ducked my head, trying to make myself tiny and huddle into the angle made by the deck and the balustrade.

Once I could not see what was happening it did not feel so very awful, and the storm's power seemed much diminished. But still the ship was tossed about in both the vertical and horizontal dimensions, and still there was the sense of vaporous fingers clutching at me, first to tear and then to choke, and I knew that my sword was as impotent as my mere hands to turn them back. I stretched out my legs, trying to hook my feet into small gaps in the wooden face where they might help to anchor me. The bow and the quiver which I had not yet tried to use were pinned beneath me, their awkward shapes digging into my flesh as I tried to force myself down on to the deck.

I could still see Myrlin clinging to the wheel, refusing to let his giant frame be cast down by the angry wind. I could not see the goddess, but as the moaning of the wind paused for a fleeting moment I heard her, screaming at the storm with all the wrath which she could rouse to meet it. She was not screaming wordlessly—nor, I quickly realised, was she screaming impotently. Although the wind's imperious howl tried hard to reassert itself when the brief pause was done, it could only enter into competition with her, and it seemed almost as if her voice now drew strength from the maelstrom of sound which whirled about us, as if the turbulence which was shaking the very foundations of the world added to her power instead of undermining it.

I raised my head, gaining confidence that I did not need to shrivel myself up in search of a hidey-hole, wondering if I might not fight too, if only I had words to do it with. I opened my mouth, and found it full of rushing, strangling air, which drove from my mind any thought of trying to form a coherent sentence—but I would not be silenced, and I shouted against the wind with all my might.

There was a brief moment when it seemed that the shout might empty my lungs and leave me helpless in the grip of the wind, helping it in its determination to choke me, but such sound as I produced seemed only to need a spark to set it alight before it grew of its own accord, plundering the force of the storm which tried to staunch it. There was a moment's struggle, a second's balance, and then I found the power to sustain the shout, to amplify it, and turn it into a cry of triumph, and I realised that Myrlin was shouting too, and that his stentorian voice was somehow adding its support to mine as we laid down a carpet of sound on which the goddess' words could dance . . . and the louder we shouted, the clearer her words became, and though they were in some primitive, forgotten language which I did not know, they had meaning enough to terrify the wind which had come to pluck us apart.

There surged through me a sense of triumphant authority as I realised what power I had on which to draw. Magic was there to be worked, and although I had no knowledge of its working, the necessity which was the mother of improvisation could bring it forth. I could defend myself, not only with the curious weightless sword but with the sheer force of wishful thinking.

For the first time in my life I felt truly free, a commander of circumstance.

The boat plunged through the tiny eye of the storm, through the arch of rosy fire, and came out the other side, bursting from the thick and ruddy cloud into the thinner, sparkling mist once more.

Water rained down upon us as we passed beneath the vortices which sucked the water up, but they could not close upon the sides of our craft, and could not break our oars—and the water was only water, which could not hurt us in the least.

Our howls of wrath extended themselves into a long ululating cry of pure elation, and when I had come to my feet I saw that we were all three looking back at the dying thing behind us, whose fury seemed now only to be consuming itself, as the red that was not like blood faded to a pastel shade of rose, and finally evaporated in the silver mist.

"Did I not tell you?" she called, when at last we stopped our yelling and drew breath. Her voice was cracked, and it was an effort for her now to speak, but the elation in her words was clear to be heard, and it was obvious that this was a conflict she was delighted to have won. We knew now that she had underestimated the enemy, but we had the compensating hope that we might have underestimated ourselves. She turned to face us, while I staggered to Myrlin's side, and we both leant on the wheel while we watched the storm expire in the bubbling waters far behind our stern.

I gasped for breath, thinking to join in the round of mutual congratulation, when I saw the expression of joy which was in her eyes begin to die. She opened her mouth to say something more, and when no words came I knew that it was not simply shortness of breath that would not let them come.

I turned, quickly, steadying myself upon the wheel, to look beyond the bows of the ship, at whatever terror now was to be thrust into our path.

Had I never seen it before it would have been a dreadful sight, but it was something I knew from the dream I had had when concussion had freed that parasite which clung to the underside of my soul.

Sailing directly toward us out of the mist was a ship four times the size of our own, which stood twice as high in the water, and looked as if it would break us in two if it could ram us squarely.

Its hull was made from strangely-knotted strands whose nature and origin I could never have guessed, had I not had my dream—but in that dream I had not had to guess, and had known what it was.

This was the ship of the dead, whose timbers were made from the fingernails of corpses, which had continued to grow long after the bodies were safe in their tombs, and whose fine white sails were woven from hair of the same strange kind. On the deck were its crew, who were made from the bare bones of the resurrected dead, all skeleton and sinew, eyeless, lipless, and heartless, yet bearing arms and fervent with the lust for life.

To the horror of the sight itself was added a sudden thrill of panic, as I realised that here was a figment of my imagination, a nightmare based in the ancient stories I had recalled. Such images had been seized and appropriated, it seemed, by the tapeworm in my mind, and now they were accessible to the others, whose object was my destruction. A moment ago, I had felt such a power within me that I had almost reckoned myself a god. Now, I remembered all too well that in the riot of *Gotterdammerung* the gods had perished, wiped out by the giants and their macabre armies.

Myrlin's huge hand cast me roughly aside as he sought to spin the wheel, but there was not a doubt in the world that he was already too late. Although he steered the ship into a turn as sharp as she could possibly take, all he could do was to make the collision a glancing one. Our gleaming spur barely had strength to scratch the hull of the other vessel, and although the gorgon's head which was mounted on our prow stared with baleful eyes at the host assembled in its bows, the enemy warriors had no eyes of their own by which her power could be known.

And as the honest timbers of the one ship grated harshly against the eerie fabric of the other, those skeletal warriors were already swinging on ropes of silvery hair, pouring like a troop of horrid insects on to the deck of our small, frail craft.

It took some thirteen hours of driving through the dead world to reach the next drop-point. I hoped that it would take us a long way down, because the horizontal sort of journey was no fun, and didn't take us a single centimetre closer to where we wanted to be. If we had to drive a thousand kilometres sideways just to reach a point which would only let us go a couple of kilometres downwards, the journey to the centre was going to be a very long one, and we'd all be old before we got there.

I had been nursing the hope that whatever was inside Tulyar's head knew the location of a dropshaft which could take us all the way down in one long, slow fall, but I'd been around Asgard too long to take it for granted that there was any through road from top to bottom, or even from middle to bottom. I knew that we had to be prepared to drive sideways across three or four more habitats, maybe for quite some distance. If the deck was really stacked against us, it might be ten or twenty, or a couple of hundred.

I wondered whether the thing which had taken over Tulyar's body had undisputed sovereignty by now, or whether the Tetron was still in there, conscious of what was happening, struggling to recover the empire of his own soul. It was a morbid preoccupation, because I had no way to be certain that I wasn't destined for the same kind of fate. At any moment, I might cease to be me, and become a warrior in some aeons-old conflict whose nature we had hardly begun to understand. To make myself feel better I imagined

John Finn having to sit next to the pseudo-Tulyar, maybe realising by now that he'd been played for a sucker, and that even the Star Force would have looked after him better than the regiment in which he was now enlisted. I couldn't find it in my heart to feel sorry for him—it was easier to ill-wish him with the thought that he had amply deserved the very worst fate which could possibly befall him.

Eventually, we came to the wall where both the tyre-tracks and the olfactory trace disappeared as if by magic. From where I sat the wall looked smooth enough, but there had to be a doorway there—an airlock guarding a shaft which was probably evacuated.

It was time for the clever suitcase to do her bit. She was hooked into the transporter's systems by means of half a dozen leads; under her guidance the truck now began to extrude similar feelers from some secret place beneath its central headlight. I watched with some fascination as the feelers began to explore the wall, invading invisible seams and searching out hidden mechanisms. I have no idea what they did, or how, but it only took a few minutes. There was a sudden drain on the power-unit, and a section of wall retreated from the rest, and then slid sideways, after the usual fashion of Asgardian doors. As I had anticipated, there was a big airlock backed by a second door. The lock was only just big enough to take the transporter, and I couldn't help wondering what would happen if and when we found a doorway that was too small for it to go through. Urania had assured me that we had more economical transporters stored somewhere in the back, but I hadn't seen them.

Once we were inside the lock Clio closed the doors behind us, and set off the command sequence which would open the inner door. Urania confirmed that there was, as expected, no air in the shaft. At least some of the levels which it served must have reducing atmospheres. The shaft was easily wide enough to take the truck, but there was no platform on to which we could drive it.

"Well," I said, drily, "We could hardly expect them to send it back up for us, could we?"

"Can we call it back?" asked Susarma. "How long will it take?"

Urania's nimble fingers tapped away at the keys on the outside of her small, square sister. Clio had no screen to display words, but she was communicating with Urania somehow.

"We cannot bring the platform back," she said, calmly. "It has been immobilised."

I felt a bad mood creeping up on me.

"Can she tell how deep the shaft is?" I asked.

"Yes. It extends downwards for twenty-five kilometres."

It wasn't as big a drop as I had hoped; it was still one very tiny step toward the Centre, even if it did take us down further than the Nine's robots had ever gone before. On the other hand, even that tiny step would be a giant leap for a man—and when he reached the bottom, the impact would reduce him to a very thin smear.

I had learned by now not to underestimate the Nine. They were used to this kind of problem.

"How do we make a new platform?" asked Myrlin.

"No need," said Urania, simply. "We will descend by the usual method."

"What's the usual method?" asked Susarma, with a certain wariness in her voice.

The usual method of descent into a lower level for humanoid scavengers operating in the upmost four levels had involved the rigging of a block-and-tackle and climbing down a rope. She'd seen that for herself when we followed

Myrlin down Saul Lyndrach's dropshaft. But we were talking about a hole that was twenty-five kilometres deep, and it didn't take a mathematical genius to figure out that we'd need a hell of a lot of very strong cable to lower an armoured truck that far.

"I guess we walk," I said. "The way climbers go up and down chimneys. Brace ourselves inside the shaft, and let ourselves down, slowly." I saw the expression of horror flit across Susarma's face, and quickly added: "Not *us* as in you and me—the entire package. The truck can put out limbs as well as feelers. How many?"

"Eight," replied Urania. "Four will hold us at any one time, while the remaining four seek a lower hold. But they will not have to brace us; the limbs are flexible, and can use organic adhesives to bond us momentarily to this kind of surface, and dissolve the bond with equal ease. Even so, it will be a long climb, and not so very comfortable."

"Think of it as a new experience," I said to Susarma. "We can be the first humans ever to get seasick while descending a drainpipe in the belly of a robot spider."

"You must try to rest, Mr. Rousseau," said the scion, solicitously. "There is nothing you need to do. Clio and I will manage the descent. You should rest too, Colonel Lear."

It sounded like a good idea. I was all in favour of new experiences, but somehow I didn't passionately want to be in the cab when the truck moved into the shaft. I was happy to believe that its extruded "legs" could secure us safely, but it was the kind of belief that might not be able to quell the anxieties triggered by one's sense of sight. I could easily imagine my stomach turning over as we were picked up and drawn inexorably into position above that twenty-five kilometre drop. Anyway, I was hungry and thirsty.

There was just about room to stand up in the back of the truck, but if three or four people tried to move around all at once, the crowding quickly became absurd. There were four narrow bunks, two on either side, and as soon as I had a tube of food-concentrate and a bladder-pack of something to drink, I eased myself into the upper left. Susarma took the upper right, and Nisreen, who had been dozing in the lower right, went forward into the cab to join Myrlin and the Nine's two ill-matched daughters.

I looked across at Susarma as I chewed my way through the flavoured concentrate. It didn't taste any better than Tetron-manufactured manna, but it didn't taste any worse either, and it was what I was used to. The colonel, to judge by her long-suffering expression, was still accustomed to food that did more favours for her palate. I sympathised, thinking how awful it would be if every single meal I ate conjured up memories of some long-ago feast the like of which I was unlikely ever to taste again.

"Does it strike you, Rousseau, that we're a trifle redundant here?" she said.

"I don't think it would constitute a fatal breakdown of Star Force discipline if you were to call me Mike," I told her. "I tell everyone to do it, but no one takes a blind bit of notice. You have to expect formality from Tetrax, I guess, but *you* could surely make an exception."

"Why break a habit just to pretend we know one another?" she countered. "Hell, Rousseau, I don't know the first thing about you, for all the time I've been forced to spend in your company. Anyway, what I mean is, it seems to me that this fancy robot truck could do the job all on its own. It doesn't need us to drive it, or to shoot its guns—that goddamn suitcase could do it all, couldn't it? Even if the levers we finally have to pull are mechanical, the suitcase and the furry hermaphrodite could do the job. Why are *we* here, Rousseau?"

It didn't seem to be worth pursuing the matter of my name, or even following up her point about how well we could claim to know one another.

"We're here," I said, "because the Isthomi find this whole situation just as puzzling as we do. They don't know what the hell to expect in the lower depths, but there is one fact about Asgard—and, for that matter, about the universe—which leads them to harbour the suspicion that we poor creatures of flesh and blood must, in the final analysis, be good for something."

"I'll make a deal," she said. "I'll try to remember to call you Mike if you promise not to conduct conversations as though they were guessing games. Never mind the build-up—just skip to the punch line."

"The Isthomi," I said, in a faintly injured tone, "are very clever. They're also very handy. They seem to be superior to us in every way—which is why we occasionally get this feeling of redundancy. But what Asgard is mostly full of . . . and what the galaxy beyond Asgard's walls seems to be mostly full of . . . is beings like us. What the Isthomi can't understand is why, if beings like themselves are so bloody clever, the universe isn't full of them. They keep looking over their shoulders in the hope of catching a glimpse of their Achilles heel. Maybe they already got shot there a couple of times, during their contacts with whatever is loose in Asgard's software space.

"The Isthomi are so powerful that they seem to us to be godlike, but they aren't really gods. They're vulnerable in all kinds of ways. We blasted our way through the hostile hardware that came after us, but that wasn't the real war. It was just a throwaway move. We may yet have to withstand an attack much more insidious than the fireworks which were left to entertain us at the bottom of the first shaft—an attack by hostile software. Every time Clio puts out feelers to pick a lock for us she could open herself up to the kind of devastation the Nine suffered when they went exploring in the heart of Asgard's software space. When it comes to the crunch, there might be no one left to carry this fight forward except the likes of you and me. So look after that Scarid crash-gun you've taken to wearing—one day soon. . . ."

I was forced to pause in my melodramatic discourse because the truck lurched, and I had to brace myself against the ceiling of my bunk space as we wobbled drunkenly. It seemed that we were under way, and that the mechanical precision of the bendy legs which were walking us down the shaft was by no means perfect. I sighed, unable to fancy my chances of getting a good night's sleep. I wasn't sure that I wanted one, anyhow—I was still apprehensive about dreaming, and the fact that the biocopy foisted on my brain had now been recopied into something more like its natural form in harness with my *alter ego* didn't affect the fact that it was still lurking in the shadows of my soul.

On the other hand, I could hardly stay awake forever.

"That explains why the Isthomi are prepared to entertain us," she admitted, after a pause for thought. "But what are *we* doing here, Rousseau . . . Mike?"

I looked at her in mild surprise. She was, after all, a volunteer. Her orders had been to return to the surface, and though circumstances had conspired to prevent her obeying them, she'd already decided that she wasn't going back. I realised now, though, that her motives for making that decision had been almost entirely negative. Her orders had seemed to her to be bad ones, inspired by forces that did not have human interests at heart, and her instinct had told her to disobey them. She hadn't thought it through much further than that.

"We're trying to save the macroworld," I reminded her. "If we needed a reason, we got it when the power was switched off. Before that, we had the fact that I seemed to have received a cry for help . . . and before that we had simple curiosity: the desire to solve the biggest puzzle that fate had ever thrown our way—excepting, of course, such commonplace mysteries as the origin of life, which may not be unrelated to it. Isn't that enough?"

"I guess so," she said. "But I can't help feeling that we may be biting off more than we can chew. Whatever the scheme of things is really like, creatures like us are very, very tiny, aren't we?"

I'd always known that. I realised that somehow, she'd never quite got hold of the idea before. I remembered the way she'd conducted herself when she first arrived on Asgard, blithely suggesting that she could always bomb Skychain City into slag if she didn't get her own way. I supposed that active participation in the virtual genocide of the Salamandrans had given her inflated ideas about the importance of *homo sapiens* which were only now being deflated to a true sense of proportion.

"Well," I said, "it was a virus whose individual particles can be measured in Angstrom units which destroyed the Scarid empire of twenty billion humanoid beings. Nothing's insignificant, if it's in the right place at the right time, doing the right thing."

I felt embarrassed about sermonising, but as I repeated my own words back to myself for reinspection, I couldn't help feeling that, as sermons went, my little homily had its merits. Unfortunately, Susarma Lear was in the mood to export a little of her newfound sense of deflation.

"The problem is," she said, pensively, "that as you kindly pointed out to me up above, we really don't know what we're doing, do we?"

I'm sure that I could have thought up a convincing reply to preserve a few of my delusions of grandeur, but I was saved from the responsibility by the fact that at that precise moment in time something very big and very heavy landed on top of the truck with an almighty crash, and broke our hold on the walls of the shaft.

What had been sideways suddenly became down, and I was catapulted out of the bunk. The only thought which my brain could then accommodate was the terrified realization that twenty-five kilometres was a hell of a long way to fall, and that even the low-gee wasn't going to save us from being comprehensively pulped when we hit the bottom.

✦ 18 ✦

It was time for our blond Vikings to come to life and do their stuff, but there was one awful moment when they simply stood, inanimate, while the walking dead streamed all over them.

"The bow!" cried Myrlin as I reached reflexively for the sword at my belt. I knew that it would be useless to protest that I had never fired an arrow in my life, from a longbow or any other contraption; not knowing what magic had gone into my present making, I might easily discover myself a match for Robin Hood.

I snatched up the quiver from its resting place and slung it over my shoulder; then I snatched up the bow and notched the first arrow in the string. It was a stoutly-timbered weapon, and I could well imagine that it was first cousin to the one which Penelope's suitors had toiled in vain to bend, but it offered little resistance to me as I drew the string back and took aim at one of the skeletons which had a little more flesh on it than most, and which had established a coign of vantage on the figurehead. I loosed the arrow, and saw it fly with a speed that belied the apparent slackness of the string. It hit the bone-man square in the sternum and exploded his entire rib cage, sending slivers of bone in every direction.

The Vikings were moving now, lashing out with their swords and spears. A couple were whirling battle-axes around their heads, and wherever the blades met the brittle skeletons the bones came apart with satisfying ease. Automata our fighting men might be, but they were none the less fearsome for that—they never hit one another, and they commanded nearly every square metre of space on the deck with their flashing blades. The skeleton men poured from their macabre craft in such profusion that they seemed sure to overwhelm our forces by sheer weight of numbers, but they were mostly smashed to bits as soon as they came within range.

One bony warrior leapt to the mast, and climbed like a gibbon to a place of relative safety, then grabbed a spear right out of the hand of one of our burly supporters. It made as if to hurl the weapon at the deck where we stood, but Myrlin knocked it from its perch with an arrow that went into its eye-socket, plucking its steel-helmed skull from the vertebral column and carrying it over the side into the sullen water.

The scraping impact of the two ships had brought us to a virtual standstill, and the entire length of our small vessel, save only for the afterdeck, was alongside the hull of the other. The platform where Myrlin, the goddess, and I were standing was not quite as open to attack as the main deck below, but it was no longer beyond the reach of the corpse-like warriors as they swung on their silvery ropes. The bow was no longer any use and I cast it down again, drawing my sword from its scabbard. I had to swing it with unseemly haste as two of the vile things came swinging through the air at me, reaching with their own rusted blades. I caught them both between the pelvic girdle and the bottom rib, and cut them in half.

I couldn't help feeling that it was all too easy, and that these creatures, for all their revolting ugliness, were far too feeble to be used as serious instruments of intimidation. But then I saw a blond swordsman stagger, and watched him pulled down by groping hands which had no right to be active at all, and I realised that it was not enough to break the skeletons, because the scattered bones were somehow able to reconnect themselves, reassembling new bodies from the shattered parts of the old.

The automata had cut down so many opponents in such a brief space of time that the deck was already littered with bones of every kind, and from that debris a new generation of enemies had already begun to form. Rising unheeded from the timbers they had struck more than one deadly blow at our defenders, and even those which no longer had swords to wield were ready and able to grapple and hinder their opponents.

Upon our raised afterdeck things were not yet set to become so troublesome. The bones which I had scattered had mostly fallen to the lower deck or gone over the side. Better still, Myrlin was wielding his great hammer now, whirling it about him one-handed, striking with such force that the creatures he assaulted were not merely broken but pulverized. But there was danger nevertheless in the detritus which threatened to accumulate about our feet as skeleton after skeleton dropped from above, eager enough to be broken, and equally avid to rise again.

One cannot truly kill the dead.

There was no point at all in trying to cry a warning to the Vikings below, who surely could not heed it, but I looked wildly about for the goddess who was our guide, wondering if she knew an answer to the kind of menace we were facing. Only she had the wit and skill to produce some magical effect that might turn the tables yet again, as she had when the fiery arch had tried to swallow us up.

She stood alone at the furthest corner of our tiny fortress, wrestling with the bow I had discarded. She was struggling to fire an ungainly arrow whose tip was wrapped in lacerated cloth. The trailing tatters made the task unduly difficult.

I did not know what she was doing, but I saw immediately that she needed a defender, because a skeleton bearing a dagger clenched between its rows of rotted teeth was scuttling like a monkey along the rampart, ready to pounce and drag her to the ground.

I lashed out with the flat of my sword, not trying to cut the thing in two but endeavouring instead to thrust it whole over the edge and into the sea. I caught it as I had intended and swept it away, but even as I did so I felt a bony arm wrapped around my neck as one of the creatures closed on me from behind.

I could not strike backwards with my sword, but as the fingers, slimy with decayed flesh, closed upon my windpipe I reached back with my free hand to hook my fingers into the vacant eye-sockets of the thing, and heaved upwards with all my might. The creature had hardly any weight, and I pulled it up with ease, twisting to hurl it over the parapet in my determination not to strew the deck with deadly litter.

When I turned again to strike at another monster that was groping for the goddess, I saw that she had managed to draw the bow, and I watched her loose the arrow. As it passed within a metre of my head the fibres loosely wrapped about its head burst brightly into flame, and I spun around to watch it bury its point in the weird carcass of the giant ship.

The flames leapt from the arrowhead along the knotted lengths of keratin, and within an instant had caught the edge of one of those great grey sails. The sail caught alight as though it were tinder-dry and hungry to burn, and the entire rigging of that remarkable vessel immediately became sheeted in blue fire, the ropes falling about the decks in eerie cataracts of flame. Those skeletons which were still crowding the decks of the huger vessel, ready to swarm down upon us, were wreathed and cloaked by the burning fabric of the tumbling sails, and thrown into dreadful disarray. Although their brown bones would not easily burn, the fire seemed to attack whatever spirit it was which held the bones together and gathered them again if they were parted. The skeletons aboard the ship of the dead seemed almost to melt as they fell in disarray.

There were others which had already attained the platform on which we fought, but Myrlin was striking out now with tremendous force. The hammer, far more effective in his hands than any mere sword, wrought a destruction as complete as the woman's witchfire, and the giant paused only a moment more before leaping over the parapet to the deck below—one giant coming to the aid of an entire company. He danced a complex path between the stabbing blades of the harassed automata, striking downwards and across to splinter skulls, crush fingers, and shatter leg-bones, so that wherever a new warrior tried to rise from the relics of those struck down, there was insufficient substance to give it effective shape.

One last skeleton heaved itself over the rail, sword high in hand, and struck at the goddess, but I shot out my own sword to intercept the blow, then lashed out with my boot to bundle the thing over the side and into the water.

The whole of the attacking ship was now sheathed in flame, and the heat was intense, but our oars were working furiously to draw us away. Those which had been trapped between the hulls had somehow lost their rigidity, and were thrusting like the legs of a desperate insect to push us away from the fire.

The expanse of water which appeared between the two hulls seemed to have an anger of its own, roiling and swirling as the oars whipped its surface, and the ships *did* come apart, slowly at first and then more quickly as the oars, free to operate with all their power, skated our smaller vessel away from the burning wreck.

The warriors in the horned helmets, despite the fact that they were not sentient, did not lack the intelligence required to begin sweeping the remains of their erstwhile attackers into the water, to prevent any chance of their forming again to renew the assault. Half a dozen of the blond defenders had been struck down and had taken fatal wounds, but no more, and what was left of the mock-men of bone and sinew could pose no further threat.

I dared not pause to relax, but made sure that our own enclosed platform was quite free of cadaverous parts. When this ugly task was finished, my first instinct was to look again to the sea before us, lest another enemy should already be rearing its ugly head from the waters. But there was nothing to be seen save for another bank of cold grey mist, and that some distance off.

"Is it over, for a while?" I asked our patroness, as she put down the bow and scanned the scene with her radiant eyes.

She shook her head. "They need not give us time to rest or confer," she said. "We are unlimited by the heaviness of matter and the emptiness of real space, and so are they. I have no doubt now that they are clever, and that they have established a bridge of common meanings across which they may launch their assaults. Whatever is hidden within that bank of fog will be just as anxious to destroy us as the things which we have so far faced, and it will be upon us very soon."

I managed a small but humourless laugh, and asked:

"Are we near to our destination? Can we hope that help will come?"

"I cannot tell," she replied. "I do not know what strength we have, let alone what the enemy will use to draw it from us. We have spun the fabric of this world from the thread of your wayward dreams, Michael Rousseau, and none of us can be sure just what our present state will permit, or how it might be conclusively disrupted. They are exploring the imagery of assault, and we the imagery of defence. There is no way to know what ingenuity they have to bring to bear, or what we have within us to defy it. Do what you can, and time will tell us whether we have done enough. Remember that you may be the most powerful of us all, with assistance already given to you."

As I turned to face the mist that waited to swallow us up, I could not help reflecting that this was poor encouragement. This might be a world concocted out of my dreams, but it was nevertheless a world where I felt myself to be a stranger. If I had ever been here before, in my waking fantasies or my deepest slumbers, I was not aware of it, and I had so far seen little evidence that my subconscious resources were uniquely fitted to the magical metaphysics of this realm. My sword might be a featherweight in my hand, my aim with the bow as unerring as my heart's desire would have it, and my voice the forceful instrument of my will, but I was still a man in a world where forceful spirits moved which had more power than I could ever muster. Behind the appearances which we must fight to maintain were entities which had brought Asgard itself to the brink of destruction, and they did not need to understand us wholly in order to crush us as comprehensively as Myrlin's magical hammer had crushed the rotting bone-men.

The mist closed about me, then, forcing a shiver from

my body. I felt by no means tireless as the damp greyness chilled the sweat of exertion that stood upon my forehead.

For a moment, I felt our movement through the fog as though it were a wind, but then that movement slowed abruptly as the ship seemed to be gripped by a giant vise, which closed upon its hull and held it tight—and though I could not see the oars straining to pull us on, I knew that they strained in vain, and that we were caught fast. However close we might be to the mysterious shore ahead of us, we had ceased to make progress toward it.

◂ 19 ▸

I had an uneasy feeling that I had been dead to the world for a long time—and by "the world" I do not simply mean the world of material objects, but also the private world inside my head. Ordinarily, of course, the fact of my unconsciousness would have rendered meaningless any reference to that private world, which could not be said to exist independently of my perception of it, but my existential situation was no longer ordinary. Like 994-Tulyar, I was harbouring a mysterious stranger, which could take advantage of any loosening of the grip of my own personality to increase the measure of its own dominion within my brain and body.

Because of this curious state of affairs, I awoke from oblivion not once but twice—first into a dream which seemed not to be my own. I experienced it only as a spectator, from a perspective more remote than any I had ever experienced before, in normal dreaming or under the influence of a psychotropic drug.

The dream that I interrupted was a dream of Creation, but I cannot say when it had begun, or how long it had been going on. I was too late to witness the birth of the universe, if that had indeed been its starting-point; nor was I in time to study the intricate dance of the atoms which must have long preceded the origin of the complex organic molecules from which the first living systems were built. I do not know whether dozens or hundreds of self-replicating molecular systems had already been born and superseded, or how those systems had been propelled up the ladder of evolution by whatever chain of cause-and-consequence overruled the logic of random chance. When I invaded this dream the youngest stars of the nascent universe were long dead, and in their explosive dying had given birth to scores of heavier elements which decisively altered the context of opportunity in which the adventure of life was due to unfold. There was already a molecule in existence which was a rude ancestor of DNA, and others which joined with it in an intricate game of transferred energies.

The habitat of these molecular game-players was not to be found on the surfaces of worlds, but in vast hetero-geneous clouds of gas and dust extending over distances of such magnitude that light took years to traverse them. These clouds were the wombs of new stars, and it was in the energetic haloes created by such births that the molecules of proto-life pursued their game with the greatest avidity. Elsewhere, their more ingenious trans-actions failed, and darkness stilled their enterprise; but the players and their game were rarely obliterated, even in the least promising regions of space; they merely waited patiently for the light of new stars to renew their efforts. With each new sun-birth, the molecules came closer to producing the phenomena of authentic life, and each sun-death would blast the spores of proto-life into distant regions of every cloud, destroying all but a few, but leaving those few to resume their unfolding story at some future time.

As aeons passed, true life—the life of DNA—was born, a by-product of the creation and destruction of the stars which was the rhythmic history of the universe it-self, the fundamental alchemy of all things.

Life was not everywhere in the universe; it had come too late for that. It emerged here and there, and there again. Similar processes of chemical unfolding produced nearly identical chemistries again and again in different regions of space. Every time life emerged, it would begin to spread, its own molecules—organised now into the first primitive cells—discovering abundant food in the vast clouds ripe for their predation, and discovering in the light of suns the powerhouses which would drive the motor of their future growth and evolution.

Eventually, life discovered *worlds:* planets bathing in the light of suns, whose gravity-wells offered the opportunity for molecule-systems to congregate very densely, and play their games with an intimacy and an intensity of competition hitherto unthinkable. Worlds were not conquered easily, for their surfaces were very violent places, but in the clouds of gas-giants life often found a refuge, and in the oceans of water which sometimes surrounded rock-worlds life discovered the most zestful of all its games, where competition was fiercest of all and the ladder of evolution reached out to new heights of complexity and cleverness.

It seemed to be only a matter of time—albeit time measured in billions of years—before life *did* fill the universe, extending its seeds into every last corner where they might one day grow, so that it was potentially present in every region where a new sun might be born, ready to take advantage of whatever opportunities were opened up by the material system which formed around each coalescing star. There seemed to be nothing that could inhibit the infinite and eternal extension of the great game, whose play would become the universal project, the strategy of existence itself.

There *seemed* to be nothing. . . .

But there was *something*.

It was something whose nature I could not quite grasp. I had to struggle for a way of understanding it. I did not even know whether it was something that came into being long after the story of life had begun, or whether it had remained hidden and dormant all the while. Was it, I wondered, another kind of life, which had its own incompatible game to play with matter, space, and time? Could it be conceptualised as a force which was the very antithesis of life—some elemental principle of destruction, or at least of *deconstruction?* Was it something opposed in essence not merely to life but even to matter, like the antimatter built of positrons and antiprotons?

I could not tell, and as I struggled to understand what message the dream was trying to deliver to my own intelligence, I felt the perspective shifting from what had seemed (only seemed?) to be a literal representation into a mythical one, where life became a generative god, father and mother of all things, while whatever adversary it was that threatened life became demonic: Satan, Beëlzebub, Ahriman, Iblis, Tiamat.

But this mythical framework of understanding would no more come to a stable and graspable point of resolution than the cosmological vision had, for simple dualism was quickly hedged with alternative images and doubts. I caught glimpses of giants which my memory was quick to name Ymir and Purusha, but they were mere shadows on the cave-wall of my skull, cast by some inner light that was flickering already under the threat of being extinguished. They overlapped and all but drowned out a host of other shadows, some with humanoid form, some with animal form, and some built from eccentric combinations of the two.

I tried to give names to all the dancing silhouettes, but it was a hopeless task, because they were already fading away. I felt like an avatar of Tantalus, condemned to stand beneath the fruit of the tree of knowledge, but never able to take a bite. I struggled desperately to find something sensible and meaningful in the chaotic whirl of impressions, but it was too late.

The communicative bond was shattered. I woke up.

I had one hell of a headache, which was not so much my previous headache doubled, but my previous headache raised to a new order of magnitude.

I opened my eyes anyway, and found myself back in the bunk from which I'd fallen. Opposite me, suddenly attentive, was the scion Urania.

"Please lie still for a few minutes, Mr. Rousseau," she said, before I could open my mouth to speak. "Your skull is not fractured, but you were badly concussed. The powers of self-repair which my sisters awakened in your flesh will preserve you, but you must rest."

It was one of those occasions when only clichés will do: "What happened?" I asked, quickly following up with: "Where are we?"

"A trap was set for us in the shaft," she said. "I fear that we were careless—we did not think to investigate the space above the access-point. A heavy mass was dropped shortly after we began our descent. Fortunately, we were able to release our grip on one side of the shaft before impact. When the missile hit us, we were already swinging, and the blow was a glancing one. The extensors which had let go were able to seize the same side of the shaft as the remainder, so that we were able to withstand the ripping away of three of the others. Then we resumed our descent. No one was seriously injured, although 673-Nisreen sustained a broken arm. He does not have your augmented powers of healing, and the injury will prove troublesome."

She glanced down as she said it, and I realised that the Tetron bioscientist must be in the bunk below me. I would have craned my neck over the edge to catch his eye and say hello, but my head wasn't quite up to it.

"You are sure that this is me, I suppose?" I said. "Not something else borrowing my body?"

It was a feeble attempt at humour, but it was far too near the knuckle. She gave me an anxious, speculative look, obviously giving the hypothesis serious consideration.

"It's okay," I said, swiftly. "It really is me. I think the other guy had sole control for a while, there, but I'm definitely back now. It didn't try to take over. It was trying to tell me something—to explain what this is all about."

"If you had a further dream-experience," she said, taking on the interested tone of voice that her mirror-land parent had adopted in similar circumstances, "I would be most interested to hear a description of it."

"It was nothing much," I muttered, sourly. "Just a history lesson. We never got to the end of it, and I think I was too stupid to get the point anyway. All I'm sure of is that it was trying to explain to me that there's a war going on—not just in Asgard but throughout the universe. We already suspected that."

But while I said it, I was wondering. Was the thing in my brain an independent intelligence, trying to tell me what this whole affair was all about? Or had the experience been some kind of programme playing on automatic, on which I'd just happened to eavesdrop? If the latter was the case, did it mean that the thing inside me wasn't anything like a

person, but more like a bundle of non-sentient programmes
. . . game-playing programmes? Maybe Tulyar wasn't so much
a victim of demonic possession as an ambulatory automatic
pilot: a zombie lodestone or a golem direction-finder. The
possibilities, alas, were still endless. There were too many
names, too many metaphors queued up like idols in some
bizarre marketplace, none of them quite able to grasp the
essence of the problem.

"Oh, *merde,*" I said with feeling. "I think I'd rather not
have woken up at all. Do you happen to know if I finished
my supper?"

She handed me a tube and a bladder, both half-full—or
half-empty, if you happen to be of the pessimistic turn of
mind. I took a long pull from the bladder-pack, and felt a
little better. The headache was clearing fast, and I guessed
that I'd already been supplied with medication.

"How long was I out?" I asked.

"According to your measurement," she said blandly,
"about fifty-two hours."

This was not as much of a shock as it might have been.
Lately, I'd been losing vast chunks of my life right, left, and
centre. If I'd still been condemned to the traditional
threescore years and ten I'd have begun to feel aggrieved,
but Myrlin and the Nine had assured me that their tinkering
with my personal biotechnology had increased that potential many times over. If I were careful, I'd outlive Methu-
selah. I could afford to spend a few days in suspended
animation every now and again.

The truck rocked slightly, and I became aware that we
were traveling horizontally. During the two days and a bit
I'd missed, we'd obviously had plenty of time to get to the
bottom of the shaft, and for all I knew we might have
climbed down another just as long.

I eased myself out of the narrow bunk, ignoring Urania's painstaking mime of anxious disapproval. Her big brown monkey-like eyes had no difficulty at all in signifying sadness, but I wasn't about to be blackmailed into feeling guilty by an accident of anatomy.

I worked my way forward into the cab. Myrlin was in the driving seat but he wasn't actually driving. The truck was making its own way, with a little help from the intelligent suitcase resting on his lap. Susarma Lear was on the other side of the front seat, her left elbow wedged into a convenient cranny so that she could prop up her face on the heel of her hand. She was staring moodily out at the way ahead. She looked round when I moved into the space behind the seats.

"In the Star Force," she said, "we like to think that we're always ready for action. We do not take fifty-two-hour naps." But she said it lightly, to let me know that she didn't really mean it. She had about as much chance of learning to be witty as I had of absorbing the true Star Force spirit, but at least she was trying.

I looked past her at the landscape that was dimly illuminated by the headlights. There was nothing much to see—just a sea of fine sand or dust, silvery grey in colour. It wasn't flat, though its undulations were shallow. The air seemed to be full of tiny particles shimmering in the beams of light that preceded us. The truck wasn't making anything like the speed it should have been, and I guessed that the wheels were sinking into the dust. We must have been kicking up one hell of a cloud behind us.

"Dead?" I asked, as I eased myself into a position between Myrlin and Susarma Lear.

"Apparently not," said Myrlin.

"But well on the way," added the colonel.

They both sounded glum.

"Something wrong?" I asked.

"We're having difficulty following the trace," Myrlin explained. "The small quantities of organic material leaked by the other truck seem to be disappearing very quickly. It's possible that they're simply adhering to particles that are then scattered by the disturbance of its passage, but I think it more probable that the molecules are actually being metabolised. We have a bearing, of course, but it is not certain that the other vehicle will hold a straight course. If it deviates, we might have difficulty picking up the trail."

"Metabolised?" I queried. "You mean the dust is full of bacteria?"

"Ninety percent organic," said Myrlin. "Millions of species in every handful."

"The usual story," said Susarma. "Ashes to ashes, dust to dust. It's just that this level has no middlemen." It was a cleverer joke than I'd ever heard her make before, and the first sign that a bit of me was rubbing off on her.

"Is this the same sort of stuff that the rings of Uranus are made out of?" I asked. "Has anyone told Nisreen?"

"He's asleep," said the colonel, laconically. "Sedated. Got a broken arm."

The truck lurched slightly as it came over the top of a bigger-than-usual undulation. One of the wheels spun free for a second or two, but then it got a grip again. The air seemed so thick with the dust that it was difficult to see where the ground ended and the space above it began. To say that visibility was poor was an understatement—we might have been driving through a dense fog. I wondered whether this really was a level full of the kind of dust that could be found in the gas-clouds where second-generation stars were found—a sample of the primeval life-system which seeded the seas of every world where water could exist as a liquid. Who could tell? Maybe it was a different kind of system altogether—a very old one. Perhaps metazoan life was only a passing phase which biospheres went through, and in the end it all came full circle. As Susarma said: ashes to ashes, dust to dust.

My funny dream had left its imprint on my waking self. I had the history of the universe and the destiny of all flesh very much in mind. The pain in my head was ebbing away, but it didn't leave me feeling normal. I had that medicated feel you sometimes get when your pain-bearing nerves have been switched off—as if it was low gee outside my skull and zero gee inside it.

"Well," I said, "as it's all so utterly boring, I might as well go lie down."

I should have known better than to tempt fate like that. We crested another rise and were suddenly heading downhill. All four wheels had lost their purchase—which wasn't surprising, because we were riding a landslide and the dust was traveling faster than we were. It was coming up in front of us in great billows that cut visibility to absolute zero, and for all we could tell the ground might have swallowed us up entirely.

For all of five seconds I wasn't in the least worried. After all, I was used to levels that had twenty-metre ceilings, where even the deepest lake would barely cover your head if you walked across its bed. I assumed that the slope couldn't go on for long, and that we'd be bound to hit bottom any second.

Then the five seconds became ten, and I knew we were in trouble. For all I knew, this was the laundry-chute that would take us all the way down to the bottom of the world.

In a way, it wasn't so bad—after all, the bottom of the world was exactly where we wanted to go. But how many tons of dust would we be buried under, if and when we got there? And how in hell were we ever going to pick up the trail that we'd very nearly lost even before we fell into the hole?

⤳ 20 ⤳

The mist was slowly clearing, as though to let us witness the extent of our predicament, and we stood by the rail, morosely inspecting the expanse of weed which was thus revealed to us.

We were stuck fast. Though the oars still struggled to find some purchase amid the choking fronds of the weed, we could see that they were fighting a hopeless battle. It seemed that there was weed of every kind and texture—kelps and wracks, filamentous green weeds and rubbery brown weeds, were all tangled together into a straitjacket overlaying the surface upon which we traveled. There was not a hectare of clear water to be seen, and there were many places where the bulk of the weed was so great that it formed hillocks and mounds in the water. It looked as if we might descend from the ship and walk upon it, so thickly was it clustered, but I would not have dared to trust that appearance.

"What now?" asked Myrlin, sourly. "Will they send an army of giant crabs marching across this desert sea to attack us? Will other monsters gather beneath its shield, invisible until they thrust themselves up all about us?"

"A better question," I said, "is whether they need to do anything at all? Why should they trouble to find a means of destroying us, if they can hold us immobile? Wherever our goal might lie, it seems to me that we can come no nearer to it unless we can find a way to break out of this trap they've set to catch us."

We both looked to our guardian goddess for an answer,

but it was plain that she was temporarily perplexed.

"I confess that I had not anticipated this," she admitted. "Whatever it is which acts against us, it has found a way to confine us. I do not know how this has been done, and without knowing how, I cannot see a way to escape."

I had laid down my bow and sheathed my sword. I was not entirely ungrateful for an opportunity to pause, because I felt that I had hardly begun to come to terms with this hallucinatory realm, but I knew that any delay could only work to the advantage of our enemies. Their hostility had so far been relatively impotent; they had not yet learned the ontological rules by which our natures converted the raw material of software space into experience—the magic of our being still held good. But they were the natives of this space, and it could only be a matter of time before they gained full measure of the demonic powers they were anxious to possess in order to turn our little fantasy into a full-blown nightmare. Myrlin and I did not belong here at all, and even the lovely goddess in whom the Nine were embodied, however much better adapted to this milieu she might intrinsically be, was a novice in this business of warfare by witchery.

"Could you burn the weed the way you burned their weird ship?" I asked.

She stared at me blankly, the light seeming dim in her eyes. The pale perfection of her features seemed too inhuman to be truly beautiful. I did not even know whether my present form was capable of any analogue of sexual desire, but I did not think her capable of inspiring it, despite her careful mimicry of human beauty.

"Perhaps. . . ." she said, dubiously.

"If it is only a matter of finding the right magic . . ." began Myrlin, but then he shook his head in confusion.

"Only," I echoed, with a mirthless laugh.

"But you have shaped this dream of ours," complained the black-clad giant, addressing himself to Pallas Athene. "We did not find this place; it came into being with our coming. Why can you not define by the force of your will the ways by which we may control it?"

"We are far from being omnipotent," she told him. "We have laid down the rules which determine how things will appear to us, and now must abide by them. If our enemies find strategies which our rules permit, though we had not thought of them ourselves, we cannot arbitrarily cancel their legitimacy."

"Is it nothing but a game, then?" he asked her, bitterly. "When I agreed to do this, I thought it something more."

"Games are merely fantasies," she said, "which reproduce the structure of experience. Yes, this is a game, if you care to call it one, but what is at stake is the life that you have here, and countless other lives, here and elsewhere. There is no more for it to be."

"Then we have only to find the right countermove," I said, "the capture *en passant* which will let us out of the trap . . . the formula of power which will burn the weed or wither it with blight, or cause a herd of friendly sea-cows to rise from the depths and consume it with avid appetite."

She was still looking at me, steadily and without resentment. "Yes," she said. "That is what we must do."

"I can't help," I told her. "You're the one with all the magical artistry at her disposal."

She shook her head. "Not so," she said. Her gaze moved at last, wandering to the hammer that Myrlin held, weightlessly, in his hand. But what use was a hammer against a Sargasso of clinging weed? I turned to look at the carved figure-head—the symbol of whatever power might be contained within *my* being, waiting to erupt. Would it do us any good to be able to turn the weed to stone? Perhaps—if the stone were as brittle as glass. But I didn't know how. I didn't even know to release whatever power I might be harbouring: I knew no *open sesame!* which might unlock the *doppelganger* of my soul.

"It is possible," she said thoughtfully, "that this was the state which the war within Asgard's software space had reached. Perhaps the opposing forces, unable to destroy one another, had succeeded only in bringing about some kind of crystallization, whereby each held the other immobile and impotent. Perhaps that state of crystallization was shattered by our initial intervention—suddenly destroyed, liberating the armies on either side. Perhaps that is the state to which things must soon return, unless. . . ."

She was thinking that while the situation was fluid, there was an opportunity for a conclusive advantage to be gained, here or in the physical centre to which my *alter ego* might now be drawing close. But there was something else in what she said that had caught my attention. She had spoken of the possible immobilisation of the contending forces as a crystallization, but the analogy which came to my mind was *petrifaction*—a conversion of the living, active flesh to rigid, impotent stone. Was that the nature of the weapon with which I had been entrusted? Was that why it appeared to me as Medusa's head? Was I the crystal-seed whose mission, in the thinking of those who had summoned me here with their cry for help, was to restore stillness and impotence to the heart of Asgard's software space?

It was not easy to work out how I ought to feel about that. I had seen enough of the levels to know what effects the long stagnation of Asgard's systems had had upon many of the habitats and their humanoid prisoners.

But what alternatives are there? I asked myself. *And have I really any choice at all in what I do?*

166

I wondered how much choice Perseus had had, pushed hither and yon by the whims of the Olympians. But the Olympians themselves, I remembered, had been subject to the workings of an implacable destiny—beyond the machinations of the gods there was the instrumentality of fate, symbolised by three dark sisters spinning the thread of time and life.

I watched the oars, still scraping the surface of the knotted weed, albeit in half-hearted fashion now. They were still working autonomically, trying to repeat the action of rowing, but they seemed pathetic in their inadequacy, like the legs of a beetle turned over on its back, unable to right itself.

The image brought an idea into my mind, and I turned back to the goddess. "How extensive is the command which you have over the ship?" I asked. "Could you alter its locomotive action?"

"We are the ship," she replied, plainly. "It is our body, as much as this is." She pointed her finger at her breastbone as she spoke. By "we" she meant, of course, the Nine, not the three adventurers whose descent into Asgard's inner depths had been interrupted.

"Then you must stop trying to swim," I told her, "and begin to crawl. Make the blades of your oars into hands, and brace the shafts like the legs of a walking insect. If the weed is strong enough to hold us, it may be strong enough to support us, provided that our weight is sufficiently spread out."

She turned swiftly to look at the oars, and I could see by the returning light in her eye that I had offered her a possible solution.

I watched with her as the oars stopped their futile pawing. The blades grew into shapes which more resembled the feet of a wading bird, and the shafts became jointed. As soon as the feet were all in position, the legs began to lift, and though it seemed for a moment that the sucking surface tension of the sea would hold us down, our hull broke free, and we were suddenly on top of the weed. One or two of the feet broke through the matted surface, but there were too many points of support to make our position precarious, and the legs began to move, a wave passing along the rank like the kind of wave which passes along the many legs of a millipede as it makes its painstaking way along. At first we walked slowly, as though fearful to fall, but we quickly picked up speed, and soon were running at least as rapidly as we had earlier been able to row.

I saw Myrlin smile, not simply because we were moving again, but because he had accepted the lesson that we *could* discover how to act here . . . that we were not utterly impotent by virtue of the strangeness of it all.

"Well done!" he said. "Perhaps they will not stop us after all."

But I was not so ready to surrender to delight. I had not failed to notice that the moment we began to move, the mists that had withdrawn themselves began to steal inwards again. The cloudy sky above us, which had become quite white and high, now seemed to descend again, and to shift and swirl with fierce uncertain winds. I expected at any moment that the weed would sink beneath the surface of the eldritch sea, and let us down to float again, as we had before—but that was not what concerned me. I knew that we had now had our pause, and having escaped the attempt to confine us, must force our enemies to redouble their efforts to destroy us. In proving that we were not impotent, we had proved that we might be dangerous, and I knew that every adversary that came against us would be stronger than the last—until, in the end, we would meet our match.

The game, if game it was to be reckoned, had hardly begun.

⤚ 21 ⤙

When we came to rest, the truck's front end was pointed downwards at an angle of forty-five degrees. We had not been brought to an abrupt stop, nor had we been bounced about very much on the way down. All in all, it had been a pretty smooth ride. I calculated that we'd been traveling with the dustslide for the best part of half a minute, but I couldn't translate that into distance. The acceleration due to gravity was pretty tame down here, and we'd had the dust to slow us up as well. We certainly hadn't got to the bottom of the world, but in Asgardian terms we could be at the bottom of a fairly deep well, buried in dirt.

I could see through the window that it wasn't just dirt that we were buried under. It was a thick, glutinous liquid. We were at the bottom of a sea of mud.

I already knew that the truck could climb down an empty shaft, but I wasn't at all sure that it could swim.

"Anybody hurt?" I asked.

Nobody answered. I assumed that could be taken as an all-round no.

"What do we do now?" asked Susarma Lear. Like the rest of us she had both hands on the ledge of the dashboard in front of her, bracing herself so that she didn't slide off the seat. The window looked like a dull mirror, silvered by the dust in which we were buried, and I could see her shadowy reflection looking at me.

Nobody answered her question either.

Then there came a strange sound, as if something was

169

being scraped along the side of the vehicle. Wherever we were, we weren't alone.

"Is the side of the truck clear?" I asked Urania, wondering whether it was only the cab that was under the drift.

"No," she said, shortly. She was fluttering her fingers over the body of her mechanical sister, her brow furrowed with intense concentration.

The sound continued, moving closer now, until it was at the side of the cab. It was no longer a single scrape but a combination, and the sounds were now coming from three different directions. As I looked at the dim reflection of Susarma's face I saw it suddenly dissolve as though exploded, and actually winced before I realised that it was the mud which had been disturbed, not the person whose image it had caught. There was something moving in the ooze, pressing against the truck as if trying to grip it.

It was like a section of segmented tubing, pale and slimy. It extended itself across the windscreen, as though it were a piece of rope that was being wound carefully around the truck.

"Oh shit," said Susarma. "It's a bloody worm. A giant worm."

I knew there was no need to be frightened—at least, not of the worm. It could be the biggest and nastiest worm in the universe, but it wasn't going to be able to break in. To judge by the scraping sounds it was either coiling itself tightly about us, or it had three or four friends with it, but it was still quite impotent. On the other hand, its presence wasn't exactly comforting.

"What do we do?" Susarma asked again, obviously hoping that someone had thought of a brilliant plan in the interval which had passed since she last enquired. I hadn't, so I looked at Urania, who was still busy communing with the magic box.

"We are extending pseudopods," she said. "There is a rigid surface beneath us, on which the pseudopods can find purchase. Then we must drag ourselves through the mud."

"It sounds," I observed, "as if that might take a long time."

We waited. Then she said: "We are close to the bottom of a cleft. There is an upward slope about thirty metres away, inclined about twenty degrees to the horizontal. With luck, it should not take too long to free us from the mud."

She didn't sound over-optimistic. That wasn't entirely surprising. We still had to pick up the trail of the other truck. With the ground turning liquid and the local bugs busy gobbling up the organic trace we were supposed to be following, that might not be easy. If we were unlucky, we'd be lost—and of all the places I could think of to be lost in, this was far from being my favourite.

"Is there anything we can do to help?" I asked.

"It will not be necessary," she assured me. "Perhaps you should take the opportunity to rest." She seemed perennially keen to make sure that I got my beauty sleep.

I didn't think the wait would be very restful no matter what I did, but I didn't like the thought of remaining braced against the windscreen, watching the worms go by. I climbed out of the cab into the hind part of the truck.

673-Nisreen had woken up when we stopped. He had turned himself around in his bunk so that it was his feet that were pointed downward at a forty-five degree angle, but he didn't look very comfortable. He asked me what had happened and I told him, as succinctly as I could. Instead of getting into my bunk I sat down on the sloping floor, in the narrow space between the two sets of shelves. It was as comfortable a position as I could find.

"How's the arm?" I asked.

"The scion set it well," he told me. "The slide jarred it, but I do not think it did any further damage." Like all Tetrax, he was committed to making light of his suffering. They consider themselves to be a very dignified race.

"I think I have another piece of the jigsaw," I said.

He didn't understand me. Obviously, the parole word into which I'd translated "jigsaw" didn't have the right connotations.

I told him about my dream. Urania was busy, but I figured that Clio would be listening in somehow.

"Whatever they copied into my brain," I told him, when I'd finished, "seems to be intended to tell us what the situation is, as well as helping us to deal with it. Comparing its tactics with what the thing that got into Tulyar seems to have done, I'm inclined to believe that we're on the side of the humanitarians—which makes it the right side, in my book. I only wish I could get a proper grip on whatever it's trying to teach me. What is this *anti-life?* You're a bioscientist—what could it be?"

He was a Tetron bioscientist, which meant that he had an inbuilt evasiveness when it came to guesswork and speculation, but I could tell that what I'd told him intrigued him a little.

"The simplest hypothesis," he said, carefully, "might suppose it to be something which has the same characteristics as DNA-based living systems—the tendencies of growth, self-replication, evolution of complexity, and so on—but with a different chemical basis. If its fundamental molecular system was a different carbon chain, this other system might be locked into a universe-wide competition with DNA for the elements of life: carbon, hydrogen, oxygen, nitrogen."

"So an Asgard-type macroworld would then become

both an Ark and a fortress in the context of an ongoing war between DNA-life and X-life for sole possession of the universe? It would be designed to collect and preserve DNA-forms, and also to seed worlds where the elements of life are available. But there are X-life macroworlds too, manned by X-life humanoids and X-life software entities, trying to do much the same thing. And each side is trying to shoot down the other side's macroworld."

"Perhaps," said Nisreen, though I could tell that it wasn't a scenario he cared for.

"What are the alternatives?"

"These anti-life entities might not be able to produce mirror-images of the life-systems which DNA has built. Perhaps only DNA produces trees, insects, humanoids . . . perhaps a system based in different molecules would produce very different forms. Perhaps it could not produce metazoan entities at all—perhaps nothing more complicated than a bacterium. But that would not explain the apparent presence of hostile software entities within Asgard. Perhaps the anti-life sequence of evolution does not involve carbon at all—perhaps it involves different elements, and begins to touch the world of life only at the point when its intelligent, manipulative entities begin to build intelligent machines whose brains are silicon-based."

"But what, in that case, would the war be about? What would be the purpose of the worldlets?"

"To collect and to seed, as you have already suggested. But it might help to explain the curious situation we find here if we suppose that the invaders of Asgard really have nothing against the organic inhabitants of the worldlets, and would be quite content to let them alone. They might envisage themselves as being in competition—and hence in conflict—only with the software intelligences. That would explain why life of our kind has never been wiped out or seriously threatened, although the attempt made by the Isthomi to explore the software space of inner Asgard invoked such a powerful reaction."

I considered the two alternatives. They both had certain attractions. I couldn't immediately see a way of deciding between them. Nor could I see any reason to suppose that they were the only two hypotheses that might be entertained.

"Can you think of any others?" I asked Nisreen.

"The game of speculation," he parried, "can be played indefinitely. There are always more."

"Tell me," I said.

"It is outside the scope of my expertise," he said.

"I don't think this is an appropriate time to get coy," I told him. "The guys back on Tetra will probably never know. You can be as wild as you like."

"In that case," he said, "we can multiply hypotheses simply by pushing the level of competition further and further back. We have imagined life based in an alternative organic chemistry. We have imagined pseudo-life based in the chemistry of other elements than carbon. If we are to exercise our imaginations more fully, we might attach the phenomena which are associated with life—replication, evolution, control of the environment—to things other than those transactions of atoms and molecules which we categorise as 'chemistry.' If there are to be no limits upon what we suppose, then we may babble about quasi-living systems and intelligences at the subatomic level, or at the level of the structuring of space itself. You have no doubt been told that if the fundamental constants of physics had other values than the ones they have now, life of our kind would be impossible. It is possible to speculate that those charac-

teristics themselves are in some way open to manipulation—
but at this point the imagination of beings like us is tested
to its limit. I, at least, can no longer construct a coherent
account of what might be going on."

I remembered that what seemed to be happening in my
dream was a failure of the imagination . . . an inability to
get a grip on things. Maybe that was the reason. Maybe any
story that Nisreen and I could think up must be false, for
the simple reason that we had to make it make sense, and
the reality didn't. Maybe the answer was so peculiar that we
couldn't even formulate it—but maybe not so peculiar that
it was beyond the imagination of an advanced software
persona. Maybe the things that were fighting this grotesque
war had reasons for doing so that we could never comprehend.
Maybe even the Nine were too primitive and too stupid:
mere godling cannon-fodder in a conflict which concerned
them hardly more than it concerned us.

I remembered the end of the dream, and the other
dreams, and the way in which a mythical framework of understanding kept imposing itself, incomprehensibly, upon
what might well be attempts by the biocopy in my brain to
help me figure out the what and why of things.

I tried to explain that to Nisreen—to tell him something
about the ideas underlying Greek and Norse mythology—in
order to ask him what dreams poor Tulyar might have had,
and what vocabulary of symbols the Tetron mind might
draw upon in parallel with my experiences.

"With us it is not the same," he said. "Your present
culture is a patchwork, made by the drawing together of
many ancestral tribes which had different languages and
different ways of thought, having dispersed geographically
long before inventing agriculture and settling down. Your
entire history is dominated by the idea of a small local tribe

surrounded by aliens . . . by enemies.

"On Tetra, our ancestors discovered agriculture and settled down before dispersing geographically, so that our gradual colonization of the various regions of our world was more like the growth of a single culture. In time, we developed different languages and other cultural differences, but our history has always been dominated by the idea of one tribe, changing and diversifying. You see the influence of this idea in our resistance to exaggerated individualism, and in our habit of numbering ourselves within our name-groups. Not until we began to travel among the stars did we find ourselves to be one tribe among many, and we have always been concerned to bind the galactic community together as a great whole, uneasily aware that it might be impossible or inappropriate to do so. That is why we take such an interest in theories of history and researches in biology that credit all the galactic humanoids with a common ancestry of some kind.

"In terms of our mythology, we were always monotheists. A single tribe very quickly produced the notion of a single god. That idea, in its turn, gave way fairly readily to the notion of a universe that, although godless, is law-governed and ordered as a great machine. Our historical scientists believe that is why the Tetrax are the most scientifically-advanced race in the galactic arm, although we are no older, in evolutionary terms, than any other.

"We have nothing in our cultural and mythological heritage which resembles the complicated notions of your ancient Greeks or Norsemen—the idea of Gotterdammerung would be entirely alien to us. We have not even the kind of covert dualism that is built into your supposedly monotheistic religions, which oppose a law-making god with an adversary or a subversive chaos. It may be, I think—for reasons which are purely accidental—that you have far better resources in the imagination for representing what seems to be going on around us than 994-Tulyar had. It may be that coincidence has helped to model your mythical thinking on a pattern which really is reproduced in the universe, in a conflict of godlike beings with which we have somehow become entangled."

My head was beginning to ache again, but not with the effort of thought. What Nisreen had said was fascinating in more ways than one. One of the ways in which it was fascinating was that it might help to explain why I was being fitted up by fate to take a part in whatever was going on around us. It suggested that there might be something about the human mind—as moulded by its historical and cultural heritage—which enabled it to adapt to the context in which the war inside Asgard could be seen to have meaning. It suggested, in fact, that my other self, copied and encrypted by the Isthomi and then sent forth upon his heroic quest through Asgard's other dimensions, might indeed be enabled to achieve something which no other humanoid could do as well.

For the first time, I paused to wonder how he was getting on, and what he might be up to in those realms of Asgard which were the true habitation of the gods. Was he yet in sight of Valhalla? Or had he suffered instead the dire penalty of *hubris?*

I didn't suppose that I would ever find out, but my insatiable desire to speculate made me think about it anyhow, until I was interrupted by Susarma Lear, who stuck her head into the back of the transporter and said: "We got lucky."

"You mean we picked up the trail of the other truck?" I said.

"Not exactly," she replied. "There's no sign of the trace it was supposed to be laying down for us, and we might easily have lost it for good—if it hadn't started transmitting a Mayday. The opposition are still on this level . . . and they're in trouble."

She was right, of course. We'd got lucky. But I wasn't about to start cheering yet. Until we found out just what kind of trouble the opposition was in, we had no way of knowing whether we could avoid the same fate.

∿ 22 ∿

The last traces of the weed had vanished. Once again the mists had withdrawn and the sea was calm, but I knew that it was only another calm before a storm. As I watched the oars dipping into the water I regretted that the goddess who was the architect of this Creation had chosen to define our environment in terms of an ocean; I thought that I might have felt more secure on solid land. She had assured me that soil and rock would have been no less eager to seize and choke us than the waters of this hallucinatory ocean, and that we would still have had to isolate ourselves in some kind of vessel, but the sea still seemed uncomfortably alien to me.

I had asked why, if unfamiliarity to our enemies was the chief criterion determining her decision, she had not elected to provide us with a void to cross and a ship like *Leopard Shark* in which to navigate it. She had replied that an analogue of stressed space would in her estimation be far easier for our enemies to come to terms with, and the shell of a starship too easy for them to crack. It was, she told me, far safer to be in a realm of uncertain magic, where the enemy could not readily estimate what deceptive power they might assume, or what power we in our turn might have to use against them.

"But we do not know that ourselves!" I had protested.

"That," she had replied with finality, "may be our greatest advantage."

I did not think that I had settled well into the identity of a man of magic. Some men might have taken comfort from the suspicion that unknown forces lay latent within them, holding the potential for a miraculous rescue even in the direst of circumstances, but it was not a possibility in which I could invest much trust. I would have preferred to know just what I was, and what I could do, and to be confident that my resources would be adequate to the task in hand. Alas, even men of flesh and blood rarely know such things, and it is a lucky man indeed who has the pleasure of certainty in regard to the last of those matters.

The next encounter began with a disturbance in the water, which was not so evident on the surface of the sea but which began to exert a marked influence upon the course of the vessel, dragging us off our bearing and away to starboard. I watched the oars as they began to fight against the drag, those to port relaxing while those to starboard tried to work increasingly hard.

"Look!" said Myrlin, pointing away to starboard.

There, far away from the boat, we could see a swirling motion in the water beginning, and rapidly increasing. What had caught us was the outer edge of a great whirlpool that was endeavouring to suck us into a clockwise spiral. It was immediately clear that whatever force was working in the water was more powerful than the oars, because our course was indeed curving away along the arc of a great circle.

Myrlin grappled with the helm, holding it hard over in an attempt to steer us to port, and the prow of the ship began to come about. Instead of taking us away from the current, though, he simply succeeded in exposing a greater target to the rushing water, which began to sweep us sideways.

Myrlin spun the wheel, trying to turn the ship back again in order that the oars could gain some purchase, but the force of the surge was now so great that he could not bring the vessel around. The oars were flailing now, as impotent as they had been when the weed prevented their dipping beneath the surface.

Once again, I felt quite impotent. The weapons with which I had been provided were quite useless in dealing with this kind of attack. I looked back at the female form in which the Nine had remade themselves, and saw that she was chanting, trying to raise some kind of magical force to oppose the one sent to suck us down.

In response to her invocation a great wind blew up, which tried with all its might to carry us in the opposite direction to the drag of the maelstrom. The automata on the lower deck were busy with our great square sail, changing its attitude to catch the full force of the wind while Myrlin threw the wheel the other way, trying to pull our stern round to face the direction of the drag.

The opposition of wind and water churned up the surface of the sea in mighty waves, and turbid spray was everywhere, lashing fiercely at our faces.

I clung to the rail desperately, with my bow and arrows held tight beneath my foot, lest they should be lost. The ship had been tossed about by the wind and the waves before, but that was nothing by comparison with the effects of the present contest of the elements. The sky had grown dark, and the clouds which obscured it were almost black. As though with an outburst of sudden rage those clouds began to pour black rain upon us, cold and stinging. The raindrops mixed with hailstones the size of bullets.

The shape of the whirlpool, which had presented itself quite clearly a few minutes before, was now lost in the tumult, and we seemed to be in the grip of chaos itself, lurching and listing without any apparent pattern.

My stomach felt as if it was turning over, and I had to go down on one knee to crouch beneath the level of the rail, trying to hide my face from the scourging of the storm. I could not tell what Myrlin was trying to do, nor what advantage was being gained in the fight between our wizardry and theirs—all that I could do was wait, and hope that if the ship capsized, I would have the strength to swim in a sea made mad by the vortex in the water and the assaults of the air.

I heard a cry from Myrlin which I took to be a cry of triumph, and thought that the ship must at last have found itself able to respond to the helm, but immediately it was followed by another cry, shot through with anguish, and knew that the enemy had found new reserves.

I forced my head up, to look out into the dark mists, and immediately saw what my giant companion had seen.

All around us, rising to the surface of the water, were the coils of some immense serpent, racing round and around. It was as though the whirlpool had suddenly come to life—Charybdis suddenly transformed into Scylla. It no longer mattered which way the ship was headed, or how it caught the wind, because there was not the slightest doubt that we were surrounded by the coils of the monster. For the moment, I could see no head at all, but merely the scaly loops lying about us, two or three times wound around, and I wondered whether the creature might have seized its own tail to seal itself into a confining ring of flesh. The scales might have shone brightly had there been light enough to make them glisten, but in the grey half-light they were dull and brown, speckled here and there with clumps of dark green tendrils which may only have been some kind of weed anchored to the body of the beast.

I snatched the bow from beneath my foot, feeling a surge

of perverse elation on account of the fact that here was something I could do—here was an enemy at which I could strike in my own fashion.

I fitted an arrow to the bow, and without rising from my kneeling position I fired at the mass closest to the starboard side. I saw the arrow fly true despite the winds which buffeted it in flight, and it buried itself in the flesh of the monster . . . but the sea-serpent made not the slightest reaction. I could see the white feathers that fletched the arrow, but no red blood, nor any other sign of hurt.

I sent forth a second arrow without delay, and hit the same serpentine coil a few yards further on, but with no more obvious result, and I cursed, seeing that the coils were drawing tighter now around the ship, which was imprisoned in an area of water no more than a hundred metres in diameter.

Then came the head, rearing up out of the spume no more than a dozen metres from the flank of the vessel, just aft of the mast. It was as though it had tried to toss us up, as a bull tosses a luckless matador, and had only just failed.

The enormous head was only a little like a snake's: it had the fangs of a snake and eyes which were entirely ophidian, but it had a crest behind its head much more elaborate than a cobra's hood, and its snout was ridged to give it a less rounded profile. It was a veritable dragon's head, with rows of swords-point teeth behind the greater fangs. Its slit-pupilled eyes, golden yellow about the dark lens, caught me immediately with their stare, and the crest swelled to present the appearance of a fan-like array of webbed horns.

It paused for just a second in the air, the head becoming steady as the eyes fixed upon their target, and I knew that it was poised to strike.

I had a third arrow ready, and fired at the open mouth as

it gaped. A black forked tongue flickered out, and the arrow caught it, embedding itself just behind the junction. There was no doubt that the monster felt this blow because the head flinched, sucking the tongue back between the fangs, arrow and all. For a single fleeting moment I clung to the hope that I might have struck a mortal blow, but then the mouth gaped again, the great curved fangs standing stark and white, and the head struck at me with lightning speed.

Had I not been crouched beneath the rail I must have been caught and killed, but my reflexive reaction was to duck, and I felt the two great fangs strike at the carved parapet to either side of me, splintering the wood, but impotent to hurt my body.

As I sprawled on the timbers I looked up into the left eye of the monster, which was incredibly huge at this intimate range, although it was only as big as a man's whole head. I sensed such venomous hatred there as to make my blood run cold.

When the head drew back again I knew that I had a few seconds to spare in which to launch another arrow, and while I notched it to the string I determined to aim at that evil eye, to rob the monster of part of its sight, perhaps even to penetrate its brain.

As the head poised itself in mid-air, ready for the second strike, I managed to get myself into a firing position, and loosed my arrow. It sped in company with at least one other, but the monster swayed very slightly, and both bolts glanced off the armoured scales behind the brow, apparently causing no harm at all. The coils of its astonishing body were coming so tightly about the boat now that the lurching and heeling had stopped, and the wind which tried to catch our sail had likewise dwindled away, so that everything seemed uncannily steady as the head struck out again.

I tried to roll to one side, but the head was simply too

big to be avoided in that way. Fortunately, it was not the gleaming fang that struck me, but rather the horny ridge above the root of the fang, which caught my shoulder and knocked me away from the protecting rail. The bow shivered in my hand, and split as I rammed its end into the timber of the deck. I let it go, and tried desperately to regain my balance.

Another arrow, which must have been fired by the goddess, pursued the monstrous head as it reared backwards for another strike, and embedded its point in the black lip between the fangs, but the leviathan cared nothing at all for such a wound, and I knew that this time it would not miss me when it struck again.

I struggled desperately with my sword, trying to haul it from its scabbard, but the scabbard was trapped beneath me where I had fallen, and I could not get the weapon out.

I stared the monster full in the face as the head paused for an instant, quite still in the clouded air while that baleful eye measured the strike.

Then Myrlin stepped in front of me, his great hammer held in his right hand, and as the vile head thrust itself forward yet again he hurled the hammer with all his might. It flew, more like a thunderbolt than a missile, to meet the serpent's head mid-way. I could not judge the precise point of impact, but I know that the hammer sailed into the open mouth, to catch the upper palate nearer to the throat than the lip.

With Myrlin's heroic strength behind it, the thrown hammer was much more powerful than the sea-serpent's thrusting head, and the impact snatched the head backwards with such violence that I felt sure the cervical vertebrae must have been broken. The monster was hurled backwards, tumbling back over its own circling coils, crashing into the surface of the water.

Myrlin cried out in exultation, and my own voice began to join in, but our anticipation of victory was premature. The great coils were still about the ship, so close on every side that they had almost caught it fast, and when the head disappeared those coils went mad, closing upon the vessel with such a convulsion that they caught it by the bow and the stern, and turned it upright from end to end.

Out of the water rose what I first thought was a second head, but was in fact a great crested tail, which struck at the thrown-up ship with all the violence it could muster.

The mast broke like matchwood, and all the timbers of the hull and the middle deck cracked and splintered. I saw the gorgon's head, severed from its place atop the prow, hurtle through the air to disappear impotently beneath the storm-tossed waves. I heard the goddess scream, and remembered what she had said about the ship being no less a part of her than the armour-clad flesh which she had put on. In that scream, I was certain, I heard the sound of her death.

But it mattered no longer to me whether the ship was seaworthy or not, for I could not help but part company with it, hurled tumbling through the air to come down, not in the turbulent water, but upon the flesh of the monster itself, near to where my first and second arrows had struck.

For one sensible moment I clung with all my might to a handhold found among the scales, as though I might seize the beast and ride him to his lair in the ocean depths, but then I was snatched beneath the waves, and hit the water with such violence that all the breath was knocked out of me.

As I struggled desperately to remain conscious I tried with all my might to gasp for air—but there was no air to be had, and all I could take in was foul and icy water, which seemed to carry a tide of noxious poison into the very heart of my being. I was still on the surface of the strange cold sea, and my red armour seemed to have no weight at all, but something was dragging at me from below, trying to suck me down into the depths. I grabbed at a spar that was close by in the water, but it was by no means large enough to serve as a raft.

Still winded and desperate for air I looked wildly about, and saw a much larger piece of wreckage bearing down upon me from the crest of a wave. Clinging to it with evident desperation was Myrlin's huge black-armoured body, and had I been able I would have yelled with joy to see that he was still alive. I stretched out my hand, trying to catch hold of the edge of the makeshift raft, but the roiling of the waters carried me away. I still could not cry out to beg for help, but I saw Myrlin lift his head and was sure that he must catch sight of me, and save me from the force that was trying to pull me under.

His eyes met mine, and for a moment there was a flicker of recognition, but the instant did not last. It was as though some kind of magical fire flared inside his head, so that his eyes were suddenly lighted from within, burning like angry beacons, and his body was seized by horrid convulsions which were determined to shake him apart.

He would surely have reached out to save me, if he could—but he could not, because the demons had him, and were destroying him even while he clung to the wreckage that had given him momentary hope of salvation.

I felt that the demons had me, too, because I was pulled down by invisible hands, deep into the awful waters, which closed above my head. I knew then that the breath of life for which I fought so hard would never come.

The last thought I had before consciousness left me was that I had discovered what it felt like to drown.

⋌ 23 ⋋

The moment our lights picked out the shape of the other vehicle Clio brought us smoothly to a halt. Susarma Lear was sitting in the driver's seat, but she wasn't pretending to drive. Urania, with Clio on her lap, was sitting between the two of us.

"Better get up to the turret," I said to the colonel. "We may need the guns."

Susarma moved back, and moments later her place was taken by Myrlin. There had been no sign of movement near the other truck, which was facing a blank wall. Its lights were reflected back from the wall to produce a halo effect around it. Its doors seemed to be sealed.

"You think they've all gone down?" asked Myrlin. He was assuming, of course, that they'd come to a dropshaft which was too narrow to contain the truck, and had been forced to go on in light suits, with whatever alternative transport the Nine had laid on for them. But he knew it couldn't be quite as simple as that. Somebody had sent out a Mayday from the truck. Either they were still inside the truck, or we were looking at some kind of trap, like the deadfall in the first shaft.

"They couldn't have known that we'd lost their trail," I said, pensively. "They had to assume that we'd catch them up anyhow, if we survived their first little surprise package. If they had to leave the truck behind, it might have seemed a cute notion to turn it into a big booby trap bomb."

"But they'd need it again when they came back," said

188

Myrlin. "Tulyar may be leading them on a suicide mission, but his friends don't know that."

It was a fair point. I could imagine John Finn's reaction to any proposal to blow up the vehicle.

"Is it possible that they left some of the Scarid soldiers behind, to shoot at us when we try to open the door?" asked Urania.

"Maybe," I replied. "But the same doubts apply. A couple of snipers couldn't expect to wipe out all of us, and even if they did—who'd want to be stranded in this godforsaken spot? If Tulyar and the others have already gone on, the rearguard would be left to its own devices, with no place to go."

"Did they have enough suits?" asked Myrlin, still uneasy. "Perhaps there were simply too many of them, and they had to leave some people behind."

"There were eight aboard," said Urania. "Enough for all of them. But the truck has light and warmth, and is well-supplied. It is by no means inconceivable that some of the party would elect to stay with it rather than descend into possible danger. They might well take the view that the truck could take them up again, if those who have descended never return."

It was plausible enough, but it still sounded wrong.

"I don't suppose they'll respond to a radio call?" I asked.

"We have been transmitting a signal for some time," Urania told me. "The robot's automatic systems are returning a signal which suggests that all is well, but I cannot tell whether there are humanoids aboard. A design flaw, I fear."

Even the Isthomi couldn't think of everything.

"It looks," I said, "as if someone is going to have to go out to take a look."

"Wait!" said Urania quickly, looking down at the suitcase, which was flashing something at her. "An infra-red scan reveals that there are two bodies outside the truck, between the front wheels and the wall. It is probable that they are hiding from us."

"But why would they hide behind the truck with sidearms," asked Myrlin, "when they have a cannon on top of it?"

"The instruments," said Urania in deadpan fashion, "cannot tell us that."

"It doesn't pose much of a problem," I said. "All we need to do is call out to them, telling them to come out with their hands high or we'll blast them with our cannon. They can hear us."

"Let's try it," said Myrlin, becoming impatient with all the talk. "It might work."

We tried it. From inside, it sounded weird; I hoped the garbling was the effect of the truck's armour rather than the inadequacy of our loudhailer.

But Myrlin was right—it did work.

Within fifteen seconds, a lone humanoid came staggering out of the bushes. It was female, and she was wearing a tight transparent suit. Before she collapsed and fell face forward into the dust we got a clear look at her face, and despite the fact that it was covered in blood we had not the least difficulty in recognising her.

It was Jacinthe Siani.

The first thought which crossed my mind was that it had to be a trap. After all, her companion hadn't come out. But the more obvious interpretation of her condition was that her companion was probably in much the same state as she was, and *couldn't* come out.

We sat in silence for half a minute, mulling over these

possibilities and wondering what to do next.

"Well," said Susarma Lear, in a tone whose mockery was not concealed by the muffling effect of her being in the gun-turret, "I reckon she was asking for trouble. One woman in a cramped truck with three Tetrax, three Scarid officers, and that bastard Finn."

It had not occurred to me until she spoke that the Kythnan might have been the victim of a rape. The hypothesis did not strike me as a likely one.

"Somebody has to go out," I said, tiredly. "I'll do it."

"Like hell you will," said the colonel, suddenly appearing again at the hatchway connecting the cab to the back of the truck. "I'll do it. I'm the one with the combat training, remember?"

I shrugged. There are times when you just have to stand aside and give the limelight to someone else—besides which, she was still my commanding officer.

While she was suiting up I watched Jacinthe Siani lying in the mud. She moved once, as though trying to get to her feet again, but she seemed to be quite unable to muster the requisite strength. If it was an act, it was a good act.

I watched Susarma approach the recumbent form, with exaggerated carefulness. She had a flame pistol in her hand. Jacinthe stirred again when the colonel touched her, and it looked as if she spoke, but there was no way to tell what she might be saying. Then Susarma stood up again, and moved around the truck to look for the other person who was supposedly lurking there.

The colonel's voice came back over the intercom, sounding tired and a little bit frustrated. I think she'd really rather have found something to shoot at. "You'd better send Myrlin out to pick this one up," she said. "He's in a pretty bad way."

"Can you tell what happened to them?" asked Urania.

"Not exactly," Susarma replied. "But they look as if they've been in a hell of a fight. They've lost any weapons they were carrying and it looks to me as if they've been very badly beaten. This guy's suit has a lot of blood swilling around in it. He may have a few broken bones. It looks to me like they both might have died if they hadn't had the life-support systems in the suits to sustain them. There are a couple of things here that look like worms cut in half— they may have been twisted round the guy's ankles."

While she was giving this report, Myrlin had moved back to suit up. The colonel was able to pick up Jacinthe Siani and carry her round to the airlock at the rear of the truck, and when Myrlin went out she was able to come back in. It took time to get them through because we put everything through a sterile shower. We didn't want the inside of the truck contaminated. Susarma eventually managed to cram the Kythnan woman into one of the bunk-spaces, and we opened her suit. The wall immediately began to put out hair-like feelers that burrowed their way discreetly into her flesh. She moaned a little, but when she tried to open her eyes she couldn't do it.

"When will she be able to talk?" I asked Urania, who was busy with Clio.

"A few minutes," said Urania. "She is not badly hurt— merely weak from blood-loss and exhaustion."

I looked at the Kythnan's head, and saw that it had taken some bruising blows. It looked like the work of a very crude torturer.

Myrlin brought the other one in. It was one of the Scarid officers, the paleness of his chalk-white skin exaggerated by the ribbons of blood that had dried upon it. He had taken more punishment than the woman, and he looked as if something rather heavy had run over the upper part of his body. His suit wasn't breached, but he'd been shaken up very thoroughly inside it. Again, I couldn't think of anything it looked like except for the results of crude brute force, liberally administered.

We managed to get him into the bunk, and the truck's systems extended their biomanipulators into his tissues.

"We can save him," said Urania, after a brief pause, "but he is very weak. We should not try to bring him round for several hours—he needs coma-rest."

We waited patiently for Jacinthe Siani to come round. We all wanted to hear what she had to say.

Eventually, the Kythnan opened her eyes, and looked around at the faces watching her. We might have appeared a little absurd, crowded into the narrow passage, but she'd been riding in a similar truck with eight aboard, and it must have stopped seeming funny a long time ago.

"Rousseau?" she said faintly. I was the one she knew best—the one she was used to recognising in unexpected situations.

"What happened?" I asked in parole, coming straight to the point.

"I couldn't get him into the truck," she whispered. "I got in to send out the Mayday, but I had to try to get him in too. I got him up the shaft, but I couldn't . . . too weak. . . ."

It wasn't what we wanted to know.

"What smashed you up?" I asked. "And where?"

"Down below," she said, answering the second question first. "Creatures . . . big . . . tentacles. . . . Couldn't get into the suits . . . tried to pull us apart. . . ."

"The others?" I asked, falling into the same clipped style.

"Don't know. Some dead . . . some maybe got through
. . . we fired, but the bullets . . . no good . . . needed
flamers. . . ."

I was quite ready to believe her story. Nobody would
take that kind of a beating just to add a little plausibility to
a set-up.

"Went down in groups of four," she said. "Took equipment. I was with the last group. Dark . . . they didn't look
like anything much . . . then the tentacles . . . like whips
and cables . . . grabbed at us . . . couldn't go forward . . .
got him back to the shaft . . . they did too much damage . . .
unconscious by the time we got to the top . . . got into the
truck . . . went back for him . . . couldn't . . . no one else
came. . . ."

This was where we'd come in. I put my hand on her
shoulder, to signal that she didn't need to go on.

She stopped, and closed her eyes again.

Susarma Lear had her helmet off by now, but she didn't
make any move towards getting out of the suit.

"Well," she said defiantly. "Nobody said it was going to
be easy."

"But what do we do now?" asked Myrlin.

"We say a prayer for the wise guys who stole our truck,"
she told me. "And thank them for discovering the trouble-
spot."

"You're ready to go down there?" I said. "After what our
favourite traitor just told us?"

"Sure," she replied. "But I think we ought to send them
down a little surprise package first. I don't care how many
tentacles they have—if they're made of flesh, they'll burn. If
scorched earth is what it takes to get us through the door,
let's start scorching."

"Can we do that?" I asked Urania. "Could we send

down some kind of robot bomb that will blow whatever's down there to hell and gone, and still leave the elevator car in good enough shape to come and fetch us?"

"Something of the sort might be done," she replied. "It should not pose insuperable difficulties."

It looked as though the old adage about forewarned being forearmed might pull us through. I wasn't particularly cheerful about it, though. Next time, there might be no one to forewarn us, and it looked as if we had to go the rest of the way tourist class, without our suit of robot armour to protect us.

"What do we do with these two?" asked Myrlin, indicating the two invalids.

"Put them in the other truck," said Susarma Lear, making decisions with the swiftness of one used to operating in difficult circumstances. "Leave them to it. Lock them in, if we can, and knock them out. We may want to come back this way. Unless you want one of us to stay, and mind the trucks."

"That should not be necessary," said Urania, calmly. "But we must prepare carefully. We must discover precisely what equipment 994-Tulyar removed from the other vehicle, and make our own preparations with that in mind. We will need a little time."

I went back to the cab, more to get out of the way than because there was anything that I could usefully do there. Susarma, still suited up, came to join me. I could see that there was a feverish light of action in her eye, and knew that she was going into existential overdrive. I'd seen her that way before, and was convinced that it would one day be the death of her.

"This is it, Rousseau," she said, tautly. "Better get your arse suited up and your adrenaline in gear."

195

"Sure," I said, lightly. "This is it. Marked down in my diary: *appointment with sudden death, survive if feasible.* Do you think you could possibly call me Mike?"

"It's not the Star Force way," she told me. "And I suspect that now is the time when we have to start doing things the Star Force way—don't you?"

The Star Force way consisted, in essence, of trying to reach the target by torching everything in the way. Bearing in mind what might be waiting for us, though, I had an unwelcome suspicion that she could be right. From now on, things would probably have to be done the Star Force way, all the way to the Centre.

24

I passed from my unreal state of consciousness into a dream within the dream. I was still in the grey water, though it seemed calmer now and not so cold.

The armour I wore was hardly heavy at all, but it was slowly dragging me down. I tried to lash out with my limbs, with some idea in mind of bringing myself back to the surface, but all my actions were unnaturally slow and heavy, as though the water had the thickness of honey.

I tried to blow out the water that I had taken in, but I had no strength with which to do it, and in any case my lungs were no longer desperate for air. My feebly thrusting arms became entangled with the waterlogged cloak that had been swept around me in a great arc, so that I could not make any sensible attempt to perform the actions that were demanded by my entirely theoretical notions of how to swim. Gradually, I ceased struggling.

Once I had surrendered entirely to my slow fall into the depths, I became disentangled again, and the cloak streamed out from my body almost as though it were a great black parachute retarding my descent. The water was quite still now, and as the surface receded into the distance above me it took on the aspect of a great white-lit plane of crystal. Below me, by contrast, there was a dark abyss with no hint of illumination.

The coldness had by now gone out of the water—or perhaps my flesh had adapted to it—and the viscosity too was no longer so noticeable, so that the experience of moving through it was more like falling through empty space. I could have imagined myself adrift in the lightless void of interstellar space. There was a silence more profound than any I had ever experienced before.

I found it possible to open my mouth, but could not feel anything moving in or out of it. My chest was quite numb, and I had no sensation of breathing. Nor was I aware of any internal pulse-beat; it was as though time had stopped.

As the last vestiges of light faded away, leaving me in total darkness, I was swept by a feeling of unutterable loneliness, which drowned out all thought and memory for an unmeasurable pause. I felt that I was shrinking into a curious vanishing point—that every last vestige of my soul was evaporating, lost and irrecoverable.

I was certain that this was my experience of the moment of death. I believed that I had drowned, and would be no more as soon as my last moment of sensation was exhausted. I felt a small surge of gratitude that the moment was unmarred by pain or terror, and was calmly ready for extinction.

Whether extinction came, requiring me to be somehow resurrected, or whether my acceptance of death was premature, I do not know. I was next aware of a small *presence of mind*. I do not know how else to describe it, because I am sure—however paradoxical it may sound—that it was not an awareness of anything save that I was aware. Perhaps it was that irreducible quantum of certainty which Descartes tried to reach, imaginatively, with his dictum: *Cogito, ergo sum.* There is a thought, therefore there is a thinker.

Strangely, though, I remained in doubt as to whether the thinker was me, or whether I was merely the thought in the head of some enigmatic god or giant. I was not sure whether I was still dreaming, or whether I was now *being dreamed*. But work of some kind was going on: work of re-construction, perhaps of re-creation. Something was taking shape, and although I was part and parcel of that shaping, I could not honestly say that I was doing it. If there was any part of me actively involved, it was a subconscious part.

I am not sure how to describe what was being built, because it had that absurd property of entities in software space that what it looked like depended entirely on the eye of the beholder—it was itself pure essence. When I tried to see it, I had to decide what I would see, and I had no basis for making any such decision . . . no basis, at any rate, within my conscious mind.

It may mean nothing, therefore, to report what images did come into the burgeoning mind that might or might not have been mine. I will have to take the chance, and say what I can.

Perhaps it was a web spun to span the darkness by an invisible spider—across and across, then around and around, in a curving spiral. The anchor-points of the web were not arranged in a circle, but were instead the points of a tetra-hedron, so that the web curved in all three dimensions, and then was slightly hollowed like a net, as though the centre were being dragged away at right angles to everything else—into the fourth dimension, I must suppose.

Perhaps I caught brief sensations that might have been echoes of the dancing feet of the spinner as it whirled around its web, but perhaps those tremors of vibration were part of the life of the web itself.

The web caught nothing, and though it might have shuddered in some kind of breeze, it was never stretched taut at any point.

Perhaps the web was spun between the branches of a great tree—though I had the impression that the tree grew up to bear the web, shaped by the necessity of bearing the web. As I began to perceive the tree there must have come into existence some kind of light by which to see it—my experience of the web had been entirely tactile—and the radiance quickly increased as the tree expanded its dimensions. A whole universe seemed to be expanding around me, hyperspherically. The tree was everywhere; it was the whole of creation, the very structure of existence. Its trunk grew in entwined circles, like a knot of infinite complexity, and its branches radiated into all the space which would otherwise have been undefined, bearing foliage and multitudinous blossoms of every colour in the spectrum, which poured out silver pollen in never-ending streams, and reached out their star-shaped styles to bathe in the deluge.

There was a thought, and the thought was: *This is the magical universe, in the process of its Creation. This is all that is and ever shall be.*

Then there was an awakening.

I do not say that it was I who awoke. I cannot be sure of that. It was, however, my hand that felt the moistness of the sand and the warmth of the sun, my head that felt the sickness and the dizziness of a painful return to consciousness, my limbs which ached with exhaustion.

There was a sitting up—and that is the truth of it, though there is little point in continuing this narration by means of such circumlocutions.

For the sake of convenience, then, *I sat up.*

I was saved. I had been rescued by something that had caught me at the very moment of destruction and preserved me—or remade me, perhaps more in its own image than I had been before.

I looked around, and found myself on a sandy beach. The ocean, whose waves still lapped the sand about my booted feet, was blue with the reflection of a bright and cloudless sky, in which a golden sun blazed directly ahead.

I got slowly to my feet, and examined my body. I was still clad in the red quilted armour, but my cloak was gone. My sword was still in its scabbard at my waist. I was bare-headed. The feeling of intoxication and unreality that had attended my first incarnation in software space was entirely gone now. I felt, however paradoxically, like the *real* Michael Rousseau.

I looked inland, to see what kind of shore I had been brought to. There were many trees, so closely grouped that they presented a considerable barrier. The space between their gnarled trunks was filled with their own thorny branches, and with the spiked leaves of flowerless plants that grew between them. The trees were strange in the extreme, because their trunks were moulded in the approximate form of human beings with arms vertically upraised, like wooden people rooted at the ankles. The branches of the trees were extensions of the fingers of these luckless imprisoned souls, growing madly into a tangled leafy crown. The faces etched into the upper part of every bole each had the appearance of a man or woman sleeping, with eyes closed and expression-less. They ranged in colour from ivory white to ebon black; some seemed polished, others very rough.

I was standing on the sand, with the waves lapping at my heels. The wall of vegetation was no more than three metres away. I could see no obvious way into the thicket, but I approached anyway. The spiky leaf-blades of the plants that made up the undergrowth were very supple, and they seemed to writhe away from me as I approached.

When I came closer still, the tree-people appeared to wake from insensibility; the eyes opened, and though the faces were fixed in wood, and should have been incapable of expression, they seemed to look at me with such pain and horror that I flinched. Only the eyeballs moved within the sockets—the mouths etched in the bark apparently could not open to display teeth or tongue, nor could they contrive the slightest of smiles. And yet I was in no doubt at all that here were souls in some perverse state of torment—souls which were alarmed by my approach. The foliage of the trees rattled as if the boughs were being shaken from within, and the sound had the semblance of a childish language, as though the trees were babbling in a hopeless attempt to tell me something.

I stepped back from the edge of the forest, and turned away from the staring eyes to walk along the beach, hurrying to a place where the faces still slept. I did not try to approach too closely again, and when I glanced back I saw that the faces I had left behind had closed their eyes again, and gave every appearance of having returned to their dream-filled slumber.

Many of the trees carried fruit—bright bulbous things coloured yellow or red—but they were high in the crowns, and none had fallen to the sand.

I did not know where I was going, but I strode out purposefully, never pausing. I do not know how long I walked. The sun did not move in the sky; it remained directly overhead.

There were outcrops of black rock about me now, some of which jutted four or five metres above the sand. Etched into the surfaces of these rocks were outlines representing various kinds of animals: horses, deer, some kind of cattle. I half-expected to see these beasts open their eyes as I passed, but they never did.

I had become very thirsty, and was glad to see among these rocks a pool of water, surrounded by wet mud in which I could see the tracks of many animals, though there were none in sight, and I could see no trail by means of which they might have come from the forest. I went to kneel by the pool and dipped the fingers of my left hand into the water, carrying a little of it to my lips—but it was brackish, too salty to be drinkable.

I turned back to the wall of vegetation that prevented my moving inland. It seemed that no good could come of moving along the line of the shore. I did not want to approach again, bringing those awful faces to baleful life, but I did not know what else to do. I was alone, without guidance of any sort. If those who had helped me required something in return, I did not know what it was.

Directly in front of me there was the trunk of a tree which stood straighter and thicker than the rest. I looked at the closed eyes engraven in its thick black bark, and felt a creeping unease rise inside me.

I looked down at the hand which I had unthinkingly used to bring water to my lips, and saw that the fingers were swollen. The skin was beginning to peel from the under-lying flesh, which was an unhealthy colour, faintly tinged with gangrenous green. I was astonished by the sight, for I had thought myself whole and healthy.

The water in the pool had become quite still again, and now I knelt down for a second time, and leaned over to look at my reflection. My face had a pallor which seemed to me disgusting. The colour had gone from my eyes, and my hair was a muddy grey. The skin had begun to peel from my forehead, too.

It came to me very suddenly that although my intelligence had somehow been preserved from the oblivion of death, my body had not. My flesh was already showing the stigmata of corruption.

Then, almost immediately, another idea occurred to me. Perhaps this was not the touch of death after all, but the beginning of a metamorphosis. Perhaps I too was fated to become a part of the curious forest, extending roots into the soil. I stood up quickly, and looked again at the tree whose appearance had frightened me.

Did I know the face that was etched into its bark?

Knowing what kind of world I was in, I had not thought it possible for me to feel surprise. It would not have startled me at all to recognise in those carved features a furious face rimmed with poisonous snakes, or the stern glare of some divine countenance more terrible than any human face. But this was not Medusa, or any other character from any other mythology of Earth. It was, instead, something rather more familiar, and uncomfortably so.

It was not a human face at all, though it was humanoid.

As I examined it more closely, I realised that it gave the impression of being *part* human, but the other part was a confusion of the lupine and the crocodilian.

I took one step forward, and the eyes opened, leaving me with no doubt at all as to the identity of the soul which had been made captive by the hellish tree.

All vormyr look alike to the untutored human eye, but there was one name which always came to my mind whenever I saw a vormyran, or a picture of a vormyran, or heard the word *vormyr* spoken—and that was the name Amara Guur.

"You're dead," I said, very calmly. I did not expect to see the wooden lips move, having formed the impression before that they could not. But the surprises kept coming.

"So are you, Mr. Rousseau," he replied silkily. "So are you."

25

There was a long time to wait while Urania and Clio cooked up a surprise package for the monsters that were lurking down below. They quickly came to the conclusion that a bomb wasn't the answer—it was likely to be very messy and wasn't guaranteed to be one hundred percent effective. After examining the bits of alien flesh which had come up the shaft attached to the battered Scarid, the Isthomi decided that a biotechnological attack would be infinitely preferable.

While they were figuring out the details of its manufacture they programmed and dispatched a small swarm of flying cameras to reconnoitre for us. These electronic eyes were no bigger than the largest flying insects, but they didn't have wings. Because they had to do the greater part of their flying in an evacuated shaft—we saw no point in sending them down in the car—they were powered by tiny rockets.

In the meantime, we opened up the other truck and carried our two invalids over there. We stripped it of weapons before depositing them, but I lingered for a while before leaving them alone. Urania had asked me to stay because she wanted to make sure that the Scarid was still on the mend, but I wanted to have a word with Jacinthe Siani anyhow.

She was more-or-less okay, physically, but she was still badly frightened. She didn't want to be left alone, and was grateful that I didn't just dump her. She hadn't expected any favours, given the way she'd dealt with me in the past, but it would have been too cruel to abandon her without some kind of reassurance.

"You're as safe here as anywhere in Asgard," I pointed out to her. "If we get through, there's still a slight chance that we may be able to get the power back on. If we don't, there's a slight chance it might come back on anyway. If it doesn't, you should soon be fit enough to try to get back to the Nine's worldlet. You have all the time you need to find the way. The Nine are the best friends you could ask for in this situation. You'll be okay. I wish I could be as confident about my own future."

"Why go, then?" she asked, in a whisper. She was a pragmatist, who didn't believe in heroism for its own sake.

I shrugged my shoulders. "I always wanted to go to the Centre," I told her. "And now something else wants me to go there too."

That reminded me why I wanted to talk to her.

"Tell me about 994-Tulyar," I said. "You do understand, don't you, that he isn't really Tulyar at all?"

"I don't know what you're talking about," she said. "He was hurt, when the machines attacked us. He wasn't badly injured, but he had difficulty talking. He got better. He says that he knows how to switch the power on."

There was no point in disputing the fact. She had no idea what had happened to me as a result of the interface with the alien. She had no idea that such a thing was possible. Even the two Tetrax, who must have been in as good a position as anyone to see differences between Tulyar present and Tulyar past, must simply have assumed that if Tulyar's body was walking and talking, it was Tulyar inside it. If it had behaved peculiarly, they'd simply assumed, like Jacinthe, that it was the result of his injuries. They might think him mad if he behaved crazily enough, but the idea that his body was being operated by a biocopy of alien software sneaked into his brain while he was fast asleep lay beyond their conceptual horizons.

"He was guiding you, wasn't he?" I asked, determined to stick to less controversial ground. "He knows the way to the Centre."

"He said that he'd seen a map," she replied. Her voice was steady now, and she had no difficulty talking.

"Did he give you a reason for hijacking the transporter?"

"He said that we couldn't trust the Isthomi—that they were really responsible for the power being shut off. He said that they were fighting a war of their own, and that we would be killed if we stayed on that level. Down below, he said, we'd find people to help us—the ancestors of the Scarida. He said that they'd find a way to restore power to the Scarid levels, once they knew the Scarida were in trouble. He said that the Nine were no friends of the Scarida or of the Tetrax . . . that they were frightened by the discovery of the Scarid empire, and the galactic community, and would like to see them both destroyed."

She paused for breath. Then she went on: "He said that the Scarida and the Tetrax must make contact with the builders of Asgard, whether the Nine liked it or not, if the humanoid population of the macroworld was to be saved. If we didn't, he said, all the humanoid races would be wiped out, and things like the Isthomi would be the sole survivors. He said they'd fooled you completely, and made you their slave."

I remembered what I'd told her about the Nine being the best friends she could possibly have if the power wasn't restored. For a moment, I wondered whether it might be true. Might the Nine be worried about the power of humanoid cultures inside and outside Asgard? Might they be acting entirely in the interests of their own kind? Might they have me completely fooled?

I didn't think so . . . but how could I be sure?

The horrible thought struck me that it might all be a put-up job. Maybe there never was any attack on the Nine. Maybe it was the Nine and the Nine alone who had injected mysterious software into my brain. Maybe Tulyar hadn't been taken over . . . maybe he had only guessed the truth. Maybe he had seen a map. Maybe I was being played for a sucker all along the line.

When I thought about it carefully, though, it didn't make any sense. If the Nine had wanted to bring down the Scarid empire and cut themselves off from the galactic community, they could have done it all by themselves. They didn't need to pretend to be injured, and they certainly didn't need me. It had to be the Nine who were telling the truth, and the thing using Tulyar's body that was lying.

Hadn't it?

"I don't suppose Tulyar mentioned dreaming at all?" I asked, weakly.

She thought it was a crazy question, and didn't dignify it with an answer. There was only one question left to ask.

"I know you didn't see much when the trouble started down below," I said, "but did you see anything at all to indicate whether any of your people got through?"

"I don't know," she replied, faintly. "It all happened so quickly. Our lights were smothered . . . then put out. I'm only certain that some of them were killed. If I were you, Rousseau, I wouldn't go down there."

"If I'd always followed your advice," I said uncharitably, "Amara Guur would have made mincemeat out of me a long time ago."

She didn't say anything in reply, but her big dark eyes were radiating injured innocence. If she had really pulled the Scarid officer out of the frying pan down there, she couldn't be quite as nasty as I'd always supposed, but I wasn't about to forgive her for the bad turns she'd done me.

"Don't worry," I told her, again. "You'll be okay, if anyone is. Maybe we'll meet again, when the lights are back on."

I left her to mull over her past life, and to wonder whether she had a future.

When the flying cameras brought back their pictures we found that her story, such as it was, seemed to be honest and accurate. The picture quality was awful—not unexpectedly, given that there was no light and our spy-eyes had to use infra-red vision—but our brain-in-a-box managed to integrate all the information and enhance it a little. There was a good deal of debris, but it didn't show up very clearly. We could make out a couple of bodies, still sheathed in transparent plastic, and we guessed that the killers hadn't been able to breach the suits. That was comforting, in a way—but it hadn't saved the poor guys inside them, who'd been broken and crushed regardless.

The predators themselves looked like a cross between gargantuan slugs and sea anemones. They were sitting still while the spy-eyes flew around, so we had no way to judge how fast they could move when the need arose, but they didn't look very quick. There were about twenty of them gathered about the doorway by now, but several had been damaged by bullets and a few were almost certainly dead. They were heaped up untidily, and though it was difficult to be sure, I got the impression that the ones on top might be patiently devouring the ones below. The fact that their prey had proved unexpectedly difficult to digest hadn't cost them their meal. No wonder they were still lurking, hoping for dessert.

"They're nothing," opined Susarma Lear scornfully. "If the Scarids had been carrying Star Force flame-pistols instead of needlers and crash-guns, they'd have mopped that lot up in a matter of minutes."

I diplomatically refrained from pointing out that we'd lost our Star Force flamers long ago, and that she too was reduced to carrying a relatively primitive handgun.

"It will not be necessary to expose ourselves to any risk," said Urania. "We have programmed the truck's organic production unit to supply ample quantities of a powerful poison which will paralyse the nerve-nets controlling the smooth muscle of the tentacles. It is sufficiently powerful that the tiny robots which carried the infra-red cameras can easily be adapted to carry a lethal dose. We should not need our guns immediately, although it will of course be necessary to carry such arms as we can when we resume our journey."

I saw Nisreen nodding with approval. The Tetrax had always believed that heavy metal was no substitute for clever biotechnics.

When our fly-sized shock troops had completed their mission, we set out ourselves. We had a certain difficulty crowding five of us and all the relevant equipment into the car, but it was possible. The pseudo-Tulyar's party had divided themselves into two fours only because it was a split down the middle, not because four was the car's maximum capacity. I guess we were crammed in pretty tightly, but we'd been crowded in the truck, and it wasn't particularly claustrophobic.

The ride down was very long. The flow of time felt different now that we were out of the truck—the vehicle had been a comforting cocoon, where the minutes that passed were naturally dead and empty. Now I was in a light suit, with a small cargo of weapons and equipment to carry, every second was pregnant with hazard.

I hadn't asked Urania exactly what Tulyar's party had taken from their own truck, and much of it was already packed up in satchels. It was all too obvious, though, what kind of transport we would now be expected to employ. No doubt they were sophisticated robots in their own right, but they looked to me like glorified bicycles. Susarma was used to going into battle with whatever came to hand, and didn't seem too worried about the prospect of riding one, but Myrlin was anxious about their small size and apparent frailty, and 673-Nisreen—who still had his right forearm immobilised by a plastic sheath—seemed on the brink of asking to be left behind. I made the suggestion that perhaps he should stay with the truck, in case it was only pride that was preventing him, but he said no. The Tetrax had something of a reputation for exaggerated discretion, but if the entire race could be judged by Nisreen, they were certainly no cowards.

The long descent was a severe trial of my peace of mind. By the time we reached the bottom I was so eager to move, so eager to act, that it was almost a disappointment to find that our advance guard of mechanical wasps really had stung to very good effect, and that there was not a monster in the vicinity still capable of raising a tentacle.

I consoled myself with the thought that Susarma Lear must feel ten times worse about the absence of a meaningful target at which she could blast away.

The ground on which we found ourselves was dead white and very flat, which seemed to me unnatural until I realised that it was actually the chitinous epidermis of some

vast thermosynthetic organism—a living carpet which probably extended throughout the entire worldlet, having sustained itself until the switch-off by drawing off energy from
the real "floor." No doubt the chitinous tegument was to
protect it from herbivores, which—equally undoubtedly—
would have evolved ways of drilling through it in order to
sustain themselves, enabling them in their turn to supply
the tentacled predators with their natural sustenance. It was
the classic ecological pyramid that defines the structure of
life-systems everywhere. It would have been pleasant to
chat to 673-Nisreen about the aesthetics of it all, but we
were too busy.

Now that we could search more carefully, we found four
bodies. Two were Scarid soldiers; two were Tetrax. 994-
Tulyar wasn't among them, and neither was John Finn, but
those two were all that was left of the eight who had set out,
and we now outnumbered them five to two—six to two if
we counted the brain-in-a-box called Clio, which was
strapped to Urania's shoulders like a knapsack. I wondered
if Finn had yet figured out that Tulyar wasn't Tulyar and
that he was being played for a sucker. I thought not. Despite
his cleverness with electronic gadgets, John Finn was essentially a cretin.

The ground was far too hard to show obvious tracks, but
the heels of the suits Finn and Tulyar were wearing had
been rigged to leave a trace for us, and it didn't take long to
confirm that there was indeed a trail to be followed.

It took us about a quarter of an hour to organise the bits
that we'd crammed into the elevator with us, but eventually
we had them assembled into five two-wheeled vehicles with
power-cells in the space between our knees and luggage
compartments behind the saddle. I'd ridden similar vehicles
in the suburban streets of Skychain City, where there were

no moving pavements, but the fact that the gravity was so much less down here—and for the first time it seemed noticeably less than it had been in the Nine's home level—made me a little anxious about keeping my balance.

Just as we were about to set off, our lights picked out three more of the slug-things, gliding with surprising swiftness over the great white carpet, but while Susarma Lear was eagerly pulling her crash-gun out of its holster our little flying friends were zooming in for the sting, and they still had poison to spare. The slugs were thrown into desperate paroxysms, and were rendered helpless within a matter of seconds.

"You'll get your chance yet," I consoled her, hoping that she wouldn't. Then I looked at Urania, who had charge—via Clio—of the olfactory sensor that could pick up the trail we had to follow. She led the way once again into the desolate darkness. Susarma Lear and I followed in single file, with 673-Nisreen behind me, and Myrlin bringing up the rear.

It didn't take me long to get saddle-sore, and to begin hoping that the next drop we would face would be the last.

ᐱ 26 ᐱ

When I told him he was dead, and he said that I was too, I half-expected a needler to materialise somewhere in the branches of the monstrous tree. I winced in anticipation of little slivers of metal tearing me apart. The branches that were his fingers rustled ominously, but nothing happened. The relief was momentary—it dawned on me that if he didn't mean that he intended to kill me, then he must mean something else.

"I don't feel very dead," I told him defiantly. It wasn't true—I did remember the sensation of drowning, which had seemed horribly like dying at the time, and I was uncomfortably aware of the evil condition of my flesh.

"Nevertheless," he told me, in his barbarous parole, "your attempt to reach the core of Asgard's software space is over. You have been immobilised. Your body is already beginning to disintegrate. Do not be misled by the fact that you retain consciousness—this is Hell, Mr. Rousseau, and you are with the condemned."

I looked again at my hands, to examine my peeling skin more closely. There was little feeling in the fingers, and the strips of skin which were coming away were melting into liquid at the edges. The discolouration suggested that gangrene was beginning to spread in the deeper tissues. It was getting worse as I watched, and I became suddenly anxious about the power of suggestion. Might this be no more than one more attack, more subtle in kind? I didn't have to believe him, and I made up my mind that I wouldn't.

I thought about what he'd said, and wondered why it appeared to be Amara Guur who was speaking. The fact that he was appearing in that form was something to do with his being my idea of the archetypal enemy, but had the entity that confronted me chosen that form, or had I imposed the identity upon it?

"You're just a figment of my imagination," I told him.

"My outward form is a figment of your imagination," he agreed. "It is the way you have translated my presence into a visual image. Your consciousness is too limited to apprehend me in any other way. All of this is a figment of your imagination, Mr. Rousseau. It is a dream, which you now must dream alone. Everything you see is transfigured by your mind into a set of visual symbols, but it is happening. Dream or reality, you are doomed."

I heard a keening sound, and looked up to see a company of predatory birds wheeling in the sky. I looked up at the tangled foliage, at the poisonous fruits lurking amid the branches. I thought about being on an island in the middle of an infinite sea: marooned. But if I was already doomed—trapped and condemned to Hell—why would he be bothering to tell me?

I knew then that this was just a new phase of the contest. The gods had preserved me from the cruel sea, and the giants had found a way to talk to me, but the battle of which I was a part was still raging all around me, as yet unsettled.

"It's all just a posthumous fantasy," said Amara Guur. He was trying too hard to make the point, and I was determined to resist the power of the lie. "You're on your way to Hell," he went on, "but don't worry about the route. You don't have to go anywhere. It will all come to you."

Deciding not to believe him didn't help me to figure out what to do next. Should I run? Or should I try to cut my way through the barrier, to penetrate the interior of this alien shore? Or was there an opportunity to learn something here, which might yet be turned to my advantage?

It was possible, I thought, that the enemy knew as little about me as I knew about them. Perhaps they were trying to find out more about me, and perhaps they would reveal something of themselves by so doing.

"What are you?" I asked, with an edge in my voice. I deliberately didn't say "who."

"I'm the thing you're most afraid of," he replied. "I'm Nemesis. I'm the one who brought you to the edge of death before, and would have destroyed you, save for the fact that the Nine gave me a gun that didn't work. This time, I've been shaped by a very different armourer, and there can be no escape. No android; no star-captain; no magic-workers. I'm Amara Guur."

"You're a part of whatever invaded the macroworld. You're the infection that blighted its systems—a software virus set to injure and destroy its programmes. You're part of the thing which is trying to destroy Asgard."

The mouth, shaped in the bark of the tree, had teeth within it—the white, sharp teeth of a predator. The tree smiled.

"I'm that too," he said, still looking more like a cross between a wolf and a crocodile than a human being. "This is the twilight of the gods, and the halls of Valhalla are cold. The clarion has sounded at Bifrost bridge and the gods ride to their destruction. Thor has met the Midgard serpent and has gone to his fated death. Fenrir has broken his bonds and shakes the world-ash Yggdrasil with his howling. The fire-giants are free, and their flames will consume the vault of heaven. Odin is dead. Heimdall and Loki will destroy one another. All the great gods are dead, and the many mankinds which live in Asgard are given to the darkness, waiting for the end."

It was all straight out of my mind. He was still speaking in parole but all the names were in the original Earthly language. Did it mean that the invaders of Asgard had picked my mind clean, the way the Isthomi had tried to do when I first fell into their inquiring hands? Or was this creature some kind of magic mirror, reflecting my own ideas back at me?

"But it begins again," I said. "In the story, it begins again! There is no final end."

"Oh yes," he said, "it begins again. In other galaxies, other macroworlds, in every little Earth-clone planet which wheels in its track around a yellow star, it begins again and again and again. But for every beginning there is an end, and this is the end of Asgard. Surt will consume it all."

That was one symbol I had no difficulty in decoding. Surt was the king of the fire-giants, whose fire turned the battlefield of *Gotterdammerung* to ashes when all the killing was done. Surt could only be the starlet at the heart of the macroworld, which would blow Asgard apart if it went nova. The products of a thousand Creations—and what did it matter whether those Creations took place on planetary surfaces or inside macroworlds?—would be destroyed and wasted in such an explosion. Ashes to ashes; dust to dust. Was that what the invaders of Asgard were trying to achieve? Were they a software suicide squad?

"But you'd die too," I said. "The plague which kills the sheep leaves the wolves to starve. The destroyers go to their destruction with their victims. Why?"

He laughed. "You have made me a humanoid in order to see me," he said. "But you know that is not what I am."

"It's not what I am, either," I retorted. "I'm just a

bundle of information, like you. I'm just a shadow on the wall of the cave, lit by Platonic fire."

"Precisely," he said. "We are all shadow-selves, sent into combat by our archetypes. Perhaps that is what you are *really* fighting, Mr. Rousseau—the archetypal predators. Your Amara Guur is a very pale imitation of the real thing. You have no idea how limited your imagination is."

"Predators kill for food," I told him. "Amara Guur was a fake. He used his predatory ancestry to justify behaviour that would never have been tolerated in a wolf pack."

"You mistake me, and you mistake your own kind," replied the thing which looked like Amara Guur. "The predator kills for many reasons: for food, to defend his territory, and for pleasure, too. For pleasure, Mr. Rousseau. It is a sentimental view that says the predator takes no pleasure in his killing. The predator is prudent, the predator deceives, but the predator loves to kill. Only a fool believes that it could be otherwise."

"Territory," I echoed. "Is that what this is all about: territory?"

"Or pleasure," he riposted. "You are trying once again to omit the pleasure."

"Despite our petty squabbles," I said, trying hard not to think about destruction and decay, "all the humanoid races have their DNA in common. The Tetrax are right, aren't they, to be ambitious for galactic brotherhood? They're right to try to bind us into a community. Whatever you're a copy of, it isn't made of DNA, is it? This cuts deeper than meat-eaters versus leaf-eaters. This is competition between alternative biochemistries."

He laughed again. "Mr. Rousseau," he said, "do you really imagine that biochemistries care? Your thinking is anchored to your imbecilic point of view. Do you really think that you have the intelligence to understand, when the power of your dreams can do no more than this? How can you believe that you ever had a chance to understand?"

He was shifting the ground of the argument, leading me first one way and then another, and I suddenly wondered why. If I were dead and on my way to Hell, immobilised and facing inevitable disintegration, Amara Guur would not be here, teasing me and taunting me. Suddenly, I began to believe that I was doing the wrong thing in letting him delay me. I had to get past him—I had to go on.

I looked again at my arms, which were mottled with grey, the flesh rutted and scratched. There were several ulcerous sores, slowly turning fire-red, beginning to suppurate. The sores reminded me, strangely, of the fruit on the branches of the humanoid trees. But I knew that it didn't matter whether I was "dead" or not—what mattered was that I was still active, still thinking, and still some kind of threat to whatever strange army it was that sought to keep me from the heart of the macroworld's systems.

I drew my sword, and raised it high above my head, ready to slash at the branches blocking my way. No expression of terror came into those crazy staring eyes—it was rather as if they mocked me, challenging me to do my worst. I hacked at the tangled branches and the thorny undergrowth, scything through it with my bright, sharp blade, going against him as fiercely and as recklessly as I had gone against him once before, when he tried to use me as a shield to save himself from the Star Force.

As I moved forward to pass him, the spined leaves thrust at me, and I felt the thorns plucking at my armour, but they could not penetrate it to rip my flesh. It was as though the wall of thorns dissolved beneath my attack, evaporating on contact with my wrath and my warmth.

I forced my way through, leaving Amara Guur to return to his wooden slumber, and went on into the dense thicket, which became dark as the branches above my head obscured the sun. There was a foul, dank smell all around me, and all of a sudden there was no green at all but only shades of grey, and the signs of decay and corruption were everywhere. It was as though I were hacking my way into the body of a gigantic corpse. There was no sign of another side to the wall, and I felt that I was tunneling into the heart of something horrible.

Too late I was seized by doubt, wondering if I had been tricked. Perhaps this was not the path that the enemy had tried to prevent my taking—perhaps this was instead the way they had wanted me to go, so that I might deliver myself into their hands.

I turned, and looked back.

There was no sign of the path by which I had come—no tunnel back to the sandy beach and the sunlight. On every side of me there was nothing but a tangle of white, soft, rootlike things, dimly lit as though by furtive bioluminescence.

I looked wildly around, and while I stood still the tangled knots drew more tightly about me, until I was confined in a circular cage with no more than a metre of space around my spoiling flesh. There was still a frail, faint light to see by, and I watched the knotted things in front of my face writhe like maggots as they wove themselves into a tight, confining wall.

I raised my sword, and slashed wildly at the confining threads, trying to cut my way through. For a moment, I thought they might not yield, but the sharpness of the blade prevailed and the cage in which they had tried to confine me was breached. I shoved my body into the gap, pushing through to the other side. I was still in the forest and the branches still writhed in a determined attempt to block my way, but I broke into a run, hacking madly at whatever was in my path.

My arms ached and my head hurt. I felt dizzy, but I dared not pause for an instant lest I give the malevolent vegetation a second chance to imprison me. Branches grabbed at my arms and rootlets tried to seize my feet, but while I was moving they were impotent to establish a hold. I did not know how long I could go on, or how long I would need to, but I was determined not to be beaten while there was strength in my body, and despite the gathering discomfort I had no sensation of nearing exhaustion.

How much time passed while that strange contest went on I have no idea, but the forest began to thin again, and I saw brighter light ahead of me. Encouraged by the prospect of an end I dashed forward, and the assailing branches fell away. There were no more groping tendrils, no more stabbing thorns.

I came out of the forest into an open space, and threw up a protective arm as I was momentarily dazzled by the glare of an unnaturally bloated yellow sun. But there was a pavement beneath my feet, and the air was filled with sound emitted by countless clamorous voices, and I knew that this was no desert isle, but a busy place.

When I dropped my arm again, and looked to see where I was, I found myself confronting a ring of men, each one as tall and as muscular as Myrlin, and each one armed with a gleaming sword. They were like enough to one another to be clones, and I realised that they were probably automata like the ones that had manned the deck of the magical ship on which I had approached this shore.

I took half a step forward, and they brought up their

weapons, pointing the blades at my torso. I glanced sideways, and could see no end to their array, so I turned on my
heel. There was no sign of the forest through which I had
come—the pavement was all around me, and so were the
warriors. There were sixteen of them in all, and they had
me completely hemmed in.

"You have done well, Michael Rousseau," said a voice,
which spoke in English rather than parole, "but we know
you now, and you are at our mercy."

⤜ 27 ⤛

For the first few hours the ride was a veritable nightmare. It wasn't so much the slug-things, which were too slow to bother us once we were alert to their existence. Nor, for that matter, was it anything that was genuinely dangerous. In the light suit, which seemed so much more fragile than the cold-suits I was used to, I felt virtually naked. The last time I'd worn a suit like that to cross an alien wilderness, Scarid stormtroopers had been on my tail, and they'd come within an inch of killing me. That kind of experience is enough to make anyone feel paranoid, and though I'd been assured that I was now a superman, I hadn't yet seen much hard evidence of my superhumanity.

The headlights of our motorbikes attracted flying things: mothlike creatures bigger than any I had ever seen before. They came at us in great swarms, clumsily bumping into one another as they tried to get into the light. Some of them would stall in the confusion and fall into my path, and I couldn't help running over them, feeling their soft bodies busting beneath the bike's tyres. They continually spun out of the beam that lit my way, colliding helplessly with my helmet like balloons filled with flock.

The low gravity here made gliding easy and powered flight was to be had on the cheap, in energy-economic terms; these things didn't need wings a metre across to bear them aloft, even when they had bodies the size of my arm. Their wings were coloured in exotic patterns, although I couldn't see them to their best advantage as they jostled one another to flit through the beam. Their eyes weren't compound, and reflected the light like cats' eyes, but their mouth parts were insectile, with jaws and palps like cockroaches. The combination seemed bizarre, and though I'd recently seen enough of alien life by now to know how very ingenious DNA can be, the creatures still appeared to me to be monstrous and unnatural.

The trees were no better, if "trees" was the right word for the elements of the forest through which we rode. They were rooted top and bottom, to the ceiling as well as to the floor, and their foliage formed a curious double canopy. The thermosynthetic tegument covered the roof of the world as well as its floor, and weight was such a minor problem that most of the organisms made little distinction between up and down. I saw that the slug-things were just as happy wandering across the sky as the ground, held tight by their big suckers, and there were a couple of occasions when I had to ride directly beneath one, with tentacles snaking down at me from above. They couldn't quite reach me, because they were used to catching taller prey in that fashion; the indigenous herbivores on which they fed had taken equal advantage, in their range of forms, of the low gravity.

The local fauna leaned conspicuously toward molluscan and arthropodan forms; the branches of the double-rooted trees were swarming with things that looked like a cross between a beetle and a crab. Anchored to the tougher boughs were creatures the size of a man's head, which had tough shells shaped like barnacles. They opened their tops periodically to shoot out "limbs" like the tentacles of the slug-things. They didn't look big enough to be a threat to anything but the moths that were their prime targets, but I did my best to keep clear of them anyway.

The larger herbivores looked like giant lobsters, harvest spiders, and walking radio masts, but they were easily spooked and ran away from our lights when we came close to their herds.

We rode for hour after hour without a pause. We weren't going very fast, though it wasn't too difficult to find a clear, flat path between the trees. We probably averaged about fifty kilometres per hour, though our route had twists and turns enough to ensure that we covered less than two-thirds of that distance in a hypothetical straight line.

My mind gradually settled into an acceptance of the surroundings, and I stopped caring about the moth-like things bouncing off my helmet. I concentrated on keeping my eyes fixed on the tail-light of the bike ahead, following the route which it mapped out for me. I must have settled eventually into a kind of trance-like state, because I lost all track of time. I really have no idea how long we had been riding by the time we arrived at our destination.

I had been expecting another wall and another airlock. I had paused to wonder whether the bikes could clamber down an evacuated shaft as easily as the larger vehicle had, but had simply shelved the question, knowing that there was no point in worrying about it ahead of time. The Nine had so far been equal to everything, and there would be time to worry about the limits of their competence when we found them out.

It *was* another airlock, but it wasn't set in a wall. It was set in the floor, and it was big, like a vast drain-cover. It was in the middle of a patch of bare ground, which had a protective fence around it, presumably to keep the local wildlife away; we approached with care lest it should still be electrified, but it was harmless now, and presumably had been since the power went off. There was still the possibility of another booby-trap, though, and we didn't throw caution to the winds. We checked all around the fence—a perimeter of nearly a hundred metres. We located the point at which Tulyar and Finn had gained access, and found their vehicles abandoned outside the fence.

Urania took the magic suitcase into the compound and got to work. I arranged the bicycles in a semicircle, with their headlight beams pointing out into the darkness. They didn't show us much because they were still attracting swarms of the flying creatures, and I went to turn them off, but as I did so I noticed something odd about the trees that were faintly illuminated by the beams. They grew more thickly there than on the side from which we'd approached, and there were evident slash-marks where someone—or something—had widened a pathway through them.

I showed the evidence to Myrlin. "You think Tulyar met some friends here?" I asked him.

"Not necessarily," he said. "Someone switched the power off, and if your logic is correct, that someone needed hands to do it—it wasn't just a trick of the tapeworms. Perhaps Tulyar's friends were already down there, waiting for him."

It made sense enough, and it wasn't very comforting. I had been taking comfort from the fact that we outnumbered Tulyar's party, but for all we knew there might be a robot army down below as strong and as nasty-minded as the one which had tried to blast the Isthomi's worldlet.

"If they already have hands down there," I asked, "why do they need Tulyar at all?"

It wasn't a rhetorical question, and I would have been very grateful had Myrlin been able to provide me with an answer, but he couldn't. Only Tulyar—the thing that once had been Tulyar—knew what he was doing, and why.

By this time, Clio had managed to pick the lock that protected the gateway to the underworld. The outer wall of the airlock had already been persuaded to slide away into its bed. As soon as I got close enough to look down, I knew that it was something very different from the portals we had previously used.

The chamber within the lock was huge and deep. It was about twenty metres in diameter and fifteen metres deep. Around the lower perimeter was a horizontal ledge about eighty centimetres wide, with a protective fence and guard-rail. Within that outer circle there was just a plain floor. There were elaborate control-panels set into the walls of the chamber, and four ladders leading down to the ledge.

There were several pieces of equipment scattered about the ledge between the fence and the wall—994-Tulyar and his sole remaining companion had apparently decided to travel light. But they hadn't left their guns behind.

We let ourselves down to the circular ledge, and Urania plugged Clio's brainbox into the nearest control panel. By now, she was a master in the art of interfacing, and Urania was immediately able to tell us that there was an atmosphere beyond the lower door, and that it had oxygen enough to be breathable—though we kept our suits on as a matter of course, to defend ourselves against dangerous organics.

As the circular floor began to slide away I already had some sort of notion of what I was going to see. I knew this was no elevator shaft, and my hands had a tight grip on the guard rail as I tensed myself in anticipation of vertiginous dizziness.

It wasn't utterly dark down there, but there wasn't a great deal of light either. There was something there, directly below us, but it was impossible to tell how far away it was or what it was like. The tiny, glimmering lights were very faint—it was like looking at a distant cloud-nebula through a powerful telescope, or looking down at a city from a high-flying plane on a night whose clarity was marred by a certain amount of hazy cloud. The light, such as it was, was concentrated in a fairly small area directly below us.

There was no shaft going down from the airlock. Our descent through Asgard's levels was over, and we had reached the bottom of that part of the macroworld's structure. From where we stood now, there seemed to be nothing but empty space separating us from another object—a world within a world, very distant and very small.

I quickly realised that it might only be the lack of light which made it appear that way, and that the tiny sphere which was Asgard's core must in fact be connected to the outer part of the macroworld by dozens of threads or girders. We could see nothing of those connecting spokes, but there was no doubt at all that they must be out there in the darkness: the ribs of the macroworld, carrying the power cables and the neuronal chains which were the corridors of Asgard's software space.

I peered hard into the Stygian gloom, thinking that at least one such rib must be close at hand, to serve us as a bridge. But then I realised, belatedly, that if we were to try to cross that vast empty space by means of such a thread we would need something like the teardrop elevators which had connected Skychain City to the orbital satellite—and that there was now no power to drive them. It was difficult to imagine that the motorbikes which had brought us here could be adapted to such a purpose, even if we could reach the upper anchorage of one of the connecting threads—and Tulyar and Finn had abandoned their machines here.

"Jesus Christ!" whispered Susarma Lear, who was

standing beside me on what was now a narrow balcony, looking down into the heart of the world. "What is that?"

"At a guess," I said, "it's a baby star in high-tech swaddling-clothes. There must be bases down there where the builders live—or where they once lived—but there are no more levels."

"It is the starshell," Urania confirmed. "Inside it is the fusion reactor which supplied Asgard's power. We are looking down into the last of the levels, and the largest one of all. Remember that there is air here; there may well be life too. None of the levels above is more than fifty or sixty metres deep, but the fact that this one is many thousands of metres deep does not necessarily mean that we should regard it any differently—this too may be a habitat."

"Well," said Susarma, "there's one way in which it's different. I can't tell how far down it is, but it's one hell of a drop, and we certainly don't have an aeroplane in our luggage. So what are we supposed to do now?"

I stared down into the awesome pit, realising that I could now *see* the Centre—that mysterious Valhalla which was the home of whatever godlike beings had built the macroworld. It hung there suspended, like some kind of magic ball, gleaming oh-so-faintly with tiny lights that sparkled and twinkled uncertainly. I wondered whether they were continually being eclipsed and revealed by the passage of whatever shadowy monsters we still had to face.

"Tulyar's still *en route*," I said, quietly. "He's still out there, ahead of us. And whatever he took from the first truck, we took from the replica. We can still follow him."

Susarma Lear turned to look at Urania, who was on her other side. "What did you pack in those bags?" she asked. Her voice was still little more than a whisper, and I could hear the strain in it.

"There is no need to be afraid," replied the scion, with the air of one quoting the obvious. "The gravity is very low now, and with the exception of 673-Nisreen we have bodies better equipped to resist injury than those we are following."

But Susarma Lear didn't find these reassurances entirely convincing. "Are you trying to tell me," she said, icily, "that we're going to jump?"

"We appear to have little alternative," put in Myrlin, who didn't sound particularly enthusiastic about the idea himself. I couldn't blame him.

"Hell, Colonel," I said, my own mouth more than a little dry. "You can hardly complain. You're the only one of us who's ever used a bloody parachute."

"What is a parachute?" asked Urania, mildly. I looked at her in amazement, having long since accustomed myself to the fact that the Nine, one way or another, had soaked up absolutely everything that humans knew. But the scions were only partial personalities, created in the days before I began the intimate interfacing which had given the Nine fuller access to my memories. And everything they knew from experience about habitable worlds was based on their acquaintance with the levels. No one uses or invents parachutes when the solid sky is only twenty metres away.

"You mean," I said, "that those bags you packed for the bikes don't contain parachutes?"

"No, Mr. Rousseau." She stopped there, perhaps offended that I hadn't taken the time to reply to her question.

"So how are we expected to get down there?" I asked, satirically. "Do we strap on wings and learn to fly?"

I could tell by the way she looked back at me that it wasn't as witty as I thought.

Susarma Lear seemed paradoxically pleased by my

discomfort, though she would surely have preferred, had she been thinking rationally, a method of descent which made some use of her training.

"Don't worry," she said, with a feeble attempt to imitate Urania's calmly infuriating tone. "Flying can't be *that* difficult. Insects do it all the time."

I looked her in the cold blue eyes, so that I could watch her reacting to what she'd said as the implications sank in.

"In the Star Force," I said, maliciously, "we really have to be ready for anything, don't we?"

✦ 28 ✦

I was quite ready to believe that I was beaten, but I felt that I had to give resistance a try. After all, I had no idea how good I was at swordsmanship. Perhaps I was d'Artagnan as well as Robin Hood.

I moved forward, striking as best I could at one of the warriors. His own sword came up to meet mine, and when the two clashed, my blade shattered as if it had been made of delicate glass. I was left holding the hilt, foolishly looking down at the broken end.

The remaining fighting-men had remained quite still, their animation still suspended. The one I'd lunged at resumed the same position. Another man came between two of the warriors, and stood before me, looking me up and down with what seemed like frank curiosity. He bore a slight resemblance to John Finn, but the similarity was very superficial. This was a much taller and more handsome man, and though he had a Finnish slyness about him, he had also a self-confidence—a kind of authority implying aristocratic habits—which the sole remaining representative of the humble house of Finn could never have carried off.

He smiled. It was a nasty, cruel smile that reminded me of Amara Guur.

"I don't know you," I said, rather stupidly. I felt dreadful, and I knew that if I were to look down at my body there would be little to see but rags and tatters of putrefying flesh. I was quite convinced now that they really had beaten me. The language of my constitution was no longer arcane

232

so far as they were concerned.

"No, Mr. Rousseau," he said, in an oddly mellifluous voice which didn't seem to fit his wicked face. "You've never seen me before—not even in your dreams. And yet, I am no less a figment of your imagination than the others. The appearance which I have is one which you have bestowed upon me."

I didn't know what to say, so I said nothing. I didn't even know why the game was continuing—there was no obvious reason why they would want to talk to me before they destroyed me.

"We are at home here," said the tall man, sounding not unfriendly. "This is our world. You had power here, but you did not know how to use it efficiently. You never really had a chance of surviving here, and your friends the Isthomi were over-ambitious in what they tried to do. Believe it or not, we bear you no animosity. Our war is not with your kind, but we must do what we must do. Think of it only as a dream, Mr. Rousseau. The pain which you suffer here is not the pain which flesh is heir to. It is a mere passing incident."

When a sleeping man is close to wakefulness while he is still dreaming, there is a moment when he can exert the power of his returning consciousness within the dream, to shape and control it. I longed for such a moment now, wishing that I could do something to change the emerging pattern, but I could not even lift my arm to offer some futile gesture of defiance. I was frozen into stillness like those unhappy souls held fast by the trees of the forest, and all I could do was look about me.

I saw that we were in a city—a city built from grey stone and white marble, almost incandescent beneath the blazing glare of the huge sun. The buildings were very tall, decorated with tall arches and mighty colonnades, their façades

decorated with sculptured images of battle. My own position was in the centre of a vast square thronged with people,
but the pavement on which I stood was raised, so that I and
the circle of swordsmen who surrounded me were above the
level of the crowd by half a man's height. There was a great
deal of noise as the people in the crowd moved about, chat-
tering and shouting. I could make no sense of the few words
that I caught within the cacophony, which were in some
alien tongue that I could not understand.

Not everyone was looking at me, but I was the centre of
attention here; it was as if I was a prisoner brought out for
ritual humiliation and execution. This was the seat of judgment to which I had been summoned—dead or alive—in
order to hear my condemnation. The elements of the city's
architecture had been dredged from my vague and ill-
conceived notions of what the cities of ancient Earth must
have been like, which owed far more to antique movies than
to any real knowledge. It seemed oddly appropriate that I—
the merest pretender to godhood—should go to my destruction on the set of a low-budget epic. My other self had only
been capable of dreaming second-rate dreams, and I was
suffering now from the absurdity of his meagre pretensions.

Somewhat to my surprise, I felt a desperate desire to
know the answers to a few questions, although I did not
doubt that I would take those answers with me to oblivion
in a very short space of time.

I looked the godlike man in the eye as I had looked
Amara Guur in the eye, and said: "Will you tell me what it
is that I have been a part of? Will you tell me what I was
supposed to achieve, and why you fought so hard to stop
me?"

He smiled, wryly. "You could not begin to understand,"
he said. He must have known what an infuriating answer

that would be. And he added: "It was not such a hard fight. The Isthomi are very feeble, as godlings go."

"They thought I might find friends here," I said weakly, "who would come to my aid."

"Poor fool," he said, not ungently. "You have tried to intervene in a battle whose nature you could never comprehend. You have no friends here, but only those who would use you. Your flesh-and-blood counterpart is no better off—he too is just a pawn, and he cannot even be certain which side he is on. He does not know whether the passenger in his body intends him to save the macroworld or to destroy it."

"Do *you* know?" I asked, with as much insolence as I could muster.

He spread his hands wide, as if to say that it could not matter. I could not tell whether it was simply an act of casual cruelty, or whether there was some point in this dialogue. I wondered why he was delaying, if he intended to destroy me, and I noted that although he stood less than two metres away he had made no attempt to touch me. Was I still dangerous, in some way that I could not quite fathom?

I stared hard into his face, wishing fervently that looks could kill, but I could not move my arms or my legs. My limbs had so far submitted to the forces of decay that they had no way of responding to the signals sent by my brain, and I had the sensation that the brain itself had little left of its own order and power. Yet the end was not yet come, and I felt sure that there must be some reason for the delay. If they had been able to blot me out, utterly and entirely, they would have done it. They had not yet attained that final dominance which would permit them to administer the *coup de grace*. Perhaps there was still hope—still something I could do if only I knew how.

But the only thing I could do, it seemed, was talk.

"Who are you?" I asked, trying with all my might to be contemptuous.

He laughed. "What answer can I possibly give?" he countered. "The appearance which you see is in your eye, the identity which I have is in your mind. I have no way to answer you save by reference to your ideas, your characterizations. There are no gods, and yet I am a god, because you have no way of thinking about the kind of being I am, and the powers at my disposal, save by linking them to your myths of gods and giants. The builders of the macroworld were humanoid in form, and their nature is already pregnant in the parent being from which you were copied, in the quiet DNA which is unexpressed within your every cell, but you have not the power of their imagination, and you cannot conceive of the nature and power of the beings they created within their machines—or the nature and power of the invaders which have come to displace them. We are not gods but you must dress us as gods in order to have any image of us at all. You named the macroworld Asgard, because it seemed to you the creation of godlike beings, and you have translated the danger that threatens it into the vocabulary of *Gotterdammerung*, because there is no other way in which your petty minds might encompass it.

"You ask me who I am. I can only say that in *your* mind's eye I am the one who guided the hand of the blind slayer of Balder; I am the one who freed the great wolf Fenrir and rode with him at the head of an army drawn from the Underworld where the dead denied Valhalla groaned beneath the burden of their misery; I am the one whose call roused the fire giants and plotted the course of the ship of ghosts—you must call me Loki. Are you any

wiser now, small creator of gods? Do you understand now
what your little thread signifies within the infinite tapestry
woven by the Norns? No, my human friend, you do not.
You understand nothing—nothing at all."

"Forget Loki, then," I said. "Strip away the mythic
mask. You're one of the invaders of the macroworld: a tapeworm, programmed to disrupt and destroy. Why are you
trying to destroy Asgard?"

He smiled. "The macroworld is in danger," he said,
coolly, "but we do not intend that it should be destroyed.
We have other plans for it. We have sent our ambassadors
to save it, and they will do so, unless your fleshly self inter-
venes. If anyone intends to let the starlet go nova, it is the
ones who oppose us—the guardian gods of Asgard. What
passenger they have placed in your counterpart's brain we
cannot tell, but we know only too well that those who fight
against us would rather blow the macroworld to atoms than
let us possess it. You do not know what kind of beings they
are who have summoned you to this fight. You do not understand the game in which you are a pawn, and you owe
no loyalty to those who have used you."

He seemed to be working hard to make that point, and I
wondered whether my acceptance of ignorance and confusion, or some fatal weakening of my resolve, was yet necessary to the final victory of the forces which were labouring
so hard in the work of my destruction.

"You switched off the power," I accused him. "It was
the invaders, not the gods made by the builders, which
sought to condemn thousands of worldlets to death."

"Yes," he said, without hesitation. "We switched off the
power. The Isthomi's probing disrupted the stalemate that
had long held us impotent, and we took advantage of it. But
the robots which penetrated the starshell were of necessity

very crude, and that was the only thing which they could achieve—the real space inside the starshell is too hazardous for *our* kind of being. We have no flesh-and-blood legions at our disposal, as the guardian gods once had, but the balance of power is more equal now. When we struck again at the Isthomi, we seized our chance to conscript a little flesh to our own cause. When we have won our victory, you may be sure that the power will be returned to the levels; we have need of Asgard, if we can only dispossess its jealous gods. But you, I fear, must be destroyed. We cannot tell what the clever Aesir may have made of you, and we must protect ourselves."

There was an obvious hypocrisy in his regretfulness. He still wasn't absolutely certain that I was harmless. He was still trying to delay while the forces of corruption worked their careful way with my rotting body. I knew that I couldn't move, but I also knew that I could work magic. I had helped to calm a storm with the power of my voice, and though I knew no spells or words of power, I knew that there must be some key to unlock the forces in my mind.

"Loki died too," I whispered—and my voice, though weak, sounded oddly loud over the clamour of the crowd who were waiting to see me killed. "On the field of Ragnarok, *they all died!* When it all began again, there was a new race of gods, unknown save for Balder, whose murder was undone. You're all going to die. Do you hear me— *you're all going to die!*"

My voice rose as I spoke to what I intended to be a stentorian shout, but it came out more like a cracked shriek. The effect was entirely ruined, and the person who called himself Loki, far from being intimidated by my defiant curse, laughed again, with every sign of genuine amusement. The crowd joined in with him, and suddenly the random noise generated by the throng coalesced into a single continuing sound: the sound of joyous laughter.

I burned with humiliation, and I tried with all my might to focus every last vestige of my waning spirit into a hot surge of pure hatred. I was certain that I had the power to raise my arm, to fight back. In that moment, the sheer magnitude of my rage made me feel like a god—like one whose power simply could not be denied.

But passion wasn't enough. My arm wouldn't come up, and when I looked down to command my flesh with the power of my gaze, I saw why. The maggots were already busy in my flesh. They had devoured me almost to the bone. Where once there had been white skin there was now a grey tegument like ragged cloth, pallid and writhing, foul to behold.

Helplessly, I looked up again into the vicious grey eyes of my accuser and executioner.

He had a sword in his hand now, whose mirror-bright blade shone like liquid fire in the angry sunlight. As he raised it to sweep it around in a deadly arc his lips drew back from his teeth in a way that linked him incontrovertibly with the predator whose appearance he had worn in his previous manifestation, when I had engaged him in debate before. Perhaps it was then that I had unwisely given him the opportunity to learn to understand me.

He was Loki the traitor; he was Amara Guur; he was the devil incarnate—and I had nothing left with which to resist his evil.

He reached out with his left hand to grab a handful of my scaly hair, and held me tight while he brought the sword across to cut cleanly through my neck.

My rotting body fell to the ground, seared by the heat of the sun-warmed stone, while he held my severed head aloft, displaying it to the assembled crowd. He let loose a great wordless howl of triumph, which said as clearly as I might have wished that he *had* still feared me, and that there *had* been something I could have done, if only I had known the way, but that I had failed to discover it.

✦ 29 ✦

At first glance, they didn't look like wings.

In fact, the things which Urania pulled out of the bags she'd thoughtfully packed for us looked so much like screwed-up balloons that I thought I'd got hold of the wrong end of the stick and we were going down Montgolfier-fashion. No such luck—they were wings all right, but they were made out of artificial organics, and they spent their inactive time huddled into tight little balls.

"What exactly are we supposed to do with these things?" I asked Urania, as I took up one of these unpromising objects and weighed it in my hand. It felt distressingly light and fragile.

"Think of them as another kind of robot," she suggested. "They are not so very different from the tiny things which we used to carry cameras and poison darts down to this level. But these are adapted for the purpose of carrying humanoid beings. It will not be necessary for you to do any-thing—they will hold you securely, and have an expertise of their own which will enable you to glide down safely. They can cope with any movements which you make, but it would be as well if you tried to remain still, spreading out your limbs horizontally until you touch down on the shell which surrounds the starlet."

Susarma Lear was no more enthused than I by the sight of these creations, which certainly seemed less elegant in design than anyone could have anticipated. As inventors went, the Isthomi were easily a match for the legendary

241

Daedalus—their home level had a labyrinth to put his to shame, and minotaurs would have been a mere finger-exercise for their biotech skills—but I remembered only too well what had happened to poor Icarus.

"Do not be afraid," said Urania to Susarma Lear. "There is nothing to fear. At least, there is nothing to fear from the fall itself."

Until she appended the last remark I had almost managed to reassure myself.

"What is there to fear?" I asked.

"There is breathable air in this space," she reminded me. "Perhaps it is there only to facilitate the kind of descent which we are about to make. On the other hand, it may well support a complex life-system, which would presumably have its predators."

I looked down at the void, and contemplated the faint, uncertain lights that marked out the disc of the starshell. With the central power-supply cut off, those lights were most probably the product of natural bioluminescence. The outside of the starshell was a planetoid in its own right—though it was like no other planetoid in the known galaxy. An asteroid that size couldn't hold on to any atmosphere to speak of because it would be too light, but this one had air by virtue of being in an enclosed space. The combination of very low gravity and relatively high atmospheric pressure must be unique, and the life-system native to such an environment would probably be highly idiosyncratic. But everywhere there was life, there were predators and prey—and the hunters, presumably, would be well used to the darkness.

Myrlin handed me something else which Urania had taken from our luggage. It was a handgun—a needler. He gave one to Susarma, too, although she still had the Scarid crash-gun holstered at her waist.

"Carry it," Myrlin suggested. "But if you have to shoot, try not to point it in my direction."

She favoured him with a nasty scowl. She had chased him half way across the galactic arm with every intention of murdering him, and had thought for a long time that she had succeeded. She had probably never felt so good in all her life as when she thought she was gunning him down, and though she was a trifle saner now than she had been then, she hadn't exactly learned to love him.

673-Nisreen refused the offer of a weapon, excusing himself on the grounds that the injury to his arm would prevent his using it effectively. The long ride on the motorcycle hadn't done the broken limb any favours, and he was obviously feeling more than a little discomfort. But he wasn't about to turn back; he was determined to be in this to the bitter end.

I watched Urania place a mass of folded flesh on Myrlin's back, and I saw the thing beginning to unwind, sending tentacles around his neck and torso in a complicated web. It looked strong, but it also looked rather sinister, and I couldn't help remembering those tentacled monsters that had come so close to stopping Tulyar's party. No wings spread out as yet from the pulpy lump that was left. It just rearranged itself on either side of the life-support pack that was hugging the android's spine between his shoulder-blades.

Myrlin inspected the bits of it he could see apprehensively. He knew the Isthomi better than any of us, and was usually inclined to trust their word without the slightest hesitation, but it takes a lot of faith to accept unquestioningly the assurance that when you jump into an enormous hole, a rubbery pink mess will promptly convert itself into a set of wings which is already trained to keep you safe.

673-Nisreen looked even more unhappy, despite the reputation the Tetrax have for inscrutability. Myrlin told him that he would try to stay close to him, and I ventured the opinion that we had all better try to stay together, although we would perforce have to be very careful if we had to start shooting.

The thought of having something to shoot at usually lifted Susarma Lear's spirits, but she looked very grim now. She had a special frame of mind that she reserved for combat situations, but she hadn't yet been able to define this as a combat situation.

"Go carefully," I told her. "The guys with the headlamps are on your side. Chances are that if there's anything big down there it'll be no more lethal than those moths that mobbed us up above. It may be wiser to save our ammunition for 994-Tulyar and his friend."

When we were all kitted out, Urania simply vaulted the barrier and launched herself into empty space, hugging Clio to her chest. She didn't have a gun, but she had shown not the slightest sign of apprehension or anxiety. When she had put on frail flesh she clearly hadn't acquired all the hang-ups that fleshy creatures usually have. She was of the Nine, and she had their perfect faith that what was properly planned would always work.

It would have made me feel a lot better if I could have watched her wings sprout and seen her dive flatten out into a graceful soaring glide, but she was leaping into darkness, and she was out of the reach of our feeble beams of light before the thing on her back had a chance to get its act together. I was prepared to wait, figuring that once her equipment had got itself into gear she might fly back up and favour us with a brief glimpse of her new accomplishments, but she didn't.

673-Nisreen looked around with an expression that said: "Who's next?"

I didn't rush to volunteer. I looked at Myrlin. He was a little preoccupied, perhaps mulling over the fact that he was more than two metres tall and weighed something over a hundred and fifty kilos—at least twice as much as the scion.

"Okay Rousseau," said Susarma Lear, in her most frigid She-Who-Must-Be-Obeyed tone. "We go together on the count of three, and if either of us chickens out he gets busted to corporal. One. . . . Two. . . ."

She was already scrambling up on to the top of the protective fence, balancing herself on the guard-rail. She wasn't even looking at me to make sure that I was doing as I was told. In the Star Force, officers take that kind of thing for granted.

". . . Three!" she said, and jumped.

Somewhat to my surprise, I found that I had jumped with her. Maybe it was the influence of Star Force discipline coming out at last. Maybe it was my latent superhumanity taking over in the moment of crisis. Either way, I found myself tumbling in the air, watching the circle of light that was the airlock slowly dwindling in size. There was one horrid thrill of pure terror, like a fire alarm going off in my nervous system, and then a flood of intoxicated relief as I realised that nothing was happening to me. I was floating free, and remembered that while in free fall I was, of course, quite weightless.

It was not completely dark, but all the light I could see was emitted by distant pinpricks that were very remote, so I had no real sensation of movement or speed. No doubt I was accelerating with whatever alacrity the weak gravity could muster, but I could not feel it. Instead, I felt utterly isolated, out of touch with the entire universe . . . almost alone.

Almost.

For a couple of seconds I was on the brink of lapsing into a kind of trance—a dream-state. I was very nearly there when I realised what was happening, and snatched myself back. It was a sensation like many I'd had before, when snatching myself back from a doze induced by warmth and relaxation, but I knew that this time was different. Something was in my head—something which had nearly taken advantage of a moment of shock and confusion. Maybe its intention was innocent; maybe it only wanted to show me a bit more of its psychic movie about the history of the universe. But I'd seen it wearing the face of Medusa, and I was frightened of it. I wanted to hold on to my presence of mind at all costs.

I made a deliberate effort to assume the position that had been recommended to me, adjusting the attitude of my body so that I was face-down, with my arms and legs spread out. It was easier than I thought, but when I then tried to look back over my shoulder to see how much I resembled an angel I found myself rolling over slowly, spinning about two different axes. A moment's dizziness confused me further, and then I righted myself again.

I still couldn't sense the velocity of my fall. The darkness was near-total, and the suit I was wearing prevented my feeling the friction of the air against my skin. I had a dreadful suspicion, though, that my wings hadn't grown yet. In fact, I had a dreadful suspicion that they weren't going to grow at all.

I tried to calculate how far I might have to fall. I'd done sufficient mental arithmetic while we were coming through the levels to have some vague idea of the distances that were probably involved. The radius of the macroworld was something on the order of fourteen thousand kilometres, from which one had to subtract the depth of the levels and the radius of the starshell. I figured that if I called those seven and four thousand I probably wouldn't be too far out. That meant that I had something in the region of three thousand kilometres to fall. The gravity here was probably about a ninth or a tenth of Earth-normal, and I figured that that would lead to an acceleration not too far away from a metre per second. On the other hand, that neglected air resistance, which would in the circumstances be considerable. It also neglected the effects of friction on my suit. I couldn't quite see how to go about the job of calculating whether and how quickly I would turn into a meteor, and whether that could possibly happen before I actually landed. It did seem very unlikely, but the whole situation was so bizarre that I really didn't feel able to discount it.

"Is everyone all right?" asked Susarma Lear, startling me somewhat. In trying to absorb myself so deeply in my silly calculations I had somehow let it slip from my mind that we could still talk to one another with the aid of radio.

"I don't know," I said, truthfully. "I can't see or feel a thing. Maybe I have wings and maybe I don't."

"You have wings," said Urania. "I have Clio with me. She has you all under observation."

"I feel fine," Myrlin assured me.

"Nisreen?" I asked.

"I am quite well," the Tetron assured me, and if the smoothness of his parole was anything to go by, he was telling the truth.

"Unfortunately," the scion's voice chipped in again, with a sudden hint of urgency, "it seems that we are not alone. There are other winged creatures, in considerable numbers, approaching from below. We will be among them in a few minutes."

"Can that brain-in-a-box tell us what they are?" demanded Susarma Lear.

"Only that they are very large; they have masses considerably greater than our own."

"I can't see a thing," she complained. I could imagine her finger tightening about the trigger of her needler, desperate to find a target.

"How can *they* see *us?*" inquired Myrlin, with a similar note of desperation.

"Perhaps they can't," I ventured, hopefully, peering into the night and bringing my own gun round to aim at the gloomy void which still separated me by thousands of kilometres from the tiny sparkling worldlet which was Asgard's heart.

"I fear," said Urania—who would, of course, be the first to encounter danger if danger there was—"that they may not rely on light."

My mind, unprompted by any conscious effort, conjured up the image of a host of gigantic vampire bats homing in on us unerringly with the aid of their sonar, avid for our blood.

Urania made a noise, then. It wasn't a scream—I don't believe that she could ever have produced a scream—but it was a sound that had shock in it, and maybe terror. I hadn't thought her capable of terror, and that small sound suddenly seemed dreadfully ominous.

"What is it?" asked Susarma sharply.

She received no answer.

Then, I caught sight of the swarm of shifting shadows, silhouetted against the diffuse light which was still far below them. As they eclipsed the pinpricks I formed a hurried impression of their number, which was far more than I could count, and though in that first brief moment the shadows seemed quite small they were growing with terrible rapidity.

"Oh *merde*," I murmured, as I tried to brace the hand

which held the needler, and prepared to fire.

But I never had a target to aim at. The tiny light on my helmet showed me flickering wings, but they were too far away, moving far too quickly relative to my own downward course. I longed to let loose a stream of needles, though I could hardly begin to believe that such trivial missiles could be effective against the mothlike leviathans which whirled like a Stygian maelstrom from the starry mass of the mysterious Centre. Every time I tried to line up a shot, the flicker of leathery wings snatched the targets away.

I still had not fired a single shot when I fell with distressing smoothness into the gaping maw of a monstrous shadow, and was grabbed with sufficient force to knock me senseless yet again.

⌃ 30 ⌄

Being beheaded is not very pleasant, even when it happens to a dream-self that can take it.

I didn't know that I could take it when the blade sliced through me, so I was able to savour the unpleasantness to the full. I was in the process of trying to utter a few last words—nothing, I fear, of any particular note—but discovered that without a throat I could only gurgle wetly. My mouth opened and my tongue tried to wrap itself around a syllable of protest, but no sound came out.

Surprisingly, though, the stream of my consciousness continued on its weary way without any hint of interruption. Indeed, the effect which my beheading had on the people who were watching seemed to be far greater than the effect it had on me.

I already knew that I was not a pretty sight, and I did not suppose that my transformation into a bodiless head held aloft by a malevolent godling would improve my image, but I was quite unprepared for what actually happened.

The laughter which had been echoing around the great plaza died away. The faces which had been full of amusement had just time to change, as a wave of pure horror spread through the multitude, signified by dilating eyes and hands brought swiftly upwards in hopeless defence. Thousands of mouths opened to speak—or to howl with anguish—but were no more capable of giving vent to sound than my own impotent lips. Silence descended like a curtain, and all movement ceased.

The thing which had mockingly called itself Loki had turned my gaze away from his own when he struck the crucial blow, but I could still see him out of the corner of my eye. His pale complexion was even paler now, and the paleness had quickly claimed his eyes and his hair. He was as still and silent as the rest.

Like them, he had been turned to stone.

The only sound I could hear was the hissing of serpents, and the only movement which remained was the stirring of those same serpents as they writhed around the stone hand which grasped them, making the head to which they were anchored rock and sway.

The Nine, interpreting my dreams with casual confidence in their ability to do so, had told me that I had been given a weapon, which might be used against the forces which had injured them. They had not been entirely accurate in their judgment. The biocopy which had been thrust into my brain hadn't been designed to *give* me a weapon when my persona was re-encoded—it had been designed to *make me into* a weapon.

I had found Medusa, and she was me.

The invaders of Asgard's software space had never realised precisely what tactics were being used against them. I knew now why the one which had appeared as Loki had still been hesitant, playing for time until he felt safe—until he had seen my body decay to a point where he thought that it posed no further threat. He had been anxious, and rightly so. The enemy had been bluffed and deluded into contriving my capture and my apparent destruction, not knowing that my destruction would trigger their own. I was a booby-trap bomb . . . a Trojan Horse . . . a gorgon in sheep's clothing.

I couldn't yet begin to understand what difference this

little surprise package might make to the war that was going on in Asgard's software space. I had no way of knowing whether what had just happened was Armageddon or just a minor skirmish. To tell the truth, I wasn't particularly interested in trying to figure it out. What concerned me more was what would happen to me.

Despite the fact that I had apparently slain my enemies in one fell swoop, I was still in something of a predicament. I was reduced to the status of a severed head, with snakes instead of hair and a truly poisonous glare, dangling from the clenched fist of a stone statue. I still had my wits about me, but the problem of figuring out what to do next was more than a little vexatious.

For all I could tell, I might be condemned to hang there for all eternity, keeping my captives still and safe with my poisonous stare. Maybe that could be construed as a noble fate for a self-sacrificing hero, but it wasn't one that I could contemplate with any relish.

I had been assured by my enemies that I was on the high road to Hell, and it seemed to me that if I was now destined to spend any kind of lifetime in my present condition, that would probably be hell enough for anyone.

I was still considering this awful possibility when I caught a glimpse of movement in the crowd. It was at the very limit of my peripheral vision, and for a moment or two I thought I had been mistaken, but the writhing of the snakes turned my head just enough to allow me a better sight of the relevant area, and I saw that there was indeed a humanoid figure picking its way through the densely-packed assembly.

As he made his slow and painstaking progress he moved round so that I could see him more directly, but my eyesight was blurred and I couldn't bring him into focus.

Al I was sure of was that he looked human, and rather elderly. He carried himself as if walking required unusual effort. I had a flash of anxiety in case he might be turned to stone the moment I set eyes on him, but that fear evaporated quickly. Most of the individuals in the crowd hadn't needed to look directly at my eyes before being turned to stone, and if I was as effective against his kind as I had been against theirs he should have been petrified the moment he set foot in the square.

I watched him as he came up the steps to stand beside the statue of Loki. He was a tall man, and as he finally came into focus I saw that he had a Roman nose and blue eyes. He was wearing an amused expression. I figured that I knew who he really was. He was one of the builders. He was one of those who had sent out that appeal for help that had turned me into a hero and brought me to this undignified pass. But in exactly the same way that the enemy had worn the face of my arch-enemy, Amara Guur, he was wearing the face of a dear departed friend.

He was Saul Lyndrach—the man who had sent me forth upon my epic journey.

I still couldn't speak. He saw me trying to produce sounds, and smiled. I didn't think it was so funny, and the fact that I wasn't amused must have shown on whatever nightmarish mask I was now using for a face.

"*Pardonnez moi,*" he said.

He couldn't really have said it in French, but I *heard* it in French.

Had I been able to speak, I could have produced an entirely apposite quote: *Si Dieu nous a fait a son image, nous le lui avons bien rendu.* Saul would have understood. Saul would even have understood the subtle irony of a Rousseau quoting Voltaire. For once, alas, I could not take advantage of the readiness of my wit.

"You have rendered us a great service," he said—and I heard his words now as though they were in English, and knew that he was speaking not as Saul Lyndrach but as one of the guardian gods of Asgard, whose enemies I had blighted with my stare. "You have helped us to break a stalemate that had endured for hundreds of thousands of years. You probably believe that you have been ill-used, and so you have, but you cannot realise how much this victory has owed to your own fortitude and your own strength. The scheme could so easily have failed had you yielded to the pressure of circumstance at any point along the way. You have survived experiences that would have obliterated very many entities forced into your situation. Perhaps, had you known the true magnitude of the threats that you have endured, you could not have succeeded, but your ignorance has been strengthened by courage and by a stubborn refusal to admit defeat. We thank you, Michael Rousseau."

It was a nice enough speech, in its way. We all appreciate a pat on the back, even when we no longer have a back to be patted. But I had more urgent matters on my mind than testimonials. I wanted to know what the hell was going to happen now. Could Humpty Dumpty be put back together again? Assuming that this version of myself had to live out my allotted span in software space, without any opportunity to become a real person again, was there any way I could get another body . . . and the power of speech . . . and a haircut?

"Unfortunately," Saul went on, "the dangers which Asgard faces are not yet entirely averted. The war in software space is not over, and although the balance has swung to our advantage because of what you have accomplished, there is a conflict still to be resolved. And there is a further adventure which has not yet come to its conclusion—which might, if things go badly, undo all that you have accomplished. There is another battle yet to be fought, in the actual space that surrounds the starlet.

"We are able to observe what is happening in the starshell, but the defences which we have erected around and within it, to preserve it from our enemies, are as difficult for our own machine-intelligences to penetrate as for theirs. The enemy was able to send mobile units—robots—through the defences while they were temporarily disrupted as a result of the Nine's unlucky attempt to breach them, and although they were belatedly destroyed, they succeeded in switching off the power supply to the levels. There is now a power build-up within the starlet which is destabilising it, and there is a danger that it may explode. We are trying as best we can to get our own robots into the starshell, but in spite of the fact that we have retaken control of the peripheral systems, mechanical brains simply cannot penetrate the defences surrounding the control room. Only an organic being can reach and operate the controls.

"Unfortunately, it seems that the enemy has employed a stratagem which is virtually a mirror image of the one which we employed in creating you. We copied into your brain a programme which, when retranscribed in a software persona, would bind up great destructive power in your being. The invaders seem to have copied into the brains of at least one of your kind a programme that will give him equal destructive power. The invader now using the body of 994-Tulyar would be able to destroy Asgard, if that is his intention, once he reaches the control-room of the starshell. He would also be able to damage us as severely as, with your aid, we have damaged the forces arrayed against us. Unfortunately, Tulyar and his companion are already perilously close to that destination. Had *this* victory come in time, we might have stopped them in the levels, but they have already made the jump to the starshell."

I wished that I could ask questions, but I had no voice. I could only hang there and listen.

"It may yet turn out that our stratagem was the poorer one," Saul continued regretfully. "Perhaps our purpose would have been better served had we planted a programme in your organic persona which could have equipped it to operate the starlet's controls, but that would certainly have resulted in the obliteration of your own consciousness, and that is not our way. We are the creation of humanoids, and our primary purpose is to protect and preserve humanoid life. Alas, the biocopy which remains within your other self is virtually non-functional in that form. Your other self can derive nothing from it but a few messages, which he may not even be able to read. Although he is trying hard to reach the starshell, he does not know what to do when he gets there, and it is too late to get the information to him by any conventional means. He too has made the jump, and we cannot yet tell what his fate will be."

He paused. It would have been a good time to slip in a few clever questions, and my condition was becoming more infuriating by the minute. I remembered only too clearly, now, what the invader had said about Tulyar's mission—and what he had said about the willingness of the gods of Asgard to see the macroworld destroyed rather than lose possession of it. It was a point regarding which I would have liked to seek some reassurance.

"We still may need your help," he said, soberly. "The contest is not yet ended, and there are moves which might still be made. I am sorry for the pain and difficulty which you have so far suffered, and sorry that there may be more yet to come. We do not like to use you in this fashion, without your being able to understand what we are doing, or how, or why, but we sincerely believe that you would consent, if you could understand what it is that we require of you. Our purpose is the salvation of the macroworld—and the preservation of your community of worlds.

"What I will do now is to take you from this place to another—into the very heart of Asgard's software space, where my kind is now recovering its dominion. The journey should not be very hazardous, but we dare not underestimate our enemy's ability to hit back. Then, we will do what we can to remake you, before the time arrives when we must make what use of you we can. We will reconstruct you—and though we will make of you, as we did before, an instrument, we will nevertheless preserve for you the *persona* which is your essential self. Be patient, I beg of you. We must go now, but as we go, I will try to offer you as much of an explanation as I can, and as much of an explanation as I think you can understand."

With that, he reached out a gnarled but sturdy hand, and gently pried me loose from the stone hand that held me.

I wished fervently that I could speak, or make some sign to say that there was indeed a great deal more that I wanted to know—a great deal more that I wanted explained. What I wanted more than anything else in the world just then was to be able to ask questions—not just because there was so much I wanted to be told, but also because I wanted some way to test what he was going to tell me. After all, he said he was on the side of the angels, and he was doing his very best to act like a good guy, but how did I really know that I could trust him?

It was all very well for him to say flattering things about my courage and powers of endurance. I had been exerting them mainly on my own behalf. Sure, I wanted Asgard to be saved. I wanted the lights switched on again and everything returned to what passed for normal in these parts. But in view of the deceptions to which I had already been subject, how could I be certain that it was this masquerader and his pals who had that end in view? How could I be certain that they weren't the ones who wanted the macroworld blown to smithereens?

If I was going to be used yet again, as a go-between who didn't even understand my own make-up, I wanted to be sure that I wasn't going to be the Judas Goat who would lead my other self and all his allies to the slaughter.

But I couldn't be sure.

I couldn't be sure of anything.

In the meantime, the thing that was wearing the face of my late, lamented friend tucked my gorgon's head beneath his phantom arm, and strolled off into a gathering mist of pure confusion.

↫ 31 ↬

I dreamed that my body was wrapped around by snakes, whose warm polished scales slid over my skin as they writhed and coiled around me. I was not squeezed by the coils, for these were not constrictors bent on crushing me to death, but I was held tight, unable to move. I could see their eyes glowing in the darkness, and where their heads touched me I could feel the slick forked tongues caressing me . . . *tasting* me. . . .

That dream dissolved, and took me back to one which had visited me before:

My dream of Creation, in which the life born in the great gas-clouds which drifted in interstellar space still poured into those tiny lighted wells which were solar systems, enfolding those tiny fragments of supernova debris which were planets, finding niches in the dense atmospheres of gas-giants and the oceans of water-worlds.

The cosmos was so vast that all the matter which was in it was no more than a storm of dust blown about by uncaring energy-winds, and the molecules of life such a tiny fraction of matter that all life—all that great universal ecocloud—was no more than a haunting phantom or shadow, tenuous and precarious. And then there came again that other: the thing which was not life yet threatened life, which I could not quite bring into my framework of understanding.

259

This time, my perspective continued to alter, so that I lost sight of the ocean of stars which was the visible universe, and saw instead the molecules of life engaged in the game of evolution, building themselves into more complex cells, and then into multi-cellular beings, adding new orders of magnitude to their complexity. Now I saw the pattern of life, as it extended through the vast expanding universe of space, as if it were a prodigious tree spreading its roots and branches wherever there was room for them to go, producing gorgeous flowers and fruits wherever they touched a world which provided the vital elementary seeds around which such flowers and fruits might flourish. I saw Earth as one such fruit, Tetra as another, and all the galaxies as branches bearing flowers and fruit in abundance: fruit glowing with internal light, while the flowers sang and filled infinity with their scent.

As well as its flowers and its fruits, the tree was swarming with commensal creatures of every kind—with insects and birds, frogs, and tunneling worms. Though many of these were parasites which took their sustenance from the tree and left damage in their wake, they were no real threat to the continued existence and health of the tree, and I knew that what damage they did was only part of a continuing process of death and transfiguration, wherein a kind of balance was sustained.

But then I saw that there was another kind of blight in the tree—a canker which reached out its desiccating grip wherever it could to turn the flowers leprously white and shrivel the fruit into dry husks. Many of the canker's instruments mimicked the population of the tree, appearing as tiny parasites—whatever kind of force this was, it could produce pseudo-life of its own, but in so doing it denied the possibility of balance and of permanence, for this blight was something which could only destroy or be destroyed. It permitted only two ends—either the blight would be obliterated, or the tree would die. This was true of the whole, and of each and every part that the blight had reached. There were many branches yet untouched—their flowers beautiful and fresh, their fruits luscious and sweet—but there were many that had already withered, and others where resistance held the canker's instruments in check. Ultimately, the fate of the entire tree was at stake, and any one of these tiny battles might prove crucial to the destiny of the whole. . . .

Then I woke up again, with the desperately tired feeling that it had all happened before, and would all happen again. I was no longer master inside my own skull, and every time the fragile hold of consciousness was shaken loose, my imagination was up for grabs, ready to be shot full of whatever psychic propaganda was coded into the rogue software that was gradually increasing its authority within my brain.

And yet, I was still *me*. My essential self hadn't been blighted or damaged at all.

At least, not yet. There was no way of knowing how long a thing like the one which had taken over Tulyar might lie dormant, if it was prepared to bide its time.

Under other circumstances, I might have devoted a little time to a more detailed consideration of the pollution of my dreams, but as soon as I opened my eyes such minor anxieties were displaced by more urgent concerns.

I realised that the nightmare about the snakes had considerable foundation in reality. I was trussed up tight by some kind of thick, sticky thread, wound so thoroughly about me that I was encased in a virtual cocoon, with only my head sticking out at the top. I struggled to free myself, but my arms were pinned against my side, unable to move. As I kicked against the confining bonds I found that my thighs were just as firmly held, but that I could wiggle my feet. My whole body swung as I tried unsuccessfully to bend at the waist, and I deduced that I must be suspended from above by a number of threads. I had the small consolation of being right way up, but that was the only blessing I could count in a dire situation, apart from the fact that I was still alive.

I tried desperately to shift my fingers, and contrived some small movement, but they were spread out and bound to my thighs. I must have dropped the needler, and could not tell whether I had ever managed to fire it.

My headlight was still working, and I could turn my head enough to play its beam around my gloomy surroundings. I found that I was inside some kind of chamber whose walls were dense thickets of grey, leafless branches. It seemed to be roughly spherical, but there were a number of thick threads running across the cavity, apparently rigid. These were coated in what looked like dried glue, which was occasionally gathered into globules shaped like drips that had solidified just before they began to fall.

The bottom part of the spherical enclosure was heaped with big white things like elongated footballs a metre long and as thick as a man's thigh. The heap was partly covered by great gobs of slimy stuff. They looked to me like eggs, and I shuddered to think what manner of hungry offspring might be destined to hatch out of them.

Suspended from the roof of the chamber by strands of the dried gluey stuff were a number of neatly-wrapped packages which—I realised—must look pretty much like me. Like me they all had heads poking out at the top, but none of the heads was remotely humanoid. Every one of them was probably some kind of giant insect, but like the moths on the bottommost level of outer Asgard they didn't have compound eyes, and that gave them something of the appearance of nocturnal mammals. Though their jaws and palps and antennae were arthropodan, their eyes were big and wide and innocent. Like me, these other prisoners were still alive—their antennae and their mouth-parts moved as though they were engaged in a sign-language conversation. Some, at least, stared at me while I stared at them, and they seemed—though it was surely an illusion—to pity me in my awful plight.

We were all installed in some kind of larder. We were fresh meat laid in to feed the babies that would soon emerge from the enormous eggs.

Whatever had come after us as we tried to fly down to the shell surrounding Asgard's starlet had obviously caught me. It had brought me back to its nest. I wondered whether I ought to be grateful that it hadn't simply torn me apart. Then I wondered how long it was likely to be before its eggs started hatching, and how long it was likely to take the larvae to devour me if they started with my feet and worked upwards. Then I remembered the difficulty the tentacled slugs up above had had when they had tried to unwrap their prey, and I wondered how long it would take these things to chew through the super-tough plastic in which I was encased.

I realised, with a small frisson of fear, that the life-support system hooked into the flesh of my neck could keep me alive for a long time, even if something was slowly eating me.

Then, belatedly, I wondered what had happened to the rest of our little party.

"Hey," I said, tentatively, into the microphone. "Is anybody there?"

"Rousseau!" came the explosive reply. There was only one voice, and it was Susarma Lear's.

"Susarma?" I echoed. "What happened to the others?"

"Jesus!" she said, "I thought you were all dead. What the hell are you playing at, Rousseau? Where are you?"

"I only just woke up," I told her, in an aggrieved tone. "As to where I am, I wish I knew. But I'm in terrible trouble. Whatever grabbed me trussed me up like a mummy, and I'm hanging here in what looks horribly like a larder."

"Can you see any of the others?" she demanded.

I took another careful look at my companions, but all the ones I could see were definitely non-humanoid.

"Not unless there's someone directly behind me," I said. "I can't crane my neck that far. Where are *you*?"

Before she could reply, there was the sound of a long, sleepy groan. I knew it wasn't her, and it didn't sound like Myrlin or Urania.

"Nisreen?" I said. "Nisreen, is that you?"

There was a slight pause. Then he answered. "Mr. Rousseau?"

"Where are you, Nisreen?" I asked.

There was another pause before he said: "I am immobilised. I think I am hanging in mid-air. I can see several creatures whose heads resemble moths or beetles, wrapped up as I am in. . . ."

"Shit," said the colonel, interrupting him. "That means I have two of you to look for, and I don't even know where to start. Talk about hunting needles in haystacks. I need that damned brainbox, but I haven't heard a peep from Urania or Myrlin."

"You're free, then?" I said. It was hopeful news, though it was no guarantee of my salvation.

"Yeah," she said. "Thing grabbed me. I would have blasted it but it had hold of me and I didn't fancy joining it in free fall. I played dead until it landed—then I filled the bastard full of needles. I'm in the crown of some incredibly massive tree—must be a couple of miles high, as near as I can tell. My wings got damaged and I don't dare to try to fly. There's more light here than I could have guessed when we were looking down before the jump—glow-worms of some kind are here, there, and everywhere, and the trees seem to produce light themselves. I can see hundreds of the damn things in every direction, but the forest isn't so densely packed that I can walk from the branches of one tree into the branches of another. It's going to take me half a day to get down to the floor, unless I take a risk and jump, and I don't know which way to go to look for either of you."

It didn't sound promising.

"Myrlin?" I said, hopefully. "Urania? Is anyone there?" If they'd been able to speak, they would have spoken already, and I knew it. Suddenly I felt horribly alone.

"A couple of other things have come after me, but they're very slow," said Susarma. "I figure I can make it down to the ground. But I can't see anything that looks like a helmet-light, and I'm not sure I'd be able to tell it from the glow-worms if you *were* within sight."

"Unfortunately," I said, drily, "I'm pretty sure that we aren't. I'm inside something that probably looks like a giant pumpkin from the outside. Nisreen is presumably in another one of the same kind. But we could be twenty or thirty kilometres away as easily as right next door."

"Well what the hell am I supposed to *do*, Rousseau?" She sounded very annoyed, but I knew that it was just a cover-up. Really, she was feeling utterly and completely helpless.

"I don't know," I said, feebly. "I just don't know."

"It would seem," said 673-Nisreen, "that I have little chance of extricating myself from the bonds which confine me."

"In that case," said Susarma, with a sigh, "we're in trouble."

That seemed to me like an understatement. I looked down again at the eggs. It didn't really matter what loathsome kind of thing would emerge therefrom—a monster is only an egg's way of making an egg, just like a chicken or a man. All life, if my vivid dreams could be credited with putting things in their proper perspective, was part of the same unfolding pattern, the same infinite thread darting from the spool of Creation to be caught by the loom of fate.

In being eaten by some infant creature I would merely be casting the molecules that had briefly been me back into the cauldron of life, where they would be redistributed again and again and again in the aeons to come. Even if the local food chain were blown to kingdom come when the starlet went nova, the atoms would still exist, hurrying through the infinite void until they were gobbled up by greedy micro-organisms a billion years from now, to start the story over in some other region.

Looked at in that way, it didn't seem to matter so much. From *that* perspective, hardly anything mattered.

But none of that affected the fact that poor Mike Rousseau—the one and only; the most important entity in the universe from the viewpoint of his own tiny, narrow mind—was facing an imminent, agonising, and utterly horrible death without having completed the last leg of his journey to the centre of Asgard.

For myself, I could not imagine any more grotesque failure of the moral order of the universe. It simply wasn't fair.

At that moment, my eye was caught by a movement. Part of the wall of the spherical nest was being eased aside to allow the ingress of something large and living. For a fraction of a second I nursed the faint hope that it was a friendly humanoid come to set me free, but it just wasn't a sustainable illusion. The head coming through the gap was far too big and far too ugly to be anyone I knew.

It looked, in fact, like the head of a monstrous centipede, all golden yellow in the beam of my helmet-light, with great antler-like antennae, yellow-irised eyes, and four moving jaws like outsized hedge-trimmers.

"I hate to make a depressing situation seem even worse," I said, hoarsely, "but I may have just been put on the menu."

"This macroworld, which you call Asgard, was not always in this location," said the voice of Saul Lyndrach, who still seemed to be speaking in English. "It came here from another galaxy, in the very distant past. In your terms, it was approximately a million and a half years ago."

We were moving through a cloud of silvery mist. I could no longer see him, nor could I feel the grip of his hand on my snaky hair. In fact, I could no longer feel my snaky hair. I had an uncomfortable suspicion that what was left of my flesh was still rotting, and I expected that at any moment I might lose my sight entirely as the processes of decay worked their way through my eyeballs. After that, presumably, my hearing would go and leave me isolated in the prison of my dying brain.

I still had enough cells left in that hypothetical brain to marvel at the figure of a million and a half years. When Asgard had arrived in the galactic arm—from the Black Galaxy or somewhere else—*Homo sapiens* was just a glimmer in the genes of its parent species.

"Asgard came to this region through what you call a wormhole," the voice went on. "Under certain special circumstances, the starlet can produce enough power to warp the macroworld through stressed space."

I had no reason to doubt him, but again I had to marvel at the thought. It would take a lot of energy to warp something like Asgard. A hell of a lot of energy—more than a star routinely pipes out. I already knew that there was a small star at the centre of Asgard, but its regular output couldn't be enough to shift Asgard from here to my home sun; an intergalactic trip would be out of the question.

It was as though he could read the thoughts in my head. "The power for the displacement was supplied by a controlled nova," he said. "An artificial starlet is more versatile than you might imagine, but it was nevertheless a difficult journey to contrive. Even though there was no question of planning a specific destination, the trick of displacing the whole of the extra energy of the explosion into the creation of a wormhole required considerable cleverness. There was the danger of too large an explosion, which would have converted all Asgard into a tiny supernova and scattered its mass across the desert of intergalactic space. There was also the danger that the starlet's fusion reaction would be damped down too far once the required energy had been bled into the stresser.

"The intergalactic shift was not totally successful. Asgard did what it was supposed to do, but the fusion reaction was damped down, and though the damage was reparable, given time, it put a severe strain on power-supplies to the levels. More importantly, the invasion had already occurred, and the invaders had come with the macroworld to its new location. That was when the war within Asgard began in earnest, and the reduction in the starlet's output left its defenders at a disadvantage. The upper levels had already been evacuated—now they were refrigerated. They could never have cooled so extremely by natural processes. The intention was to seal off the lower levels.

"This barrier was not to protect the lower levels, which had already been invaded, but to protect the space outside the macroworld. The builders, riding the starlet explosion, intended to remove themselves into the dark remoteness of intergalactic space. Alas, wormholes do not form randomly, and they are always attracted to gravity-wells—something which makes interstellar travel much more convenient for species like yours. In trying to remove a centre of infection from their own galaxy, the masters of Asgard simply brought it into yours. They knew that this galaxy had been seeded, and when, and they were therefore able to make a rough calculation to tell them how long it would be before interstellar travelers were likely to arrive here. They knew that they would not survive, in their own humanoid form, but they hoped that the army which fought for them in software space might win the war before that time elapsed. That hope proved false. We could not win the war—in the short term, the damage to the starlet gave the invaders the upper hand; in the longer term it proved that we could only contrive a stalemate.

"The builders considered the possibility of trying to move Asgard again, but time was against them. They could not do so immediately because of the damping down of the starlet's fusion reactor, and once the starlet's normal functions had been restored they could not make proper preparations because the war was in its most desperate phase. They judged it necessary, instead, to isolate the real space within the starshell in order to protect it from the invaders.

"The war went badly for the builders in those early years. It took such toll of their resources that they could not survive, in their organic forms. No humanoid has set foot on the starshell for hundreds of thousands of years, and those inorganic intelligences which reached the shell itself could not breach the defences protecting the control room—until the Isthomi upset the balance of things.

"The builders had built artificial intelligences to inhabit

their machinery which were much more powerful than themselves—gods, if you wish to call them that, but gods manufactured by men who were not so very different from your own kind. But the builders did not trust their servant gods as completely as they might have done. The systems that control the starlet—the systems that control Asgard itself—were not entirely under the control of the programmes inhabiting Asgard's software space. The most crucial decisions required humanoid hands in order to be implemented—clever hands with nimble fingers. Control of the starlet is by no means a trivial matter of closing certain switches, though there are some effects that can be obtained by crude destructive work—including the interruption of the power supply. In a sense, we were fortunate—the power might have failed hundreds of thousands of years ago, even without the interference of the invaders' mobiles, just as the starlet may eventually blow up without the intervention of their humanoid instruments. But as things were, the balance of things was maintained, and the contending forces were locked into a potentially endless struggle.

"Asgard is full of humanoids, and in principle any one of them might have been co-opted into the war, given the information necessary to control the starlet. But with the builders gone, the starshell isolated, and such intelligences as the Isthomi carefully sealed off, organic beings were beyond the reach of software intelligences. They lived, as it were, in a parallel world. The power of software entities to intervene in their environments was very limited, even when the builders were in control and their machine-dwelling gods enjoyed all the power potentially at their disposal. Alas, the war had weakened us, and our opportunities to make contact with humanoids were much reduced.

"I have said that the war went badly for the builders—it

went scarcely better for our enemies. The battles that we fought were of a nature you can hardly comprehend, but they were mutually destructive to the point where neither side had more than a tiny fraction of its initial resources. For a long time now it has been fought in a purely defensive mode, with either side blocking the other's moves.

"I cannot describe to you the way that the war was being fought, or why it reached the kind of impasse which it reached. But you have seen many of the levels, and you know that the majority had begun to stagnate. We could not influence them in any way at all, because the invaders denied us access as far as they were able. There are only a handful of habitats that contain races sufficiently advanced technologically to have produced their own machine intelligences; the Isthomi are very exceptional. Part of Asgard's purpose is to preserve and protect the variety of humanoid and other species, and so the Isthomi were isolated within their habitat. When they discovered that there were other habitats, and began exploring them, they initially did so by means of mobile units—robots—which moved unhindered through actual space, much as the Scarid armies did.

"Although they attracted the attention of both the invaders and ourselves, we made no attempt to interfere with them, although it became gradually more obvious that their explorations would eventually bring them close to the starshell, making them a significant factor in the war. When they attempted to reach the central systems through software space, activating the defences, inaction was no longer possible. The war came briefly to life again, with a rapid series of moves and countermoves. When the invaders struck out at the Isthomi they would have destroyed them had we not managed to weaken the blow. They took advantage of the interface which was established between the Isthomi's systems and a small group of humanoid brains, and we made our own move in parallel—both moves were hasty and perhaps ill-judged; they were certainly decided on the spur of the moment. The move that *we* made—the move that created *you*—has succeeded better than we had any right to hope. Alas, it may yet prove to be the case that the same is true of the enemy's move.

"Your *alter ego* is attempting to restore power to the levels. He believes that with the aid of the Nine he might succeed, but neither he nor the Nine know what kind of defences the starshell has. The Nine cannot survive there, and without the Nine, your *alter ego* has no idea what must be done. The problem does not end there, because the humanoids infected by the enemy's programmes surely know how to achieve the end that *they* are intended to achieve. What that end is we cannot be entirely certain, but it will certainly involve our destruction, and the achievement of their dominion within the walls of Asgard. Asgard's software space, and all of its systems, would soon be ours again if it were not for the enemy's humanoid agents, but as things stand, the invaders may yet achieve their object.

"You may have difficulty understanding what difference it would make if the invaders were to win. They certainly would not immediately wipe out all organic life within the macroworld, or within the galactic community. Nevertheless, we do believe that their ultimate aim is the annihilation of life, and we believe that possession of Asgard would offer them a so-far unparalleled opportunity to study the multitudinous forms of life, and make more efficient preparations for its destruction. So far, the enemy's experiments in the manufacture of organic weapons have been poor ones—they have produced nothing more complicated than a bacterium, and the diseases which they have manufactured have been relatively impotent. We are anxious to deny them the opportunity to improve their skills, and if it were to seem absolutely necessary, we would destroy Asgard to prevent it falling into their hands.

"You are undoubtedly curious to know what manner of enemy it is that we are fighting, but that is not an easy question to answer—we have only met their instruments, which are weapons rather than persons. I will tell you what we do know—or what we believe to be the case, but I cannot pretend that it offers any final enlightenment.

"It seems that the parent entities which made the invaders of Asgard have nothing in common with the humanoids who were the architects of its defenders. They may well have existed before life began. The universe may have been theirs before the first carbon atoms ever came into being. The orderliness of their original nature may have been built into the most fundamental structure of matter. The recurring patterns of their existence are to be found in the dance of subatomic particles and the interplay of fundamental forces. They were probably born in the explosive chaos of time's beginning, and as the universe evolved, would have grown to fill it, to bring some kind of order to the entire cosmos. But the universe was subsequently invaded by other orderly entities—the molecules of your kind of life.

"At first, we think, the presence of life in the universe must have seemed an irrelevance to those which became its enemies, but when life first evolved to humanoid complexity, and humanoids began to design intelligences of a new and better kind—the silicon gods of the macroworlds—it must have become clear to the pre-existing intelligences that if it were left to itself, this other evolutionary process must ultimately come into conflict with theirs, imposing its

274

own stamp upon the evolution of the universe. The makers of the invaders began to intervene—they sent out their instruments to destroy. They made gods of their own, to meet the gods which your kind made—and they made crude pseudo-living entities, too, with which to attack the organic fabric of life.

"All this happened in the very distant past, long before your galaxy was seeded, long before Asgard was built. The war rages across the entire universe, and may yet continue until the lifetime of the universe is complete. The battle for Asgard is no more than a single skirmish, though it may be a vital one. Asgard owes its existence to the war, for if there was no war, there would be no need of macroworlds to preserve and protect the produce of worlds, or to help in the seeding of new worlds and new galaxies.

"The initial invasion of Asgard employed organisms whose biochemistry was alien to the vast life-system of which your world is a part—the germs of a plague whose sole function was to destroy and denature DNA wherever it could be found. But such organisms were a weapon that the builders could counter with relative ease, because the invaders have never been adept in the processes of organic creation. The software personalities that came to fight the real battle were much more powerful. But in that kind of battle, too, we believe that we will prove stronger in the end. On the infinite stage of history, life will win. We have to believe that, do we not?"

His words had begun to fade. My vision was already faded and blurred, though the cloud through which we passed was so featureless that I could not properly estimate the extent of the deterioration; now I was beginning to lose my hearing. It seemed that I might have to be content, for the time being, with such explanations as I had already received, incomplete and unsatisfactory though they were.

I wondered what would happen to me when all my senses had failed—when I could not see, or hear, or feel anything at all. Would my memory then begin to fade as the lobes of my hypothetical brain became dysfunctional? Would there be anything left of me at all?

I clung to the knowledge that this strange inhabitant of software space had, after all, collected me from the place where I had done my work, and had implied that I could be reconstructed in order to be put to work yet again, in some unspecified fashion. Despite all that had happened to me, I was still clinging to what I could only think of as *life,* whatever my enigmatic companion might have called it. *In extremis* I might be, but it seemed that I was also among friends, and though the macroworld itself might be in danger, the game had not yet reached the final play.

I spared a moment to hope, as fervently as I could, that my other self had fared even better than I, and that if he too had found unexpected dangers and dreadful threats, he had nevertheless found allies to preserve him from death.

♪ 33 ♪

As the monstrosity hauled its ugly body through the gap I saw that it wasn't a centipede after all. The abdomen was rounded, a dull orange in colour and very hairy, and there were only a dozen legs sprouting from the segmented thorax. The creature had huge wings that gleamed brilliantly in the light of my headlamp; they were translucent save for the ribs that patterned them, and the way they refracted and reflected the light gave them a multicolored sheen. Under other circumstances I might have taken time out to appreciate their prettiness, which contrasted markedly with the extreme ugliness of the body that bore them, but things being the way they were my attention was monopolised by the great gawping eyes and vicious jaws. The jaws were glistening with some kind of mucus, and the palps on either side of the mouth were writhing like white worms.

I struggled reflexively, but I was wrapped up so tightly that all I could do was rock gently back and forth, like some pendulous fruit stirred by the wind.

I didn't scream, but I think I may have whimpered a bit.

The last thing I wanted was to attract attention to myself, so I stopped struggling. I wondered whether I ought to switch off my headlight—I could still reach the control with the tip of my tongue—but the idea of being in total darkness with the monster wandering around was unbearable.

The thing made straight for me. It didn't waste a single glance on any of the other prisoners. Despite the sense of imminent doom which I had, I was paradoxically glad that I wouldn't have to watch it eat something else, anticipating my own fate while I watched it rip some moth-like thing apart with those slavering jaws.

The jaws in question reached up toward my face as the thing scrambled over the giant eggs which littered the floor of the nest. The horrid head was level with my chest, and as the jaws came apart I formed a dreadful picture in my mind of my head being squashed between the pincers, the skull-bones crumpling about my brain.

But the jaws reached on a little further than that, and snipped like a pair of scissors—with surprising delicacy—at the threads by which I was suspended. Before I had time to fall the creature reared up on half a dozen of its back legs, and grabbed me with the four front ones, hugging me to its chitinous bosom as though I were its long-lost child miraculously recovered from evil kidnappers. Then, without delay, it turned back on its tracks and scuttled as fast as it could— which was not very fast, given that I was such an unwieldy burden—for the doorway.

"Rousseau!" said Susarma Lear, her voice sounding very loud in my ears. "Rousseau, for Christ's sake, *what's happening?*"

"I'm alive," I told her, though I was unable to muster an appropriate tone of exultation. "I guess I've just become the prize in a little game of rob-the-larder. I've been scavenged."

The nest-robber hustled through the opening in the wall of the chamber and hurled itself out into space, still cradling me in its forelimbs. I tried to turn my head, because the light reflected from the polished golden plates of its thorax was dazzling me. I wished I hadn't. The robbery hadn't gone unnoticed, and beyond the thin neck of the creature that had snatched me was a great tumbling shadow. My headlamp wasn't powerful enough to illuminate it all, but I got a fleeting impression of enormous size and of a spiderlike head even uglier than the head of the beast that had me in its grip.

I suppose we flew, after a fashion, but it felt like falling, as if the nest-robber were diving as steeply as it could to avoid its vengeful pursuer. As my head twisted I caught brief glimpses of other shapes hurtling past—the trailing tips of the branches of the gargantuan trees which grew on the shell that surrounded Asgard's starlet. We came too close to some of the branches, reeling in mid-air as the wings of my captor touched them. It swerved to avoid them, but not very successfully, and I treated myself to a brief moment of macabre humour by wondering if the giant fly which held me had qualified for its pilot's licence.

For fully fifty seconds the scavenger out-dived its pursuer, and I had just about decided that perhaps it had got away with its raid when our barely-controlled fall was rudely interrupted. It wasn't the pursuer that got us, though—it was something which had been waiting on one of the tree-branches, ready to catch anything which happened to be passing. When I recovered from the shock of the collision I saw immediately that something had wrapped itself around one of the segments of my captor's thorax, less than ten centimetres away from my helmet, between the fourth and fifth limbs.

The something was thick and wet and very rough, and I guessed immediately what it was. It was a tongue, and it was hauling my temporary custodian into a mouth so vast that it seemed to my befuddled brain that one could easily lose a whole microworld down there. But I only got the briefest glimpse of the pink wet throat and the dark tunnel that presumably led to a vastly cavernous stomach and an acid ocean of digestive juices.

Mercifully, the thing that had stolen me from the nest chose that moment to drop me. I didn't for a moment suppose that it had done so for any altruistic reason, and I credited my release to its instinctive urge to concentrate all its resources on a hopeless effort to save itself, but I thanked it anyway—or would have if I could have mustered the breath to speak. My throat was so tight I couldn't even whimper any more.

Susarma Lear and 673-Nisreen were both trying to attract my attention, complaining—politely, in the Tetron's case; but with some asperity on Susarma's side—that I was letting them down by not taking the time to tell them what was happening. But I really didn't feel capable of offering them an adequate running commentary.

I fell—and this time there was no doubt that I was falling as freely as anything could, with no wings at all to bear me up. I wondered, absurdly, whether the stuff that was wrapped around me was elastic enough to let me bounce, provided that I didn't fall on my head. I was under no illusions about what would happen if I *did* fall on my head. Low-gee or no low-gee, the most important bit of me would be a sticky red smear on the surface of the starshell.

Then I was caught again—grabbed in mid-air with an abruptness which shook me up badly. It wasn't as bad as hitting the ground, but it was enough to jar my brain inside my skull and knock me dizzy. For several seconds I wasn't in a position to see or feel anything at all except the kinaesthetic display of my own miserable discomfort.

When I could see again, I thought I was right back to square one, because the thing that had me in its grip now was the monster that had pursued the nest-robber in that lunatic helter-skelter dive. I could see all of its hairy spiderlike head, which had black eye-spots here there and everywhere, and vast hairy mouth-parts. It clutched me tightly between two foreshortened forelimbs, with four great fingery tentacles wrapped tightly around my trussed-up torso.

"Rousseau!" complained my two-man audience, avid for news. *"What's happening?"*

"I fell out of the frying pan," I yelled—not knowing quite why I was yelling—"and now I'm in the fire!"

And then, abruptly, my stomach turned over again. It wasn't because we had changed direction again, but because we had actually stopped. We were quite still, not because we were hovering, but because we had landed. Beyond the ugly head I could see the edges of the vast wings, which were vibrating gently. I tried to crane my neck around, to see if we were on the ground, or merely perched on a branch, but I couldn't turn far enough.

I looked up into that huge unfathomable face, wondering which of those many eyes were focused on me. I didn't know whether or not dinnertime had finally arrived, or whether the monster was just taking a breather before flying back up to return me to the larder, but I was just about past caring. It didn't really seem to matter much any more.

The tentacles placed me very carefully on the ground, feet downwards, but didn't let go. If they had, I'd have fallen over. Then something very weird snaked round the side of the monstrous head, and poked at me. It was long and thin and silvery, and for a moment I couldn't for the life of me imagine what it might be. Then it began to slice through the threads that bound me, neatly and with awesome efficiency.

"Zut!" I whispered, in sheer amazement. "I think the bastard's friendly!"

"What?" said Susarma Lear. She wasn't shouting any more, and neither was Nisreen.

"I think I made it," I told them, realising as I was cleverly released from my uncomfortable confinement that I really had made it. The pursuer that had pounced on the nest-robber hadn't been an outraged victim of theft—it had been a would-be rescuer. No doubt it had been a predator among predators when first it got involved in the little melodrama, but it must have been the one predator that was taken completely by surprise by its prey. *This* beastie had managed to snatch the agile box which was carrying the Nine's most versatile daughter, and instead of a square meal it had bought itself an artificial parasite which had run half a hundred synthetic nerve-lines through its chitinous hide to hijack its entire nervous system. The stupid monster had never had much of a mind of its own, but now it was under the dominion of a brain far superior to any other in this entire ecosystem.

Within a couple of minutes I was free, though the circulation to my feet had been inhibited and I found myself temporarily unable to stand up. I sat down on a woody ridge of some kind, and rubbed my ankles enthusiastically.

I explained to Susarma Lear and Myrlin what had happened, and told them to find a safe place to wait. "She's got some way of homing in on us," I said. "She can hear us even though she can't talk back. She's still in control of the situation. The monster's taking off again now, Nisreen—I think it'll come after you, this time. Don't panic when you see it. Just let it bring you down. In no time at all, we'll all be together again. We made it. It was a close one, but I think we made it! Hell and damnation, I think we've made it!"

My exultation died as quickly as it had come when I

remembered, suddenly, that some of us hadn't made it. Urania, who had been carrying Clio when she jumped, hadn't been as lucky as me. Whatever had grabbed her had been looking for an instant meal instead of something to save for the little ones. Even Myrlin, whose giant size had presumably made him the tastiest morsel of us all, had found his fighting prowess inadequate to the slaying of such dragons as inhabited this vile region of Asgard's inner space.

I looked around then, more soberly. I could still savour the triumphant sensation of having reached the legendary Centre, but there was a bitter undertaste that spoiled the experience. I also looked around for a place to hide. The flying spider which had Clio's brain-box perched on its back couldn't stick around to look after me, because it had more urgent work to do. It had saved me from two nasty fates, but there might be any number of greedy things lurking in the woods at ground zero, and I hadn't so much as a dagger with which to defend myself.

There wasn't much in the way of undergrowth down on the forest floor, and there didn't seem to be anything too big or too terrible wandering around between the radiating root-ridges of the trees, which extended in every direction, fusing together wherever they met. The impression I got when I shone my light around was that the actual surface of the starshell was covered in a deep carpet of woody tissue, interrupted by very many pits and crevices of unknown depth.

I found a flat place that was as far from holes and cracks as I could manage, and crouched down, trying to keep a lookout in every direction. What I would do if anything hungry and vicious emerged from one of the pits I wasn't entirely sure, but I was certainly ready to fight. Having come this far, I wasn't about to be intimidated by any humble vermin from the local Underworld.

I waited patiently for the party to be reassembled. Although we had lost Myrlin and Urania, Clio was still in the game, fighting with all her electronic might. Even if 994-Tulyar and John Finn had made it past the flying nightmares, we were still four-to-two superior, and we had the cleverest player on the field. We still had to find a doorway into the starshell, but in the space of half an hour I'd come all the way back to the land of the living, having earlier been written off as so much sandwich meat stored in readiness for a birthday party. I felt as though I was on a miraculous winning-streak.

The Centre of Asgard, where the answers to all the puzzles in the universe were waiting to be discovered, seemed to be mine to possess, and I was irrationally convinced that nothing could stop me now.

34

I fell into a kind of trance while we moved through the mist. I could no longer see or hear, and the thoughts with which I laboured to maintain my stream of consciousness were fragile and sluggish. I could readily believe that I was dead, as something wearing the appearance of Amara Guur had told me I was. I could accept that this was only a kind of afterlife: a slow shriveling of consciousness, an evaporation of the human spirit.

Whatever power I had possessed to force that which was outside of me to conform to my expectations of space and matter was gone now. I was no longer conscious of my own medusal form, and could not feel the slithering of the snakes upon my head. I struggled against the apparent erosion of my being. Although I could no longer see, I tried to picture things in my mind's eye. I was sure that my companion was still there, still engaged in the business of transporting me through Asgard's software space, and I tried to reconstruct his image in the inner space of my soul. I reconstructed him as Saul Lyndrach, but then I realised that Saul was only an appearance that he had worn, based in a whim of my expectations. I tried to picture the entity differently, then, as a valkyrie carrying my packaged soul to the Valhalla in which it was destined to rest, awaiting the possibility of some enigmatic rebirth into the grey matter of a living brain. I did not doubt that I had earned my place in the paradise of warriors; although I had been an instrument rather than a mover in all that had passed since I had been so strangely born from the grey matter of my prototype, I had surely shown an abundance of courage.

For some reason, I could not quite hold the image steady. The valkyrie I imagined was borrowed from an earlier dream, but that dream-image had itself been compounded from faces which I knew. She was not Susarma Lear, but her piercing blue eyes were certainly Susarma's, and the rest of her features seemed somehow to be struggling to acquire her whole appearance. All the female apparitions of the Nine had borrowed in much the same way—had been variations on that one basic theme—and there seemed no getting away from her sheer insistence on stamping her authority upon me. I wondered, briefly, whether I had committed the awful folly of allowing myself to become infatuated with her. It would, after all, be understandable—she was the only human female with whom I had come into any kind of intimate contact for many years.

I put that train of thought aside. There was no point at all in sexual fantasy, given that I had lost even that virtual image of a real body that I had brought into this dreamworld. I had surely transcended the desires of the flesh.

I allowed the blurred face of the valkyrie to dissolve, and let the picture in my head drift on the idle breeze of whimsy. It decayed into a sequence of surreal shapes—some of them faces or insectile creatures, but mostly abstract forms. I became hyperconscious of the fact that it was all mere illusion. The stirrings of my subconscious were somehow refracting ghostly images into my mind, but everything was feeble and unfocussed. There were echoes of memories that I no longer had the ability to recall, but there was nothing to cling to . . . nothing to help me maintain the conviction that I still existed as a whole, coherent person.

I had lost all contact with the passage of time; there was no reference point that would have enabled me to measure its progress. I had no heartbeat, no inner rhythm of any kind. Nor did the journey seem capable of an end, in the sense that we might reach something that could present the appearance of a new *place*. What change there was had now to operate within me rather than in my apparent surroundings. The images my mind had conjured up faded into darkness. There was nothing outside of me at all, and little enough *of* me.

I remembered that I had felt once before that I was making in fact the journey that Descartes undertook in his imagination. When I had drowned in the ocean that the Isthomi had created to carry us into software space I had come close to total extinction before recovering my sense of self.

Then, it had all been happening *to* me. Now, although it was all happening again, I was more self-destructively involved. I seemed actually to be casting aside all sensation of the world, and all sensation of belonging to my own body. Like a snake shedding its skin, I was sloughing off the burden of my psyche. I was not *losing* so much as *surrendering* my grip on time and memory, becalming myself in the instant of the present. But as before, I could think nothing, save *cogito, ergo sum*: there is a thought, therefore *something* exists. Perhaps it was not I who was existing, though . . . or perhaps I was acquiring a liquidity of personality which made me more than myself as well as less.

I felt, anyhow, as though I—or whatever now existed in my place—had reached the very limit of existence, beyond which there was nothing at all.

From that brink of oblivion, something gradually returned. I felt that a new "I" was constituted, and did not doubt that it could qualify not merely as a self, but as *my* self. That self, I felt, was once again gathering substance—or, to be precise, the virtual image of substance which entities in software space possessed. I was once again acquiring a body. I could see and feel nothing outside of it—my sensorium was not yet restored—but I nevertheless had some awareness of extension and solidity. More important, I was able to bring new thoughts out of the abyss of lethargy into which the old ones had sunk, savouring their strength and agility.

Was that, I wondered, what it feels like for man of flesh and blood to die? Was it possible that once the heart has stopped pumping, and all the nerves have stopped relaying information from the sense-organs to the brain, consciousness fades slowly and peacefully away in such a manner? Perhaps there was no curtain of darkness that abruptly descended—no *shock* of death to bring down a guillotine on experience. Perhaps there was always that fading disconnection—an odyssey beyond sensation, beyond pain, beyond memory, beyond self.

Previously, I had always imagined that it must be horrible to die, and all the more horrible if the moment of death were extended, savagely torturing consciousness upon the rack of pain. Now, I wondered whether existence might be kinder than that, and death a more peculiar ecstasy than any which life could offer.

But I wondered too whether my sense of self was absurdly anachronistic, still trying idiotically to conceive of itself as a being of flesh and sinew, blood and brain, when it was really no such thing. Perhaps, I thought, I should have used this opportunity to cut myself off from such residual notions, and accepted fully what was surely the truth: that I was no more like the entity of flesh which produced me than a dragonfly is like a nymph, or an anonymous egg like the organism it must become.

Perhaps, I thought, I should no longer be contemplating the idea of death. For was I not now a god among gods? Had I not been brought, like many a hero before me, to share the realm that was Asgard and Olympus, to be omniscient and undying, not human at all?

I tried to train myself in that way of thinking. I instructed my new self that it had become a kind of insect, redeemed from temporary entombment in a chrysalis. Out of the wreck and dissolution of one form another had now arisen, I said, and the new must put away all thought of the old, and learn to fly.

I told myself, urgently, that there was encrypted in my soul an inner nature beyond any which I had previously suspected, which had survived not only my "duplication" as an item of arcane software but also my annihilation in that form, providing some kind of template for my reincarnation as a second software self. I had been human, and quasi-human, but now I was divine.

Was I not?

Was I not?

I imagined myself grown again from that inconsiderable atom of thought to which I had been reduced, and tried to picture what I now might be. I *felt* that seed of being burst forth with a renewed vitality.

But I felt also that something was wrong, and that a promise was in the process of betrayal. I felt, however paradoxical it might seem, too familiar to myself.

I was Michael Rousseau, and I felt—I knew—that I ought to be more than that.

For a time (which seemed long) I could not quite imagine what form it was that I was acquiring. I deliberately played with the possibility that I might no longer be humanoid, or even animal, and imagined myself growing as a tree, like the great world-tree Yggdrasil which I had woven into the pattern of those dreams by means of which I had tried to envision the war which had been fought—was still being fought—in Asgard's various spaces.

I imagined myself also as a spore floating in the reaches of interstellar space, drifting for millions of years, awaiting the moment of coincidence which would deliver me into a place where life could thrive—into the vaporous maw of a gas giant, or the great hoop of warm cloud surrounding a condensing sun. I imagined myself as a tight-wound thread of nucleic acid, unraveling into a world pregnant with possibility, doubling and doubling and doubling to spin raw organic matter into the stuff of life, bound into organisms which could not only reproduce themselves, but which also carried wrapped in their quiet DNA the apparatus of future evolution: the templates of a million different forms, a million different creatures whose interactions would be the seed of that intricate building process which led inexorably to the complexity of mind, the humanity of man, and the creativity of whatever being it was who was quiet in man himself—in all the millions or billions of humanoid species which the spinning thread of universal life had woven on its planetary looms.

I imagined myself as both the whole and a tiny part of the thread manipulated by the three grey Fates, daughters of Night and sisters of the Seasons. I could catch no glimpse of the Fates themselves, but remembered dimly that in one representation they were one and the same with the Keres, who carried the souls of the dead to Hades, and wore therefore the selfsame faces as the valkyries who had taken possession of *my* soul. I was sensible of the fashion in which that thread spilled eternally into the darkness which was the universe, woven not into a single pattern but an infinite series of patterns, each one different in detail and yet serving the same aesthetic end.

Finally, I imagined myself as an embryo, floating in an amniotic sac, shaped and formed while I grew by an unfolding plan, sustained by a placenta which I would soon no longer need, waiting for the renewal of sense and sensation, of life of my own . . . waiting for birth, or rebirth, or a place in the vast unfolding chain of being in which birth and rebirth, duplication and metamorphosis, death and putrefaction, were all mere marks of punctuation in the sentence of existence.

All of that, I knew, belonged to the realm of the possible, the realm of the real. . . .

But I knew, somehow, that it would be denied to me.

I had been shaped for a different purpose. I had not been made ready for immortality, for life in the world of the gods. I might have become divine, but instead I had been prepared for another destiny, another mission. I was still an instrument, a weapon of war. I was helpless in the hands of those who sought to use me.

Knowing that, I realised how easy it must be for men to hate their gods, and how wise it might be not to trust them.

35

The flying spider, with Clio hooked into its nervous system like a possessive demon, returned with 673-Nisreen within half an hour. He was badly shaken, and still suffering from his broken arm, but once he was free of his swaddling-clothes I helped rub his ankles to restore the circulation. He had no weapon, so we remained defenceless until Clio and her assistant brought Susarma Lear down, but nothing emerged to threaten us. The forest floor seemed to offer adequate sanctuary from the horrors that haunted the treetops.

Clio put the flying spider to sleep before disengaging herself, leaving the monstrous thing laid out across the root-ridges, legs and wings sprawled in all directions. I had never seen such an ungainly creature, nor an uglier one, and I was glad when we hurried off, leaving it to the mercy of any scavengers or predators which cared to risk approaching it while it was too dazed to resume the normal course of its life. I rather hoped that it would survive—it had played a vital role in saving us from a particularly nasty predicament, even if it hadn't been quite itself while doing so. Who was I to minimise the efforts of a helpless instrument, drafted into a conflict far beyond the scope of its own understanding?

From her temporary vantage point high up in the trees Susarma Lear had seen many small lights produced by living creatures, but down on the surface of the starshell it was much gloomier, and we had only our helmet-lights to show us the way. I had not the slightest idea which way we ought to go, but the magic box still had matters well in hand. She climbed up on my shoulders, but refrained from running her neuronal feelers through my suit and into the back of my skull. Instead she began to send electronic signals over the radio link that we used for voice contact. She couldn't manage a voice of her own but she could understand our speech, and she could answer questions on a buzz-once-for-yes-twice-for-no basis. It didn't take long to work out a rudimentary system of communication, and to figure out which way she wanted us to go.

"How far is it?" I asked. "An hour?"

No.

"Two hours?"

Yes.

It wasn't much of a conversation, but the essentials were there.

In anything like Earth-normal gravity the journey would have been very difficult, because the ground was far from flat—the cracks in the carpet made by the root-ridges were anything up to five metres deep and ten across. As things were, we couldn't have weighed much more than a tenth of our Earth weight, and we found that we could hurdle the cracks with consummate ease, and could have turned somersaults if we'd wanted to. But we had to keep a wary eye on the trees. Their lowest branches were high above our heads, but there were things moving on the trunks, and on three occasions great winged shadows fluttered down towards us, presumably intent on investigating our nutritious potential. Susarma was always ready with her needler in case the situation became desperate, but we obviously didn't seem appetising enough and the shadows passed us by. There were creepy-crawlies in the cracks between the root-ridges, too, but they kept their heads well down and didn't bother us at all.

"These roots don't just overlap," I said to Nisreen. "They're all one system. There's only one organism here, and *all* the trees are just branches. The starshell is bedrock to a single mammoth plant."

I didn't mention Yggdrasil, the mythical world-ash of which I'd dreamed. The name wouldn't have meant anything to a Tetron—or to Susarma, who'd had a more practical education.

673-Nisreen agreed that the plant was remarkable. From a Tetron, that was a genuine concession. I think he might have entered into the spirit of the thing if his arm hadn't been troubling him so much. I felt fine again, but he hadn't gone through the Isthomi's bodily tuning-up process, and he was conspicuously less than superhuman. Bioscientist or not, a discussion of the wonders of the local ecology simply didn't warrant a place on his immediate personal agenda. I was left to marvel privately at the multitudinous scions of the single starshell-hugging tree. No doubt there would have been far more to marvel at had the light been better, but the gloom put me in mind of my expeditions into the cold levels in the quiet days before Saul Lyndrach, Myrlin, and Susarma Lear had so rudely interrupted the pattern of my life.

The journey took less than two hours—Clio had underestimated the ground that we could cover in the low-gee conditions. Our destination, it transpired, was a kind of tower built beside one of the spokes which connected the starshell to the outer part of the macroworld. The tower was built in the form of a tall four-sided pyramid with a few square-sectioned extrusions and a hemispherical dome on top. The spoke that vanished into the canopy above it was oval in section, about four metres thick on the long diameter. The dome on top of the building looked as though it ought to be transparent, but there was no light inside it now; the entire edifice was silent and dark.

There was a moatlike ditch around the building, created because the carpet of root-ridges was held back by a fence not unlike the one that protected the airlock on the level above. The ditch was about twelve metres across and five deep. We could see that there was a doorway directly across from the point where we stood looking down, and we could see that it had been opened in a rather crude manner. A way had been blasted through it by a sophisticated petard of some kind. The gap was adequate to let through a man—or a man-sized robot.

We jumped down into the ditch and approached the doorway cautiously. Susarma had the needler in her hand, ready to fire, but there was no sign of anyone lurking within.

We paused on the threshold, and the box on my back started buzzing at me to attract my attention.

"What's the matter?" I asked. "Is there a booby trap?"

Yes. No.

"What's that supposed to mean? Is there or isn't there?"

Yes. Pause. *No.*

I shook my head, wearily. Then I felt the feelers which were holding on to me relax slightly, as if the box was trying to let go.

Inspiration struck. "What you mean," I said, "is that it's booby-trapped in such a way as to make it dangerous for *some* of us."

Yes.

I thought hard for a minute, and then it clicked. It had to be magic bazookas, like the one the Isthomi had given Myrlin to blast the robot mantis. The inside of the starshell was lethal to silicon brains.

"What's going on?" asked Susarma.

"What I think she means," I explained, "is that there's something over the threshold which is intended to put mechanical intelligences out of action. Maybe that's what damaged the Nine the first time they tried to contact the Centre through software space. I guess that's why the enemy needed 994-Tulyar—or his body. They must have slipped through some relatively crude device to hit the power-supply, but maybe it couldn't carry the kind of programming required to complete the job. For that, they need an organic brain—and clever hands."

Yes, signaled Clio. Short and sweet—but none too encouraging.

"So how can we get you in there?" I asked.

No.

"I think it's trying to tell us," said Susarma, drily, "that we're on our own."

Yes. No.

"She can still communicate with us from out here, as long as we don't get too much solid wall between us," I said. "Maybe she can send some eyes in with us, too—those flying cameras that spied on the slugs. They can't carry much in the way of software."

Yes. Yes. Clio wasn't getting excited—it wasn't in her nature. She was just giving us a measure of encouragement. She might have to be discreet, lest she walk into an ambush in there, but she was still on the team. We might have to work out a more elaborate code than a series of buzzes if she was going to work out for us exactly what we had to *do* in there, but she might be able to cope. At least she might be able to tell us how to switch off the defences that were holding her back.

I waited while she disengaged herself, and I placed her

296

discreetly beside the doorway. She emitted a couple of tiny mobiles, the size one normally expects flies to be, in a world where they weigh what things that size are supposed to weigh.

Susarma took the lead, still carrying the needler in her hand. I went next, while Nisreen brought up the rear.

There were marked doors on either side of the corridor but we ignored them. At the far end there was a deep circular well about four metres across, with a spiral catwalk winding around its perimeter, leading down into the body of the starshell. We went down, in no great haste. There were more doorways, clearly marked, but I figured that our objective was down below, and that was the way we went. There was a good deal of dust on the steps, and it had recently been disturbed. I couldn't tell how many other feet had passed this way, but it seemed to be more disturbance than one pair was likely to have made, so I had to stop being optimistic about the possibility that Tulyar and John Finn were waiting for feeding time in something's nest.

The catwalk wound around and around the well so many times that I lost count. My headlamp wasn't sufficiently powerful enough to show us more than a dozen metres or so, and there was no way to guess what was waiting for us at the bottom, so we had to be patient. We were able to take big steps because of the low gravity, and we covered the ground reasonably quickly, but we were taking a roundabout route and we took a long time getting where we were going.

Eventually, though, we came to the bottom of the well.

The catwalk delivered us into a much larger open space. The wall we had been following round and round straightened out, and extended away into the distance as far as we could see.

The space at the bottom of the stair was strewn with the most amazing litter I had ever seen. Some kind of battle had once been fought here, and there were bits of shattered machines everywhere, covered in thick, greasy dust. Among the debris there were numerous humanoid skeletons, stripped of their flesh by scavengers that had long ago moved on in search of more profitable fields. I could tell that they weren't human, in the strict sense of the word, but they were certainly humanoid. If they were all that remained of the superhuman builders, then those builders had indeed been closely akin to all of us, human and Tetron alike.

There was a clear trail leading away from the foot of the catwalk, into the gloom of the cavernous chamber.

"I don't know how it looks to you," I said to Susarma, "but I don't think there are two sets of footprints there. I think there are at least three—maybe more."

She knelt to look at the scuffed dust. "There are more than two," she said, pensively. "But they needn't all have been together. Maybe Tulyar and Finn are following a trail, too—the trail of the whoever or whatever switched off the power."

It was a possibility. We moved off, following the tracks in the dust. We moved carefully, all too well aware of the possibility of an ambush. Tulyar and Finn had suits like ours, and could listen in on our conversation if there were no thick walls separating us—though that would force them to keep silent themselves. They couldn't know exactly where we were until they saw our lights, but they knew which way we'd be coming.

I wondered, briefly, how John Finn was feeling now that he was all alone with a Tetron who wasn't really a Tetron at all. Maybe he was ready to defect yet again, back to our side. On the other hand, maybe not. He was way out of his intellectual depth, and there was no telling which way he would figure out his best interests.

"Clio," I said, softly. "Are you still with us?"

There was a very faint buzz, at the threshold of perception. There was too much junk between the surface and our present position—as soon as we'd moved away from the well we'd come to the limit of our communicative apparatus. If we went on, we'd be on our own.

I hesitated, and looked at Susarma.

As far as she was concerned, she'd always been in command, and now it looked as if we would soon be catching up with the bad guys she was only too willing to take control. She wasn't unduly worried about losing contact with Clio—her objective was the strictly short-term one of keeping us alive until 994-Tulyar and John Finn were neutralized. She brought us close together, and raised a finger to the part of her helmet that was in front of her lips, telling us to be quiet. She signaled in dumb show that she would follow the tracks, while I was to move away to the left and Nisreen to the right. We had to stay close enough to see her headlight, but at least we wouldn't present a single target.

She took the Scarid pistol from her waist, and looked at her two weapons for a moment or two, as if inwardly debating their relative merits. Then she shrugged, and passed the needler to me. It was by far the more effective weapon, and I was initially inclined to refuse it, but I remembered that she'd showed her prowess with the crash gun once before, while I was by no means certain to be able to hit anything with it.

I took the needler, and we moved off. As methods of communication went, the dumb show was only marginally better than the yes/no buzzing farce to which we had been reduced in exchanging opinions with Clio, but it worked well enough. The worst of it was that once we had separated and begun to move forward, none of us dared say a word.

We moved off along a corridor between two ranks of squat platforms, each one bearing the broken remains of what looked like a plastic bubble. The platforms were about two metres long by one wide, with the corners rounded down; the bubbles were a little less than that, and added an extra thirty centimetres or so to the height of each column. The space between them was so cluttered with nasty debris that I didn't pay much immediate attention to the platforms, but I realised belatedly that they must be something like the artificial wombs which the Nine had built. This had once been a hospital—or a hatchery. Maybe this was where the builders designed other humanoids: the lab where evolution really happened, before the gardeners begin seeding the worlds with pre-adapted DNA. Or maybe it was only the place where the masters of Asgard investigated the lifeforms which they plucked from the worlds which they visited. We still didn't know whether Asgard was an Ark or a nursery, though we were pretty sure that it was a fortress.

Somehow, that particular enigma seemed much less important now. The problem was not to interpret Asgard, but to save it.

We moved more slowly now than we had before, taking shorter strides. I tried to keep one eye on Susarma's headlight, and the other on the rubbish which threatened to trip me up, with occasional glances into the gloom ahead, to make certain that nothing nasty was looming up there.

We had been on the move for about half an hour—just long enough to enable me to get thoroughly relaxed, when things began to happen again, and to happen all too quickly.

There was a sudden blaze of light from somewhere up ahead of me, which burst upon my retina like a bomb and blinded me. I knew that I was an easy target, and I let my brief Star Force training take over, diving away to my right to get behind one of the platform-wombs. A powerful beam of light chased me as I dived, and I didn't hang about when I landed—rolling and keeping low, I wriggled away through the wreckage of machinery, trying to lose myself among the shadows.

I heard the crash-gun fire, and one beam of light disappeared—but then I realised that there were at least three.

I heard another gun go off—a needler spitting its tiny slivers of metal. The crash-gun boomed again.

Then there was silence. I tried desperately hard to locate some movement around the lights, hungry for a target.

And then I heard something very strange.

"Oh shit," said Susarma's voice. "I almost. . . . Why the hell didn't you. . . ."

She didn't sound angry—but she did sound very surprised. And her voice was cut off with a sudden, sickening abruptness, swallowed up by the brief growl of a needler.

I knew that someone had shot her.

But why, if she'd seen the other coming, hadn't she shot first? Had she thought it was me?

I ducked down beneath one of the pillars, trying to hide as best I could, and trying furiously to think. Clio couldn't hear us; Susarma Lear was down; 673-Nisreen didn't even have a gun. It was all down to me, and I didn't have a clue what was happening. I tried to look over the top of the plastic bubble, hoping that my eyes were ready to see, but in the glare of whatever light it was that promptly picked me out, I could see nothing but a vast shadow heading towards me. The shadow had a headlamp just like mine, and mine must have got in his eyes just as his got in mine, though they were feeble enough by comparison with the spotlight.

I didn't have any trouble recognising him. I couldn't see his face, but I would have known his bulk anywhere.

It was Myrlin—who was not, after all, being digested in some hideous insect's stomach, but looming above me like a great big bear. I had half raised the needler, but I stopped myself from shooting, and remembered far too late what Susarma Lear had been saying when she was taken out. Enlightenment didn't save me.

It was Myrlin's body, but it wasn't Myrlin's mind. As he shot me in the belly, and sent my body hurtling backwards to collide with one of the platforms, I reflected that the Isthomi had made a bad mistake in judging that Myrlin hadn't taken aboard any mysterious software during that fateful moment of contact. And so had I.

Whatever had got into Tulyar had got into him, too. It had simply lain dormant, biding its time—and by that strategy, had won the game.

We were all down, all dying . . . and the starlet was probably all set to go nova.

36

There was a voice, although there was no image of a speaker. I still had no sense of sight, and I did not think that the voice was really heard. It was more like a spoken thought inside my mind, though it was not my thought.

We have re-established full contact with the starshell, whispered the disembodied voice. *Its own systems are virtually inert; the greater part of its software space is devastated; and its defences still prevent our moving any machine with substantial intelligent software into its actual space. But we do have eyes there, thanks to the Isthomi. And there is one move which may yet work. We are preparing.*

I had the opportunity, at last, to ask a question.

What am I? I was surprised by the frailty of my own thought-voice.

There is no time, Mr. Rousseau, the voice replied. *Believe me, there simply is no time. You know who you are, and there is nothing to be gained from a discussion of the nature of things. It is not that we wish to use you as a mere tool, understanding nothing, but the Tetron is within minutes of destroying us all. The crisis is upon us now, and desperation urges us on. Watch!*

Suddenly, there was light, and it was as if I could see, though I still had no sense of possessing a body, and the sight which I had was not the sight of human eyes. It was more like an image transmitted by a camera—transmitted into the depths of my consciousness, upon the screen of my imagination.

I could see a room, where several figures stood. One

stood alone, while three others watched him, two before him and one to the side. The viewpoint from which I seemed to be looking was somewhat above them, looking down from the side of the lone man confronted by the two, over the shoulder of the third.

The lone figure was 673-Nisreen. Directly in front of him was a second Tetron—or, to be strictly accurate, a second person inhabiting a Tetron body. That was 994-Tulyar. Beside Tulyar stood Myrlin, and the one whose back was to me was John Finn.

But where am I? I thought. *Where are Urania and Susarma Lear?*

"I don't understand," Nisreen was saying, in parole. Obviously, we had come in on the middle of a conversation.

"You cannot be expected to understand," Tulyar told him, in that soft, dead voice that had given me the creeps when I first heard it on the Nine's home level. "All will be explained, in time, but for now, there is urgent work to be done, and it is simply a matter of duty. The starlet is nearly ready; the power build-up in its peripheral systems is becoming critical."

I saw Nisreen look around, angry with confusion. "What is happening?" he asked. "Do you intend to destroy the macroworld?"

"Certainly not," said the thing in Tulyar's body. "Did Rousseau tell you that was what we intended? Is that how he persuaded you to join in this pursuit?"

Nisreen did not reply. The thing that was using Tulyar's body had much better control of it now than when I had last seen it—in a former incarnation. Now it was no longer tongue-tied, and no longer had that manic stare, it could pass for a Tetron. It was even talking about duty. I could sense Nisreen's uncertainty—the self-doubt which must be telling him that perhaps, after all, he had been wrong.

I realised, though, that *one* of those present had that zombie-like manner which I had once seen in Tulyar's behaviour. I remembered the earlier voice, murmuring away to me while I was carried through a cloud. It had spoken of humanoids infected by enemy programmes—*humanoids,* in the plural.

"No, 673-Nisreen," said the pseudo-Tulyar, "we do not intend to destroy the macroworld. It is we who intend to save it, and to save thousands of our brethren with it. The macroworld might have destroyed itself, if the power build-up within the starshell's peripheral system had been allowed to continue, but we are here to prevent that happening. You should be thankful that your human friends finally met their match—had they succeeded in killing us all, Asgard might well have been doomed."

"What is your ultimate purpose?" asked Nisreen uncertainly.

"We intend to return power to the macroworld. In fact, we intend to flood Asgard's systems with power. We will send such a blast of energy into the labyrinth that it will devastate every system through which it passes—a tidal surge of power, which will destroy the godlike beings who have opposed us in this long and bitter war. But you need not fear for our fellow humanoids; they are not the target of the assault. Some will undoubtedly be inconvenienced. A few may die as an indirect result of our action, but they will be innocent bystanders. Our real enemies are entities of a different kind. It is the artificial intelligences created by those who built Asgard—the gods which they made to guide the destinies of their creation—that we must annihilate. From here, you see, we can direct the power-surge exactly as we wish, protecting those systems that we control and destroying those that we do not. We will certainly injure the macroworld slightly, and life in some of its artificial habitats will never be quite the same, but we shall do as little harm to your kind and mine as we can. We aim to preserve life— and to preserve ourselves. If our enemies were in our place, it is by no means certain that they would act as kindly."

673-Nisreen stared at the creature that had once been his kin.

"What are you?" he asked. He seemed to be no longer angry, but simply curious.

"I am 994-Tulyar," said the other, calmly. "I do not deny that I am more than I once was, but I remain who I have always been, and I demand your obedience to my authority. When the present task is complete, there will be much work still to be done, and the Tetrax are the natural heirs of that mission. The people of the macroworld must be brought into the brotherhood of humanoid species, and the remaining enemies of that brotherhood—the Isthomi and their kin—must be destroyed. There is much for the Tetrax to do, and much for humans, too."

The last was said with a sidelong glance at John Finn. I could see that Finn looked unhappy and uncertain, but he was listening as intently as Nisreen.

"What kind of war is it that you are fighting?" asked Nisreen, levelly. "Rousseau represented it as a war between two kinds of life, or between life and anti-life. I could not understand."

"*Rousseau* could not understand," Tulyar's voice replied. "Our allies are minds, like the minds which humanoid beings evolved and then set free within their machines, but they had different makers. Their ultimate origins, like ours, must be sought in the dark dust that drifts between the stars, but for what it is worth, it was their kind and not ours that were the first intelligences of the universe. The substance of life is the stuff of second-generation stars, while theirs had its origin in simpler matter. It is of little significance now, for both kinds of mind have transcended the matter that gave them birth. Material entities created gods, and now the gods dispute for control of the material entities that gave them birth. Asgard is one battleground; when this battle is settled the galaxy will become a battleground. But what you must understand, 673-Nisreen, is that it matters not at all to entities of flesh-and-blood which side they choose; they must have one or the other, but they owe no essential loyalty to either. We are Tetrax, 673-Nisreen, and our only loyalty is to the Tetrax, and to the galactic community whose ideological leaders we are. We must make whatever alliance will serve Tetra and the galaxy best, and that alliance is already forged."

673-Nisreen seemed less than totally convinced, but he glanced sideways at John Finn. Neither he nor Finn said anything, but the glance spoke volumes. John Finn was turncoat through and through. He didn't give a damn which side he was on, as long as he was looked after. Nisreen cared, but he didn't know any longer which side was the side of right. He'd listened to my side of the story, based on what I'd experienced in my dreams—but how much could a human's dreams count for in the eyes of a sceptical Tetron?

Nisreen looked at Myrlin, then, calmly appraising the state of the android. Myrlin's eyes were glazed, and he was saying nothing, but he had a needler in his hand and he was all-too-obviously capable of using it.

The question I had asked myself before came back to mind: Where was I? Where was the Rousseau of flesh and blood, from whose brain I had been mysteriously born? As I looked at the thing that had once been my friend, I remembered the other Myrlin, and the strange light that had flared in his eye as he was about to die. In the moment of reaching out to save me, he had changed. Perhaps, if death had not claimed him, he might have destroyed me. I was overcome by the horrible suspicion that the Myrlin of flesh and blood had been used by some alien master to destroy the fleshly Rousseau.

Nisreen was looking at Tulyar again, but the thing that was wearing Tulyar's body had turned away now. He was sitting down in front of some kind of console. It had a lot of controls—manual keyboards, and mechanical levers.

The intelligence in 994-Tulyar's body took no further notice of the other Tetron. He seemed quite absorbed in his rapt contemplation of the console. He reached out tentatively to turn a couple of knobs, but then turned back again. He was as inscrutable as any real Tetron now, but I inferred that the final shot in the crazy war which had raged inside Asgard for hundreds of thousands of years was not quite ready for firing. On the other hand, he seemed to expect that the mechanical omens would become auspicious at almost any time. It was a matter of minutes rather than hours—and there didn't seem to be anything that anyone could do to stop it.

It was nice to know, of course, that Asgard wasn't going to be blown to bits after all, but if I read pseudo-Tulyar's meaning right, the blast he was going to unleash would be a holocaust to consume all those inhabitants of software space who had opposed his kin.

Including me.

And there didn't seem to be a damn thing that anyone could do about it.

But then the disembodied voice chipped in again, and

said: *No time at all, Michael Rousseau. You know what to do, even though you do not know that you know. There is no hope of establishing any physical interface by means of which we can transcribe you, and we believe that it was once explained to you that the transmission of personalities in any wave-encoded form is difficult in the extreme. There would be no hope of success, save that we are transmitting you into a brain which is already configured to contain you.*

We are going to put you back into your body, Michael Rousseau, if we can—we must fire you like a bullet from a magical gun. We do not know if it will work, and we cannot tell how badly your body has been injured, but there is nothing else to be done. You are the very last shot that we can fire. We are sorry for the indecent haste, but there simply is no time to. . . .

⤳ 37 ⤵

I awoke with a horrid, nauseous shock, as if some mysterious beam of malice had jolted my grey matter.

I felt very numb, as though I was floating. I was as high as a kite on some kind of pain-killer. That was due to the life-support system on my back, which was still hooked into my flesh. It had fed me enough anaesthetic to knock me out, and now it was letting me down again, as gently as it could.

I moved the hand that was clutching my abdomen, touching the fingertips very gently to the wound where the needles had gone in. There was a rough edge, but it was only the lacerated plastic of the suit. The entry wound had already scarred over. Whatever the Nine had done to me had given my powers of self-repair a considerable boost. I tried to sit up, and immediately regretted it. It wasn't exactly pain, but it was a dreadful sensation of nausea. The needles were still inside me, and the damage they'd done was going to take a good deal more than half an hour to make good.

I lay back against the pillar, wondering whether it could possibly do me any good to be alive. I looked from side to side, hoping to see something reassuring. My headlight was still working, but its feeble beam showed me nothing but dust and wreckage—including a skeleton which must have been sprawling in much the same position as myself, against another pillar. When I tried to turn my head, though, I realised that there was another light-source not too far away. At first

I thought that it must be Susarma Lear's helmet-lamp, but it was actually an open doorway in a wall some thirty metres away. I couldn't see inside from where I was lying, but I could hear 673-Nisreen's voice over the radio link, and I had to bite my tongue to stop myself exclaiming in surprise.

I tried to sit up, and succeeded. It wasn't comfortable, but I had a terrible sense of urgency. I couldn't quite think why, but I had the idea that I was in a hurry. I came to my knees, and then I managed, with some difficulty, to stand up.

I looked around, but the needler I'd been carrying had gone.

Myrlin—the thing that was using Myrlin's body—had taken it away.

From my new position I could see a pair of boots, attached to a body that was hidden by one of the pillars. They had to be Susarma Lear's. There wasn't the least sign of movement—if her powers of self-repair had managed to preserve her life they'd obviously had more work to do than mine.

I remembered that Susarma had had a crash-gun. Myrlin had shot her first, then come after me. He had disarmed me, but perhaps he hadn't gone back afterwards to disarm Susarma.

I wasn't sure that I could walk, but the low gravity gave me hope. Hyped up as I was, I didn't seem to weigh anything at all. When I took a step I thought I could feel the needles ripping my intestines, but it might have been my imagination. I clenched my teeth hard, determined not to give myself away by groaning.

I don't know how many steps I took to reach Susarma's body, but I got there as quickly as I could, and knelt down beside her.

The crash-gun was still in her hand.

I could see her face through the helmet. It was very pale and drawn, but her brave blue eyes were shut and she appeared to be sleeping peacefully. I knew that she wouldn't be feeling any pain, whether she was dead or not. I looked at the entry wound where the needles had hit her. She hadn't taken any more needles than I had, but she'd taken them higher up, around the lowest ribs. No matter how well the Isthomi had rebuilt her, she couldn't recover if her lungs had been reduced to tatters—but when I put my hand to her breast, I thought that I could feel a faint heartbeat.

I didn't dare wait until I was sure—I was in a hurry. I prised the gun out of her hand. Her fingers weren't rigid with *rigor mortis,* but it seemed as if she opposed me, very feebly. The reflex gave me further reason to think—at least to hope—that she was still alive, and that the ingenuity of the life-support system was equal to the task of preserving her strengthened flesh.

I checked the magazine, and found that the gun had only two bullets left. There were several spare magazines in her belt and I took two out—I didn't really think that I'd get a chance to reload if seven shots weren't enough, but I figured that I might as well have it as not.

I stood up, feeling my intestines lurch as I did so, wondering whether the superhumanity treatment the Isthomi had given me was really up to coping with aggravated peritonitis. I switched off my headlight.

I moved as carefully and as quietly as I could towards the open door. I made sure that I couldn't be seen from within the room, though they weren't likely to be able to see much looking out from a brightly-lit room into the darkness. From a distance I took a long discreet look to see where everyone was. Pseudo-Myrlin was away to the left, Finn to the right. 673-Nisreen was between them. Pseudo-Tulyar would be the most difficult one—he was sitting down again.

Again?

I shook my head to clear the strange sensation of *déjà vu* which had come over me. I felt dizzy, as though there were something I ought to remember, but there was no time to worry about it.

I paused when I got into position beside the door, leaning against the wall to gain what support I could while I gathered my strength. I looked back the way I had come, but it was too dark to see Susarma's body. I was as ready as I would ever be. Mentally, I rehearsed the shots that I would have to fire, and prayed fervently that I could aim the crash-gun effectively. It was a kind of weapon I'd never handled before.

My calculations weren't made any easier by the fact that I couldn't tell how many shots I'd have to fire. Whatever was in control of Myrlin's body might not have recaptured all his skills, but had been effective enough to take Susarma Lear by surprise and shoot her down. Myrlin's body was just as resistant to damage as mine, and wasn't full of needles. It wasn't going to be easy to put him away, even with a full clip. And how many shots would I need thereafter? One for Tulyar, to be sure—but what about Finn? Had he come sufficiently to his senses to realise that Tulyar was no friend of his? Might there be just enough humanity left in his befuddled brain to make him see that I was on his side?

I couldn't spend too long wondering. Somehow, I knew that there was no time to spare.

I slid around the edge of the doorspace, keeping my back firmly against the wall—I knew that I'd need every bit of support I could get, given that the gun would have a much more powerful recoil than a needler. I was levelling the weapon as I moved, supporting my right arm with my left, as I'd seen Susarma do. Pseudo-Myrlin and Finn no longer had their guns in their hands, but they were far from relaxed, and when Finn saw me appear from nowhere and his eyes widened in horror the giant was quick to go for the needler which he had laid down near to hand.

I fired at the invader who was wearing the body of my friend, but couldn't help wincing as I did so. It wasn't a perfect shot but he was a very big target, and the bullet ripped into him just below the right collar-bone. He wasn't braced the way I was and the bullet hurled him backwards, sending him crashing into the console behind him. I wanted to fire at him again, to make sure that he stayed down, but I could see from the corner of my eye that my optimistic hopes regarding John Finn's essential humanity were not to be fulfilled. His hatred for me had corrupted his reflexes irredeemably, and he was already going for his gun with murderous intent.

I swiveled instantly and fired at him.

I saw the terrified expression on his face as he saw me turning towards him. He had already plucked his needler from his belt, but as I shot him, a convulsive jerk of his hand sent his shots straight upwards into the ceiling.

My bullet hit him in the head, and he went down as if he'd been switched off. Blood and brains filled up the space inside his helmet, and I knew that he wouldn't be back, no matter how much work the Isthomi had done on his body.

I hadn't intended to kill him, and if I'd had the option, I really would have knocked him down in such a way that he could get up again when it was all over, but I didn't have the choice.

I also didn't have a choice about what to do next, because pseudo-Myrlin was already coming back to his feet again. The bigger they are the harder they fall, but in low gee they can bounce back with astonishing alacrity. He was braced now as well as I was, and he was bringing the needler up to fire. I tried to zero in on the centre of his chest again, and blasted away. It would have done far more good to blow his head off the way I'd blown Finn's, but that had been a freak shot and I knew better than to try for a repeat. I had to hit the giant again before he cut me in half with the needler, and if I had to hit him four more times to keep him down then that was what I had to do.

Pseudo-Tulyar should have been out of it for a few more seconds, but he wasn't. His chair didn't swivel but he had turned in it with unexpected agility, and was covered by its broad back. He must have had a gun very close to hand because it was in his fist now and he was already aiming it— but he didn't have a chance to fire because 673-Nisreen, the aging man of science, brought down upon his wrist the hard cast which was protecting his own broken arm. Pseudo-Tulyar dropped the gun, and Nisreen grabbed him, wrenching his arm downwards, using the back of the chair as a fulcrum. Pseudo-Tulyar somersaulted lazily over the back of the chair.

I had already fired a second shot at pseudo-Myrlin, who took it square in the chest. Maybe it was too square, because it seemed to have no effect at all. He couldn't be thrown back again and there wasn't enough power to stop him even in a great big bullet like that.

He fired, but the needles went wild, splashing into the wall beside me. If he'd really been Myrlin he would never have missed, but he was a biocopy of some alien software, locked in an utterly unfamiliar body—he hadn't had as much time as his brother to become accustomed to his flesh, and I realised how completely we had been taken by surprise when he first shot us down. I realised that he hadn't fired into my belly in order to hurt me more, but because he didn't know any better. It had been a mistake, and now he was paying for it.

I fired again, and again, and again.

I didn't miss once. The third bullet opened up his great big chest, sending splinters of rib deep into his vital organs. The fourth and fifth must have turned his heart and lungs to pulp.

Three or four more needles ricocheted from the floor, and one of them grazed the boot of my suit, but I was still standing, still able to fire.

673-Nisreen was down in a heap with the pseudo-Tetron on top of him. There was no way I could get a clear shot, and I had no option but to pause.

I coughed, feeling a gout of blood rising from my belly into my mouth, but I knew that I had to remain standing. Whatever else I did before I died—and there was *something* I had to do—I had to destroy the alien that had made use of 994-Tulyar's body to breach the defences of the starshell. Whatever mischief he was trying to work, he had been mere moments from completing it, and it wouldn't be enough to hurt him. He had to be finished.

I watched, impatiently, while he got his arms inside the futile grip which 673-Nisreen was trying to secure, and thrust outwards both ways. The bioscientist's grip was broken, and Tulyar threw him off. While Nisreen tumbled through the air in grotesque slow motion pseudo-Tulyar groped in desperation for the needler that he had dropped.

But in throwing Nisreen aside he'd signed his own death-warrant. I had a clear shot now, and I fired.

For the first time, I missed.

I was supposed to be the low-gee expert, the man from Achilles, but I fired the last bullet before I had quite brought my hand to a standstill, and I wasn't properly braced against the kick of the gun.

I felt a surge of nausea, but I couldn't even pause to swallow the blood that was in my mouth. I coughed again, spraying tiny flecks of red all over the hood, but hurled myself forward anyhow, knowing that I had to hit him before he could fire the needler.

I had my arms out ahead of me, and it was the gun I was holding which slammed into his helmet, but now he was the one who was braced and I was the featherweight. When he thrust out at me with his arms I began to do the same slow somersault as Nisreen. I went all the way over, and by the time I was facing him again I was staring straight down the barrel of his gun, looking failure and death in the face.

But when the needles came, they missed me again. The zombie had fired just a fraction too late, and the convulsion which sent the shots wide was caused by the impact of a stream of needles which passed through his right eye and cheek, ploughing into the brain and destroying whatever strange entity it was that had taken possession when 994-Tulyar's own real self had given up the ghost.

673-Nisreen was holding John Finn's gun. It was he who had fired. Finn was lying dead at his feet, and when Nisreen dropped his eyes to avoid looking at 994-Tulyar's corpse he looked straight at the bloody mess inside Finn's helmet. Tetrax can't turn pale, but Nisreen did the best he could, and I saw him shudder convulsively.

I thought I knew how difficult it had been for him to do what he had just done. In a way, he'd done exactly what Finn had, and taken the side of an alien against his own species-cousin, but I knew he hadn't done it for the same reason. Whatever Tulyar had been telling him when I woke up, he hadn't believed. Reason had told him which side to be on, and even though what he'd done was making him sick to the core of his being, he'd done it. It only looked like the Star-Force way; the motive behind it had been something very different.

I hadn't time to do or say anything. I took my place in the chair where pseudo-Tulyar had been sitting, and looked at the keyboards and the dials. There must have been two hundred different switches, and although every one had been shaped with humanoid fingers in mind, I couldn't make any sense at all of the symbols.

I raised my hands, feeling a frightful sense of utter frustration rising inside me.

And then some kind of bomb went off in my head.

I began to punch the keyboard furiously. There were no flashing lights or ringing bells to give evident warning of the fact that the power build-up in the starlet was about to discharge itself, and I had in fact lost all consciousness of the fear that Asgard might very shortly be turned into nova debris. I had not the slightest notion what I was doing, or how, and my self-consciousness seemed to be locked into some absurd psychostasis, whereby I could watch my hands but could feel no connection with them whatsoever.

I had not even sufficient presence of mind to wonder whether this was how Myrlin had felt when the creature lurking in his brain had sprung its sudden ambush, and made him into what he had so tragically become—the traitor who had very nearly turned the war around.

When my hands finally finished their work, they just stopped. I must have been struck rigid in the chair, frozen into stillness. How much time there was to spare when I completed the sequence, I have no idea. The conventions of melodrama demand that it be a mere handful of seconds, and I can't say for certain that it wasn't, but the simple truth is that I did not know then and do not know now.

I wondered, as I sat there, perfectly still, whether it was now safe for me to die. I was feeling no authentic pain, but in myself I felt absolutely awful. If someone had told me then that I was dead, I could not have denied it with any conviction.

When I felt a touch on my shoulder, I looked up to see 673-Nisreen staring down at me. The poor guy still hadn't much idea of what had happened, or how, or why, and he was desperate for some reassurance that he'd done the right thing.

"What have you done?" he asked, starting with one of the easier ones.

That was the moment when I discovered that I did, in fact, know what I had done. I didn't know *how*, but I knew *what*.

"I shunted the power which had built up in the starshell into a stresser, to wormhole the macroworld," I told him. "Which is exactly what they did a million and a half years ago, when the battle first reached its critical phase. The builders were still around then, in humanoid form. They didn't survive the consequent skirmishes, but at least they got the starshell sealed off, and left the war to the software gods who were equipped to fight it."

"Where are we?" he asked. I could see from his eyes that he was quick enough on the uptake to know that a thing the size of Asgard would make a hell of a wormhole. I knew he wouldn't be overly shocked by the answer.

"I don't know," I said. "I moved us, but there's no way to know where. At a guess, we've come a couple of million light-years. I hope you don't feel homesick, because we aren't ever going to see the Milky Way again, let alone Tetra. Asgard's all we have now—we might even have to practice being nice to the Scarida. There are still billions of them up there. I doubt that there are more than a couple of thousand Tetrax, or a couple of dozen humans."

The needles were churning in my guts, but somehow I had them sealed off. I was bleeding inside, but I had enough blood left in the arteries to keep my brain going. I felt light-headed again—anaesthetised.

He began to work his way up to the difficult questions.

"It *wasn't* Tulyar, was it?"

"No," I confirmed. "It wasn't Tulyar, and it wasn't Myrlin. Whatever their short-term plans may have been, they meant no good to your species or mine, or anything else that's truly alive. I don't know what it was that made them, but when it comes to the choice between our gods and theirs, it has to be ours that we go out to fight for. I'm certain of that, if nothing else."

"How did you do it?" he asked. "How did you know what to do?"

"Physically," I said, "I feel like half the man I used to be. Mentally, I fear that I may be a little bit more. The copy of my consciousness that the Nine launched into software space was somehow retranscribed into my own brain. It's been through a lot, and it's come every bit as close to extinction as my poor fleshly body, but it was strong enough, at the end, to carry another injection of programming into biocopy form—a set of instructions for moving the macroworld.

"The gods found themselves a hero, Nisreen. A demigod—whatever you care to call it. Believe me Nisreen, there's a part of me that has seen things and been things *nobody* should be asked to see and be. The penalty of living in interesting times, I guess."

I had a question of my own, though I didn't really expect

him to be able to answer it. "Is the colonel still alive?"

"Yes," he said. More time must have passed than I thought. I must have been sitting still for several minutes—time for him to take a look.

"I don't know how," he went on, "but she's still alive. I'm not sure she can survive for long, though, unless we can get help."

"Help," I said, "is not a problem. This is the real Centre of Asgard, and from this seat you can do *anything,* if you know how. The gods that the builders made to look after themselves and their creations can be summoned from the vasty deep and made to do our bidding. It's all at our fingertips, now. If Susarma can be saved, she will be. You too. Even me—although it may take a long, long session in one of the Nine's magic eggs. We're going to live, Nisreen, thanks to you. If you hadn't stopped Tulyar. . . ."

"It *wasn't* 994-Tulyar," he said, with a sudden flare of wrathful indignation of which I would never have believed a Tetron capable. "It was something obscene. *Something. . . .*"

He couldn't even find words for it, and I realised belatedly how desperate had been the decision which he'd made. Reason had only been a part of it—and maybe, in the final analysis, not the most important part. The Tetrax identify with one another rather more closely than humans do. The brotherhood of man may be nine-tenths pretence, but the brotherhood of the Tetrax is something else. The thing that had stolen Tulyar's body hadn't killed Nisreen because it thought that it could recruit and use him the way it had recruited and used John Finn, but it had been wrong. As I looked at 673-Nisreen, I realised that even if I hadn't managed to hit back—even if pseudo-Tulyar had managed to use the starlet's power to destroy Asgard's gods—the war wouldn't have been over. Far from it. The Tetrax might still be primitive by comparison with the builders of Asgard, but they were on the side of life, and they would have entered the lists with every last atom of force at their disposal.

I knew that the war was still going on, throughout the universe, but I was hopeful.

It wasn't just that we'd won our tiny little skirmish—there was more than that to help me to hope.

Whatever imagination it was had created the demons of Asgard had a hard fight on its hands if it intended to annihilate life itself, because life had men as well as gods, and hearts as well as minds, and its enemies had not.

✦ 38 ✦

I touched Susarma's shoulder, very gently. She opened her eyes, and stared up at me stupidly. She didn't know where she was; maybe she didn't even know who she was.

"Sorry," I whispered.

I let her look at me for a few seconds. Her brain had to start working in its own good time.

"Rousseau?" she said, very faintly. She smiled. Her mind was a million light-years away, and she was floating, high as a kite.

"I thought . . ." she began, and then stopped, probably thinking that she was about to say something silly.

"You thought right," I told her, calmly. "We should both be dead. But the Nine fixed us up. We're supermen, remember?"

She tried to sit up, but I put out my arm to restrain her. Her eyes widened as she felt the damage inside her. She was carved up more thoroughly than I was.

She opened her mouth to speak, but no sound came out. I had to guess what questions she probably had in mind.

"Help," I said, "is on its way. The gods of Asgard are back in Valhalla. The power is back on in the levels. You and I are hurt pretty badly, but thanks to the Isthomi we can come through it. I'm not sure that we can stay conscious, but I know we aren't going to die. The war within Asgard is over, save for a little mopping-up. 673-Nisreen is okay, and in better shape than either of us, except that he broke his arm again while saving my life.

"That's the good news. The bad news is that we're a million light years from home and we aren't ever going to be able to go back. Maybe even that has its brighter side. If the Star Force still exists, you're the grand commander—She-Who-Must-Be-Obeyed. I can't think of anyone who could play the part better. It's not inconceivable that you're the only human female of child-bearing age on Asgard, but with Isthomi biotech to help us there's no need for you to worry unduly about becoming the mother of the species—I dare say we could have a thousand kids without troubling ourselves with any greater intimacy than passing the test tube and arguing about what to call the brats."

She wasn't in any condition to laugh at the joke, and she looked more annoyed than amused. She wasn't the maternal type.

"Did you get that bastard android?" she whispered.

"It wasn't him," I told her, dully. "It was some other bastard, just using him. He never really had a chance, did he? First the Salamandrans, then the evil masterminds of Anti-Life. Given the opportunity, he'd have been a better man than you or I, but he got all the rough deals that fate could find for him."

"Did you get him?" She had a one-track mind.

"Yes," I said. "No clever illusions this time. No mistakes. I blasted all hell out of him. You'd have been proud of me. I got Finn too. And the thing that was pretending to be Tulyar. I got them all, the Star Force way. No ifs and buts . . . just blood and guts."

She looked up at me. There wasn't a trace of hero-worship in her pale blue stare.

"As of now," I told her, "I've resigned. You can keep the medal."

She smiled faintly.

"You got to the Centre," she said, "didn't you?"

I looked around. The lights were back on in the levels, but not here. We were surrounded by darkness, dust, and the dead.

"I got to the Centre," I agreed. "All the answers are here . . . and I have all the time in the world to find out what they are."

It was true, in a way. Our friendly neighbourhood gods would be only too pleased to give me a more leisurely explanation of anything and everything, as soon as someone had put my intestines back together and I was fit to be told. I could have the unedited version of the history of the universe, and all the lessons in life-science I could possibly desire. All the secrets of Asgard the Ark, Asgard the Fortress, and Asgard the Universal Landscape Gardener would be mine for the asking.

I could have long conversations with any god I cared to name, and share classes with Athene of the Isthomi.

Magnifique.

Something deep inside me echoed my ironic cheer. I was not the man I used to be, and I knew that what was lurking now in the darker recesses of my brain might yet trouble my dreams far more than any scary vision of Medusa, even though it was really only me.

Only me!

I had a lot of finding out still to do, and I knew only too well that although my perilous journey to the Centre of Asgard was over, my journey into the depths of my own being had hardly even begun.

⊁ABOUT THE AUTHOR⊁

BRIAN STABLEFORD was born in 1948 in Shipley, Yorkshire. He was educated at Manchester Grammar School and the University of York (B.A. in Biology; Doctorate.Phil. in Sociology). From 1976 to 1988 he was a Lecturer in the Sociology Department of the University of Reading, teaching courses in the philosophy of social science and the sociology of literature and the mass media. He has also taught at the University of the West of England, on a B.A. in "Science, Society and the Media." He has been active as a professional writer since 1965, publishing more than 50 novels and 200 short stories as well as several non-fiction books; he is a prolific writer of articles for reference books, mainly in the area of literary history.